Ex Libris

*Hartmore Hoffman*

# The Williamsburg Forgeries

# The Williamsburg Forgeries

## JOHN BALLINGER

St. Martin's Press

NEW YORK

Design by Judy Stagnitto

Library of Congress Cataloging-in-Publication Data

Ballinger, John.
    The Williamsburg forgeries.

    "A Thomas Dunne book."
    I.  Title.
PS3552.A47125W5      1989        813'.54                    88-30578
ISBN 0-312-02670-6

First Edition

10 9 8 7 6 5 4 3 2 1

Dedicated to Myrtle M. Cross and
her children, Martha Ballinger, Alma
Williams, June Dotter, and Ben Cross.

# The
# Williamsburg
# Forgeries

# Chapter

# 1

Jebediah took his gun out from underneath his jacket in one smooth motion, just as he had practiced it. The gun was a Smith and Wesson model 29, made longer by the addition of a silencer. Jebediah had seen one like it in a Clint Eastwood movie and had insisted on buying it over the sales clerk's objections. Now he held it six inches from the bus driver's left ear.

"Don't panic. Just pull off at the next exit."

After a year of driving the Atlantic City Express, the bus driver had seen his limit of crazy passengers. He had begun to turn around to direct his sarcastic reply straight at Jebediah when he saw the barrel of the revolver quivering in front of his face. The bus swerved into the left-hand lane, sideswiping a 1978 Horizon and sending it caroming into the metal road divider. Jebediah grabbed the pole in front of him with his free hand and maintained his balance. Inside the bus all thirty-five passengers were now awake.

"This is a holdup," Jebediah told everyone. "Anyone tries anything, I'll blow the driver's brains out."

Jebediah gave the speech with rehearsed confidence. He was now holding the revolver in his right hand with his arm not quite fully extended. The clerk had warned him about the gun's recoil, but there were other things to think about now. There was an exit three hundred yards ahead. The driver's face was beaded with perspiration. Behind the bus he could see the Horizon bounce back onto the highway, only to be struck broadside by a white Chevrolet.

"Mother of God."

"Just keep driving. Off at this exit," Jebediah ordered.

Among the passengers panic began to mount. In the middle of the bus, a heavyset woman started screaming hysterically. Then a large black man in the back row said, "Just do as the man says and nobody gets hurt." He didn't shout, but there was something about his low, modulated voice that had the subtle impact of the understated taste of a good single malt scotch. The woman's scream softened into a sob and she turned around. The black man just sat there with a quiet smile on his face. He was at least six-foot-five and must have weighed two hundred and eighty-five pounds. It was well muscled weight, and gave him the physical presence of a well-groomed Muhammad Ali in his prime. The .38 revolver he was holding like a toy in his right hand seemed incidental.

The bus was now on the exit ramp, descending from Route 95 into northeast Philadelphia. It was an old warehouse district. On Sunday morning the buildings that weren't abandoned were empty on their day of rest.

"In here," Jebediah told the driver, pointing to a driveway between two brick factories.

"I—"

"In here," he repeated more emphatically.

The bus just fit between the two buildings. After a hundred feet the driveway widened into a loading area. There was a new Mercury Cougar already parked in the courtyard, a woman sitting behind the wheel. The loading dock to the right was partially covered with a tin roof that extended out over the yard.

"Pull under there."

"If—" The driver was finding it hard to talk, looking up at Jebediah and having to focus, cross-eyed, on the tip of the silencer only a few inches away.

Jebediah twitched the gun slightly so that the driver could see directly into the barrel. "Now, keep quiet and open the door."

The woman walked over from the car. She was wearing a bold-colored designer scarf on her head and a baggy tan Alligator raincoat over a pair of loose-fitting slacks. She also wore oversized sunglasses, the kind of cheap ones you find at a stand on the boardwalk. It was a good disguise. Two of the women on the bus later told police they thought she could have been young, primarily because of the fluid way she moved, but that was the only description they could give and even that was just conjecture. She carried three empty pillowcases over her left arm.

The black man at the back of the bus took charge now. "I'm only saying this once: Everybody put your hands up on the seat in front of you. I want to see everybody's hands on the back of those seats." He paused. "That's real fine." He stood up to get a better view of the bus. "That's fine. Just be cool."

He watched as the woman in the Alligator coat boarded the bus. She laid two of the pillowcases over the armrest of the first seat and held the third one in front of her. She walked over to the man sitting in the second row. "Put your wallet in here," she said, gesturing with the sack. Along with the pillowcase, she carried a revolver, a 9-mm Baretta. The black man had doubted whether she had ever used it. "Hold it if it gives you confidence," he had told her. So she did.

The woman worked through the passengers slowly, one by one, taking the women's purses and asking the men to empty their pockets. In practice, Jebediah had drilled her on the most likely places people would hide money when they traveled. She was careful not to forget about watches, rings, and other jewelry.

A young black-haired girl was especially nervous and fidgety. The woman stopped to check her purse before it went into the pillowcase.

3

"There's only five dollars in here. Where is the rest, honey?" she asked in the harsh tone of a waitress from an all-night diner. She ran her left hand expertly over the girl's body as she began to frisk her. It stopped at the girl's stomach.

"You want to get it, or should I?" the woman asked her. The girl demurely lifted her skirt and took a wad of green bills out from her pantyhose.

While the woman worked through the bus, a fat, balding man near the middle slowly slid his right hand down from the seat in front of him and removed something from his pocket. The black man caught the movement out of the corner of his eye and quietly walked behind him as the fat man was stuffing his treasure between the seat cushions.

"That's dumb," the black man said as he brought his right hand and the gun it carried down in one rapid movement against the side of the man's head like an exclamation point at the end of a sentence. The man rolled unconscious into the aisle.

"Everybody listens; nobody gets hurt," the black man said reassuringly. He reached over and dug a cigarette case from under the cushions where the man had hid it. As he bent to pick up the case, a balding man sitting in the next seat cringed against the window, trying to force his body to melt into the bus itself. The black man just looked him directly in the eyes and smiled.

He stood up, surveying the aisle once more. "Driver, shut off the engine."

Everything was quiet now except for the sounds the woman in the raincoat made as she worked her way through the bus, one passenger at a time. Jebediah still had his revolver pointed at the bus driver's head for everyone to see. A middle-aged, foreign-looking woman left her seat and tried to help the man lying in a heap in the middle of the aisle. She scowled at the black man as she bent down and wiped some of the blood from the man's head with her babushka. The black man met her glance and without a word reached over and helped her lift him up and put him back in his seat.

Jebediah nervously surveyed the bus. "It's time," he said.

"Just about six more to go," the woman replied. Her voice was now more businesslike. It had lost some of its former harshness.

"Now," Jebediah demanded.

"Give the girl a chance," said the black man. "Wouldn't want the rest of these fine folks to feel cheated. This is democracy in action. Everybody gets an equal chance to be robbed."

Jebediah was sweating now. His eyes didn't seem to be focusing. He had to concentrate on his breathing. He could hear his heart pound, and he had to swallow repeatedly to clear the ringing sounds from his ears. The black man noticed the gun begin to tremble slightly in Jebediah's hand.

"I'll give you some help with the last six," he said to the woman in the raincoat.

Two pillowcases were already filled and sitting in the front seat next to Jebediah. They worked quickly on the third. When they finished, Jebediah and the woman took the sacks over to the Mercury. The black man stood by the driver in the front of the bus. He reached over and removed the keys from the dashboard and walked outside, smiling at everyone. "You saved yourself a whole day," he said to no one in particular. "It would take you eight hours easy to lose all that money in the casino. Now when you get to Atlantic City, you can walk on the beach, look at the ocean, enjoy yourselves. Yes, you'll be thanking me by morning."

He calmly stood next to the bus, screwed a silencer onto his revolver, and shot out all six of the tires. The Mercury pulled up next to him. "Have a nice day," the black man said, waving to the passengers, the relaxed grin still firmly fixed on his face, as they drove away.

# Chapter

# 2

I don't believe this," the woman said. She had removed her scarf and Alligator raincoat and sat in a yoga position on the motel bed. The digital clock on the night table read 11:32 A.M. "It's not even noon yet and here we are." She was glowing like a kid at Christmas, surrounded by a pile of purses, wallets, and jewelry instead of the traditional gaily wrapped holiday presents. "Twenty-four thousand in cash, and I still have one more bag to count."

"Don't forget all that jewelry and stuff," the black man said. His name was Napoleon Robespierre Jones—"My mama had this thing about French historical romances," he'd once explained. He was sitting in one of the room's two Danish modern armchairs, leaning back, his feet resting on a corner of the bed. He sipped a can of Schlitz malt liquor, staring at the girl in front of him with the disinterested demeanor of a man drinking at a topless bar.

They were in Room 125 of the El Conquistador Motel by the Philadelphia International Airport. A "Do Not Disturb" sign hung on their door. The "El," as it was known locally, was a seedy stucco affair famous for its discreet management and a two-hundred-percent occupancy rate.

Jebediah leaned on the dresser, smoking his pipe. In a natty sweater, with his long, dark brown hair parted in the middle, he looked the very image of an Oxford student, an image he had assiduously studied in every movie from Robert Taylor's *A Yank in Oxford* to *Oxford Blues*.

"What a fine, fine day, Jebediah," Napoleon said, still looking at Deborah counting their money on the bed.

"We really did it, didn't we?" Jebediah said.

"Yeah, you did good." There was an imperceptible pause until Napoleon continued. "Anyway, Jebediah, you're an A-number-one planner to have figured all this out."

"What a magnificent caper," Deborah said to him. "Come over here and let me give you a great big, wet, soggy kiss." She patted the mattress next to her.

Jebediah stood where he was, holding his pipe and his pose. It was what Robert Taylor would have done. He should have thought more about Robert Taylor during the robbery, but "the voice" started talking to him and broke his concentration.

Napoleon raised his half-empty can of Schlitz in a toast. "To Jebediah, Jeb the Reb, A-number-one planner *extraordinaire*."

The idea for what Deborah insisted on calling "the caper" actually had been more happenstance than planning: the happenstance of Jebediah's having a brief affair with an accountant who liked to gamble, the happenstance of his being invited along for a weekend at the Golden Nugget Casino in Atlantic City.

Gambling was not one of Jebediah's passions, and after a few hours of watching his friend sitting at the blackjack table singularly fixated on the cards, playing like a condemned man facing a firing squad, Jebediah broke away. He took a long stroll up the boardwalk and back down it again, absentmindedly walking into an occasional casino along the way. Between these towers of lights and glitz were the same small, sleazy shops and arcades he remembered as an eight-year-old child on vacation with his mother. The names came back to him: Steel's Fudge,

Taylor's Pork Rolls, Fralinger's Salt Water Taffy. He remembered the way his mother would scrunch up her face when he asked her to stop and let him play the arcade games. She never had approved of what he wanted, he once told Deborah, and soon he learned to keep his desires to himself, secret and apart from her and her ideal of Southern gentility, to which she had tried so long to convert him.

After a while, Jebediah tired of his memories, just as he had tired of the lights and the frenetic noises of the casinos. He found refuge a half-block from the boardwalk, down one of the dimly lit, Monopoly-named avenues where happenstance tugged on his shoulder and beckoned him into that dark bar for a quiet beer.

The bar was called the Hawaiian Café. It looked to Jebediah as if it had last been decorated at the end of the Second World War: black walls, low, indirect lighting from a line of hidden fluorescent bulbs that circled the room two feet from the dingy drop ceiling. A long, U-shaped bar dominated the center of the place, surrounded by ten tables for the more genteel customers, of which, Jebediah thought, there were probably damned few. Cardboard palm trees, faded now, were nailed to the walls and pillars. The jukebox, which had seen better days, played a country and western song. The atmosphere at the Hawaiian Café was as close to most people's vision of Hawaii as Watts in Los Angeles was to Beverly Hills.

Jebediah ordered a beer from the bartender. The bar wasn't busy, but it took the old man in his flowered shirt five minutes to bring it. He was probably the owner, Jebediah thought, just waiting to sell his bar to a casino for the right price and move to Florida.

"You live here?" a man in a bus driver's uniform asked Jebediah from the other end of the bar. He got up and came over with his beer to the stool next to Jebediah's. "The reason I asked is because not too many strangers come in here. Doesn't have all the lights and action the casinos do." He took a small sip from his mug. "Where ya from?"

"Philadelphia," Jebediah answered, looking directly ahead into his own mug of beer.

"Didn't think I saw you here before," the man continued. "Well, you picked a real local landmark." He looked around the room with a proprietary grin on his face. "Been here a lot longer than the casinos. Right, Mike?" The gray-haired bartender grunted and went on with his work.

"I've been driving buses down here since the casinos opened, and I always end up here for one drink. One drink, no more, not when I'm driving." He paused for a second. "What brings you down here?"

Jebediah stared into his beer.

"Silly question. Right? Come down to do a little gambling. Right? Christ, that's the only reason anyone comes here. The city was a regular morgue before the casinos. Mike can tell you. I'm not complaining none, mind you. Gambling's good. It pays my salary. I bring people down here every morning; take them home every night. It's a good living."

Jebediah was concentrating on sending telepathic thoughts to the driver, pleading with him to leave, but it wasn't working.

"Crazy people come here. You know, you sit driving them in a bus every day, you get to know them. I don't gamble, myself. No use for it. Never caught the bug, I guess. But these people, some of them come two, three times a week. Jesus, you wonder where they get the time and money."

Jebediah held up his empty beer mug to the bartender. "Can I get another one of these?"

"You get curious, driving down here every day," the man said, nursing his daily drink. "Just how much are they winning or losing? You know?"

The bartender brought Jebediah a second beer, more quickly this time. Probably out of pity, Jebediah thought.

"People are pretty open after a day of gambling. So I started to ask them how they did. Stands to reason they probably lose more than they win. So I ask them. Told them I was taking a survey for the bus company." He paused, considering the genius of his deception. "The first night I asked, how much do you think this bus lost? Thirty-nine people on the bus. Go on, take a guess."

Jebediah looked over at him for the first time. "I really don't know," he said laconically.

"Come on, take a guess."

"Five thousand," Jebediah said, hoping the end of the conversation was near.

"Yeah," the driver replied, satisfied now that he was talking to a reasonable man. "That's what I thought too, but you want to know how much they lost that night, just on my bus alone? Twenty thousand. The bus isn't even full and these jerks drop twenty grand. Can you believe it? Makes you think, huh?"

It did make Jebediah think, and he thought about it again and again for almost six months. If the people on that man's bus lost twenty thousand dollars, he reasoned, then they had taken more then twenty thousand in cash on the bus with them. Casinos were a cash business, especially for the day-trippers. And there it is, Jebediah thought, all that money in one place, just waiting to be had.

The driver from the Hawaiian Café said he started his daily trek at seven-thirty each morning from Altamont, Pennsylvania. Curious, Jebediah rented a car and drove to Altamont to ride the bus for himself. He arrived a half-hour before it was scheduled to leave, and immediately he felt that he had made a terrible mistake. Altamont was a gray, coal-mining town that both the coal barons and the militant labor unions had ravaged and then deserted decades before. As Jebediah looked down the main street, with its empty storefronts and its aura of desolation, he doubted that all the townsfolk together could come up with twenty thousand in cash.

Still, he boarded the bus. There was a different driver. The one he'd met at the café had probably talked himself to death, Jebediah thought. The front seat opposite the driver was empty, and Jebediah took it. He watched as the other passengers started to arrive. They were mostly middle-aged, a good many obviously of Italian or Slavic descent. He looked at their haircuts, the way the women held themselves, the polyester clothing. They were poor people, like the poor people Jebediah grew up with in rural North Carolina, like poor people the world over.

Some seemed to be regulars. They joked about the Atlantic City Express, "Ace" they called it, and they called each other "Aces" too. There was a carnival atmosphere on the bus, but underneath the bright talk Jebediah sensed lives that were as gray and lifeless as Altamont itself.

Once they arrived at Atlantic City, Jebediah cashed in the tokens the smiling casino hostess gave to each person who walked off the bus and went out on the boardwalk, where he sat for several hours staring across the beach at the ocean beyond.

True, he concluded, the people on the bus were not the affluent high rollers he'd expected to find, but they were the type who might save up far more money than they should spend on a day at the casinos, and, at least for that brief time, escape the depression of their everyday world. For some reason this thought cheered him up. He walked along the boardwalk with a lighthearted bounce and decided to buy a Taylor's Pork Roll sandwich, something his mother had scrunched up her face over twenty years before. As he ate it, greedily, he could almost see her disapproving look.

Even though his talks with fellow passengers on the return trip confirmed what the bus driver from the Hawaiian Café had told him, all of Jebediah's thoughts remained unfertilized seeds until happenstance once again took him by the hand—this time in the form of Napoleon Robespierre Jones.

Since his days at college, Jebediah had worked in the highly specialized world of rare books. He could absorb tens of thousands of isolated facts about titles and editions, then make the serendipitous connections between them. If he handled a book once, he remembered it. He knew who the best customers were and what types of books specifically interested them. He knew the desires of his collectors better than he knew his own, and, most important, he was honest. All of this made him a fine employee and bookshop manager, but after all was said and done, this was a dubious achievement. His pay was low, the hours long, and in the entrepreneurial business he had chosen, the gap between himself and his employer, created by Jebediah's lack of money, would always be unbridgable.

It was the spring after his trip to Atlantic City, and Jebediah was in New York at the Seventh Regimental Armory on Park Avenue for the annual Antiquarian Book Fair. He was helping his new employer, Brad Parker, arrange his booth at the fair. They had just flown from Williamsburg, Virginia, the night before, and Jebediah was alone in the booth trying to make order from the chaos of unassembled bookcases, trunks of books, and a dirty glass display case that looked, from the grease and grime on its glass front, as if it had come from an all-night gas station. Brad Parker had assumed the privilege of ownership and was walking around the floor looking at the books the other one hundred and five exhibitors were showing.

Jebediah was searching for a book fair worker to help him remove a table from the booth when he saw a familiar shape in blue overalls. He wasn't sure at first—the bluish-green haze from the exhaust of cars and trucks unloading books had given the Armory the aura of a painting by Toulouse-Lautrec—but as Jebediah walked toward the man, staring at his massive back, he became more certain.

"Napoleon?" he asked.

The mass turned toward him. "Jebediah Stuart," it said. "Damn. It must be ten years. Hey," Napoleon called to the man working with him, "this here's my college roommate." A wide, warm grin fell easily over his face.

They met later that evening at a Greenwich Village bar Napoleon knew.

"Ten years," Napoleon said.

"Lafayette College, Easton, Pennsylvania."

"What an armpit."

"Who was that man who paid you to play football for the school?"

" 'Wild Bill' Glitzmore, the Used Car King of Long Island. The man offered me thirty thousand a year, actually paid me the first fifteen thousand."

"Yeah, but I remember something about him trying to kill you."

"Wasn't my fault. I made all-M.A.C. conference defense—the first freshman ever to do it. Wasn't my fault that pussy quarterback of ours fell and broke his arm."

"I don't remember that."

"You didn't pay too much attention to sports back then, as I recall." Napoleon took a sip of beer. "I remember, though. The Thursday before the Lehigh game, Coach Palmyra, he calls an all-out practice. 'Game conditions,' he told us. So our quarterback sets to pass and I hit him blindside. He kinda broke his arm."

"That's why Glitzmore tried to kill you?"

"No. But he was sore. It was when he was up at the Holiday Inn with a bunch of cronies—made a weekend of the game. He found me in bed boffing his daughter. Seventeen. What a piece of ass."

"Oh."

"One hell of a crazy time."

"Yeah."

"Jebediah, you were a pitiful dude back then. You even stopped going to classes after the first few weeks."

"I stopped for aesthetic reasons."

"That's it. That's what you told them." Napoleon sat back and laughed.

"We both left after the first semester."

"Flunked out, as I recall."

"Yeah, but we shouldn't have been there in the first place."

"Amen. We were certainly two bad-ass misfits."

Jebediah told Napoleon about the way his life had progressed since Lafayette, and then listened to Napoleon.

"Been working for the International Brotherhood of Teamsters, mostly. Hard, bull-work at first till they found out I was good at helping to negotiate contracts. I just sit there. The man likes a big, black dude like me in the room to help show folks the righteousness of his cause." He stopped to pour the remainder of a bottle of beer into his glass, staring at the head as it flowed over the rim. "What I want, what I'd like, is maybe to own a bar someday. It just takes money. That's all."

They talked a little more and then Jebediah told Napoleon about his trip to Atlantic City and the man from the Hawaiian Café.

"And you checked it out yourself?"

"I did."

"Damn."

Napoleon sat back in his chair and looked at Jebediah.

"What are you thinking?" Jebediah asked.

"Same as you, I suppose. Sounds like two smart fellas could pick themselves up a little seed money. Become entrepreneurs."

"I agree."

"Forty-five thousand in cash, gentlemen," Deborah announced from the middle of the motel bed.

"And the watches and jewelry," Napoleon added.

"What about credit cards?" Jebediah asked.

"Don't have a fence for them. They could be trouble."

"Then let's just toss them where they can't be found."

"Okay."

Napoleon reached into his pocket and took out a cheap cigarette case. "Here, I almost forgot," he said, throwing it across the room to Jebediah. "This is what the fat man tried to hide between the seats."

Jebediah opened the case and turned it around to examine it. He handed it to Deborah. "What's so special about this?"

"It's no antique," Deborah said with authority. "It probably has some sentimental value."

"The fool took a big chance trying to hide it."

"You'd think he would have tried to hide his wallet. He had three thousand dollars in it," Deborah said.

"Three thousand? You sure?"

"Yes." Deborah reached into the pile of wallets and pulled one out. "Joseph Sabatino."

"How can you be so sure that's him?"

"How many people did you knock unconscious today?" Deborah asked. "Anyway, I remembered because I was surprised at how much money he had."

"Strange."

"People *are* strange, Jebediah."

"We don't smoke," Deborah said, looking at Jebediah. "Do you want this as a souvenir?"

Jebediah looked at it again. "Sure."

"And now the money, gentlemen," Deborah said in a more formal tone. "I get five thousand and you divide the rest."

"Jeb and I think we should cut it three ways," Napoleon said.

"We agreed that my cut was five thousand and you two would divide the rest. Anyway, I have a rich husband to support me."

"What do you want me to do with the money I get from the fence?" Napoleon asked.

"Keep it until we see each other again."

"We really shouldn't be in contact for a few months," Deborah said.

"The lady's right."

"We'll set a date and meet again three months from today," Jebediah said.

"Maybe we could spend a weekend in Atlantic City."

Deborah drove Jebediah to the airport to catch his plane for Norfolk. She took her own station wagon. The Mercury Cougar they had used for the robbery, which they'd rented on a phony credit card and driver's license Napoleon had bought for the occasion, was now safely and

anonymously in the Philadelphia International Airport's parking lot—
no fingerprints, no personal belongings.

"What am I going to do without you?" Deborah asked.

It was a rhetorical question, and Jebediah didn't feel the need to
answer. He sat there for another moment being Robert Taylor, his pipe
between his teeth and the strains of an Oxford school song resounding
in his head.

"I'm serious," Deborah continued. "Life won't be the same anymore."

"You'll find something. You always do."

"Nothing as exciting as this. All I have is Gerald." Deborah said it
as if she had discovered that the cat had thrown up on the table just
before Christmas dinner.

"At least as far as husbands go, it's a plus that he's a rich one."

"Rich and boring."

Deborah had married Gerald Hamilton shortly after the incident she
had labeled her "TV Commercial Disaster." She told Jebediah the story
one night after far too many black russians. It started with her leaving
home in Athens, Ohio, to go to New York City to become an actress.
Armed with a large portfolio of photographs, courtesy of a good but
libidinous photographer from Cleveland, she began auditioning and
making the rounds. After four weeks, she finally was called back for a
second reading by an executive of a small advertising agency looking for
a "Miss Safety" to represent a pharmaceutical company's new birth-
control product.

"I should have known," she told Jebediah. "No one would shoot an
advertising campaign in Room 512 of the Algonquin Hotel. But then,
I was young and naive."

"You went?"

"Yes, and of course there was no crew there. Just the advertising
executive wearing little more than his leer. You might say the cad
forcibly had his way with me."

"You might say that. I wouldn't. Nobody says 'cad' anymore."

The next day, Deborah sent two telegrams, one to the man's wife, the second to the president of the guy's agency. "I don't know how his wife reacted, but I do know that the cad was escorted from his office by security an hour after my telegram arrived. It seems that he raped me in a room he'd charged to the agency. Billing the company for the room was the more serious crime in their eyes, and grounds for instant dismissal. Anyway, I married Gerald soon after that and gave up my career."

Over the years they had been friends, Jebediah had heard many "Deborah" stories and remembered them all. In return Deborah used their friendship as a cover for a long string of affairs with enough different men to make Jebediah lose count and then lose interest.

"Doesn't your husband ever get suspicious?" he'd asked her once.

"Gerald? If Gerald suspected, he'd only try to figure out a way to make a buck off of it."

Shortly after Jebediah met Napoleon in New York, he told Deborah of his idea for robbing the passengers on the Atlantic City Express.

"How perfectly poetic," she told him. "Fleece the customers before the casinos can get their hands on them." Later she said, "Please, I can be a great help planning, and from the way you talk, you're going to need three people to do the actual caper." Deborah was always persuasive, doubly so when she was right.

Deborah drove up the ramp and left Jebediah in the area reserved for Piedmont's departing passengers.

"Take care of yourself," Jebediah said, reaching over and kissing her proffered cheek.

"You do the same."

Jebediah grabbed the overnight tote with his twenty thousand dollars cash inside, and got out of the car. He had wanted to say more, but he knew that Robert Taylor would have silently and bravely walked away. So he simply shut the door and gave Deborah a jaunty little wave and a shy, vulnerable smile.

Inside the terminal Jebediah got his seat assignment and found a bar to spend the thirty minutes he had to wait before boarding. He sat by the television set. The sound was turned low so that he could only hear some of the words. ". . . this commercial break," he heard the anchorman say, ". . . return with news . . . local bus hijacking . . . gamblers . . . Atlantic City."

The commercials seemed to take forever. The last one featured a man running in circles and shouting, "Insane." Jebediah wished it was on a videotape so that he could turn it to "fast forward"—a feature he regretted was not available in real life. He had gulped down his first beer and ordered a second before the neatly groomed newsman came back on the screen. The man's intensity told the viewer that this was quite a story. Jebediah wondered how he would react to World War Three. "First hijacking of a bus . . . three perpetrators." An artist's sketch of a woman appeared on the television. It was a nondescript face that could as easily have belonged to a bag lady as to the Queen of England. The next one was of an archetypical black with a flat nose and large lips made more real to Jebediah by the voice describing the assailant as "six-foot-six, two hundred and fifty pounds." Then, finally, a sketch of Jebediah flashed on the screen. Three new people came into the bar then, and he had even more difficulty hearing over their noise. Jebediah did make out the words "neurotic . . . terrorized . . . front of bus." He listened harder, but he did not hear the anchorman use the name Robert Taylor once in describing him. The sketch was not Jebediah's best likeness, too thin, he thought, but it was a closer image than those of the other two. The neatly dressed newscaster returned again, looking sad but forthright. ". . . bus driver . . . guarded, but stable . . . apparent heart attack." He added in still-graver tones that "the driver of the Horizon . . . struck . . . pronounced dead on arrival."

Horizons are terrible cars, Jebediah thought. The man should have known better than to buy one. He got up from the bar and left a dime on the counter as a tip, deciding to wait for his plane at the gate. A policeman stood in the corridor, and Jebediah watched his eyes closely to see if they would betray any sign of recognition from his appearance on television. They didn't, and he hurried past. He looked down at his tote bag and tried to think of a story he could tell if the policeman actually did stop him—something that would explain why he was carrying twenty thousand dollars in cash. He couldn't think of one.

His mind was still inventing possible scenarios when he noticed passengers stopping at the X-ray station just ahead of him. He absentmindedly had begun to put his bag on the moving belt. Then he remembered that he had packed his Smith and Wesson in with the money. He stopped sharply and snatched the bag back, bumping an elderly man behind him. The collision tottered the old man, and Jebediah held onto him until he regained his balance.

"Stupid," he heard the old man hiss through his dentures.

Jebediah turned and walked quickly back down the hall, rushing into the first men's room he could find. He went into an empty stall and slid the bolt to lock the door. He stood there clutching the bag and waited until his breathing returned to normal. "Christ," he said out loud.

There were sounds of footsteps and flushing urinals outside, and it wasn't until he felt alone and in control of himself again that he released his death grip on the tote bag, unzipped it, and removed the Smith and Wesson. He sat on the toilet seat and took off his undershirt, using it carefully to wipe his fingerprints from the gun. Satisfied, he put his shirt back on, using the undershirt to wrap the Smith and Wesson. It was quiet outside again and Jebediah took a deep breath before he left, dropping gun and undershirt into the trash basket by the paper towel dispenser.

He went through security once more without raising any comment. He felt even more relaxed as he was waiting for the plane. Christ, he thought. If the bag had gone through the machine, they would have pulled me aside for questioning.

Jebediah had fantasized being questioned by the police. He was a good liar, he knew that, able to keep a poker face when he talked, even believing for that brief moment that what he said was the truth. But he doubted that he could sustain one of his stories through long questioning. He would confess and end up in jail. He had thought a good deal about prison during the past three months. He had decided that if he were caught, he would kill himself rather than serve time. Napoleon had laughed at him when Jebediah mentioned this. "Wouldn't be too hasty," Napoleon had said. "Not many pretty boys like you in stir. You'd be real popular. Might even learn to like it."

Jebediah sat at the gate clutching his bag and boarded the plane when his row number was called. A feeling of relief washed over him as the plane finally left the ground. When the stewardess came around, Jebediah ordered two scotches. "Yankee liquor" his mother used to call it, in her derogatory way. Jebediah had developed a taste for it at college, along with a thousand other things he knew his mother would not approve of.

The scotches and the drone of the plane's engines made him relaxed and drowsy. Money, he told himself. It's bound to make life better, make life easier. He sat on the plane staring at the bag in front of him, half-awake, thinking now of his life as a rising spiral, rising from that sleepy North Carolina town where he was raised, rising from the genteel poverty with his mother, rising from the shame of growing up without a father, a father who'd left when he was only a baby. He had often wondered, as a boy, in the darkness of his room just before falling asleep, if his father had left because of him. But I have money now, he murmured in the netherworld between wakefulness and dreaming. The thought comforted him, and Jebediah was smiling as the airplane's wheels finally screeched against the runway at Norfolk and the plane slowed to taxi safely to the gate.

# Chapter
# 3

**B**rad Parker walked in the door of Parker's Rare Books carrying his cat, Fleder, in her red cardboard case.

"Any calls, Mrs. Johnson?"

Mrs. Johnson, the shop's accountant and part-time sales clerk, came out from the wrapping room behind the cash register, pouring the remains from a tiny bottle of what she called her "medicinal sugar water" into a cup of coffee.

"What?" she said sharply, recovering herself gracefully, like a Southern belle caught necking at the cotillion ball. "Oh, Mr. Parker, I didn't hear you come in."

"Any calls, Mrs. Johnson?" he asked again, louder this time.

"Just two. Mr. Avery called. He said to tell you he will be here just before noon to see the books."

"Here?" Brad asked, mildly surprised. Jonathan Avery rarely left his estate, but had sufficient wealth and fame to make Brad's frequent visits to him not seem like an imposition.

"Yes. He also asked me to tell you that he was going to have lunch at Rusterman's afterward and that you were invited to join him." As she talked, Mrs. Johnson watched the ritual of Brad letting Fleder out of her case. "You're not going to go to lunch and leave me alone here with that cat again, are you?"

"With poor little Fleder?" Brad cooed in the slightly higher voice he reserved for the cat. Fleder seemed to sense the situation and rubbed against Brad's hand. "Who was the other call from?" he asked in his normal voice.

"Mrs. Riesling. She wouldn't leave a message. Wants you to call her back. Here's the telephone number." She handed Brad a slip of paper. "Now, what about the cat!"

"Not to worry," he reassured her. "Jebediah will watch her."

Fleder was fifteen years old and the last remnant of Brad's earlier life. Brad felt guilty leaving the cat alone in the apartment each day, so he found a cat at the SPCA to serve as the grande dame's companion. Fleder, however, would not share her turf with another animal, and Brad was forced to take the newcomer back to the shelter. Now each morning he folded Fleder into a red cardboard carrying case and brought her to the bookshop. Fleder, for her part, seemed to enjoy the change of scenery. Her favorite spot in the store was the corner of an open bookcase in the front window. She would jump effortlessly from floor to table to shelf and lie there, motionless, watching the tourists as they walked past outside along Duke of Gloucester Street.

When she tired of the view, Fleder would bound up the stairs to Brad's office and the adjoining bathroom, where her food dish and litterbox were kept. Her only other activity was tormenting Mrs. Johnson. Never having been around cats before coming to work at Parker's Rare Books, Mrs. Johnson seemed unable to adapt. Fleder's pleasure was to pounce unexpectedly onto her lap, producing a variety of terrified screams, which seemed to satisfy Fleder immensely.

"Is Jebediah here?"

"Not yet."

"Tell him when he gets in to come up to my office," Brad said.

Brad's office was on the second floor. When he first opened the bookshop, he had worked at a small desk in the area behind the cash register. Brad liked the contact with his customers, talking about their interests and enthusiasms, but as the business grew, and he started issuing catalogs, these pleasant diversions became interruptions, and when he began thinking, more and more, of his customers as tourists with ice cream cones, Brad knew that it was time to build a separate office for himself.

He spent a month with a local architect redesigning the entire second floor of his shop. Along with the office, Brad created a Rare Book Room to hold his best books. The room was richly paneled in oak and had a parquet floor, partially covered by a large red-and-blue Karastan rug he had bought for a bargain price at a local auction. Along the walls were six glass-fronted bookcases, mostly from the nineteenth and early twentieth centuries, and one short expanse of built-in shelving. In the middle of the room was a small oak library table covered by an old tapestry that Phyllis, Brad's wife, had bought in a small antique shop just south of Sloane Square in London the year before the accident.

With his more expensive books upstairs, Brad gave a greater portion of the shop itself over to prints. There were always a few Audubons and Catesbys, handsome eighteenth-century mezzotint portraits, and colorful Currier and Ives scenes. The books on the shelves tended toward polished leather-bound sets, signed books, and unusual works on a wide variety of subjects. Since the shop was in Williamsburg, there were several sections of eighteenth-century works in their original calf bindings—books that might have been in American libraries at the time of the Revolution. Brad still was able to show some of his best books in the shop area behind glass display cases, hinting to the true collector that further treasures awaited upstairs.

The office gave him the buffer zone he needed, and he had settled into a pleasant routine, meeting other booksellers, traveling to buy new stock for the shelves, and developing a rapidly expanding mailing list of new customers. Now he could meet them one at a time and give them the personal attention they deserved. The office was the most worthwhile investment, aside from the business itself, that he had ever made. It kept him sane.

Brad went into his office and dialed the number Greta Riesling had given Mrs. Johnson. "Good morning, Greta. Brad Parker," he said cheerfully. There was a long silence.

"Carl died last night," a flat voice finally answered. The coldness in her voice somehow mirrored Carl Riesling, her husband, himself. Brad pictured the heavyset, bearded enigma, wearing one of his many sweaters and looking slightly disheveled. He remembered the sour odor that hung around him. Never a close friend, Carl had still been a fellow bookseller.

"Oh, Christ." Brad recovered slightly and asked, "Are you all right?" Then, "Is anyone with you?"

"Yes. Mrs. Woods from next door is in the living room." She was silent again; Brad knew she was collecting herself and mentally rephrasing her thoughts from her native German to English. "Carl told me, if anything ever happened to him, to sell his books to you. He said you were a fair man."

"I'm sorry about Carl, Greta." He wanted to ask her how Carl had died, but something in her manner put him off. There was another, longer pause. Finally Greta asked, "When can you come out and make an offer on the lot? I want to sell the stock and the reference library both."

"Greta, now's not the time."

"There is no better time. I want to clean up this business."

Brad said patiently, "I'm not sure that you know, but I lost my wife and two children in an automobile accident five years ago. I mention this because I understand a little about what you must be going through. Now is a time for mourning; business can wait."

"I know what I am doing," Greta said, her German accent thickening as she talked. "I must have the books removed before I can put this horrible house up for sale. That I want to do as soon as possible."

Brad realized that the telephone was not the place to continue this conversation.

"So I ask again, when can you come here?"

"I'm tied up at the shop until after lunch," Brad finally said. "I can be there at four if that's convenient."

"Four is fine."

Brad held the telephone through another long pause, until he heard Greta gently hang up her receiver. He listened to the silence on the line until it was replaced by the sound of the dial tone. He remembered his own family now and felt the deep pain and emptiness of the past, terrible feelings he thought he had buried or merely outlived. He was close to tears, but then he abruptly became aware of Jebediah standing at the door with a supercilious expression on his face and his pipe firmly clenched between his teeth.

Brad had come to regret hiring Jebediah. While he respected him as a bookman, he could never envision liking him. He had discovered a sneakiness and arrogance in Jebediah and a cold, snobbish aloofness that made it impossible for anyone to get close to him. It was a feeling several of his customers shared about his young assistant, and Brad knew he would eventually have to do something about it. For this one particular moment, though, he was grateful for the interruption.

"Sorry I'm late. Had to stop off at the bank first. Rent a safe-deposit box."

"That's okay, but before you do anything else, would you get the books we have been saving for Jonathan and put them out on the table in the Rare Book Room? He'll be here in less than an hour."

"The great Mr. Avery is gracing our humble commercial establishment with his presence?" Jebediah said with mock solemnity.

"Yes, and I haven't had a chance to go over the books myself. You'll have to do that for me. Make sure any old prices are erased, spiff them up—you know the procedure."

The telephone rang and was answered downstairs. Then the intercom buzzed on Brad's desk. "Miss Frye is on line one," said Mrs. Johnson, "and Peter Eastrovich is here to see you."

Brad looked up at Jebediah. "You know what to do, then," he said.

Jebediah nodded.

"Mrs. Johnson," he said into the intercom, "give me a minute before you send Peter up." With that Brad picked up the telephone. Jebediah was still standing in the door with a vague smile on his face, as if he wanted to say something to him. Brad cupped the receiver with his hand and asked, "Yes?"

"Nothing. Nothing, really," Jebediah responded vacuously, and walked away.

"Hello, Brad."

"There you are, Miss Frye, on line one as promised."

"But you only have one line, my dear."

"Mrs. Johnson has great expectations for this business," Brad said. "It's good to hear your voice. When did you get back?"

"Last night, but I was too tired to call. I thought I did see Jebediah at the airport, though. Where was he?"

"He had the weekend off, but he didn't say anything to me about going away."

"Oh, well. It could have been someone else."

"When can I see you?"

"How about dinner at my place tonight?"

"Sounds fine, Sam," said Brad. "Oh—"

"What's wrong?"

"I don't know if I can. Greta Riesling called. Carl, her husband, just died. I have to go out there at four."

"Riesling? Did I ever meet them?"

"I don't think so. Carl ran a book business about five miles outside of town."

"How did he die?"

"You know, I never even asked."

"You couldn't have been close friends, or I would have heard about them."

"I don't think anyone was close to Carl. He was a rather unpleasant character, actually. I'm not looking forward to going."

"I've never heard you say anything bad about another bookseller before. He really must have been gruesome."

"He was."

"How did he manage to stay in business?"

"It was totally mail order. He issued catalogs—low-grade scholarly stuff mainly. He seemed okay enough over the telephone, but no one ever stopped at his place to buy that I was aware of. He wouldn't let them."

"Have you ever been there?"

"Once. He came across a library of private press books and sold them to me. He had to let me come out and take a look at them."

"I've got an idea," Samantha said. "How about if I knock off early and go out there with you? Then we can have dinner when you're finished. Maybe we can even have some Liebfraumilch after the Rieslings. Vat do you say?"

"I say it sounds delightful; especially the part about coming home to port. I'll want to leave around three-thirty; can you meet me here?"

"Shop . . . three-thirty," she repeated.

As he replaced the telephone receiver, Brad could hear Peter Eastrovich in the corridor outside his office where the reference library was and the books Brad held on quote for his mail-order customers. Over the years Brad had made it a practice to send out letters offering his customers a book he thought they might like before it appeared in one of his catalogs.

"I see you found it," Brad said. Peter did not look away from the seventeenth-century book of aphorisms Brad had told him about. He held it barely four inches from his eyes, scanning an engraving in it.

"The only good thing about being as nearsighted as I am is that you don't have to carry a magnifying glass with you for occasions like this," Peter said without looking up.

"It's a nice, fresh copy, isn't it?"

"That it is," Peter acknowledged, finally glancing at Brad and bringing his glasses down from his forehead.

Peter Eastrovich reminded Brad of a slightly overweight Lenin. He had a sharply trimmed goatee and a severely receding hairline. He was in his early forties, and during the three years Brad had known him his face had become more round and jowly. Peter's eyes sparkled whenever he talked about books. They were his passion, and he pursued them with zeal and fanaticism.

"Anything exciting happening at the college?" Brad asked.

"The present administration has seen fit to cut my budget by twenty percent," Peter said. Eastrovich was the Rare Book Librarian at the College of William and Mary.

"Sorry to hear that."

"Well, I'll just have to work harder to find some endowment money, won't I?" Peter spoke flatly; he obviously lacked the force of resolution needed for fundraising.

Brad had felt for some time that Peter Eastrovich was a minor genius who had never found his particular niche in life. His work at William and Mary had become a war with the administration. He was good at what he did—in fact he was very good. He had the right blend of enthusiasm and knowledge for developing the rare book collections under his jurisdiction. His successes spurred him forward to new ideas and projects, at a speed that was increasingly out of sync with the activities of his supervisors and the college. A certain amount of national publicity had brought on the usual peevish reactions from his peers, and when Peter looked higher in the local political structure for support, he'd found that no one cared. The last thing anyone in authority wanted to do was to explain to a state legislature why the college spent increasingly larger sums of money on rare books.

"You have good collections here," Peter had told the head librarian. "If you want them to be great, you have to fill them in when the opportunities arise, and when a really great book comes along, bite the bullet and buy it." The message was clear, but the money was not forthcoming. Over the years Peter's frustration had turned to anger, and this anger isolated him at the college, where he had few friends.

At one time Jonathan Avery had been looking for a librarian to oversee and develop his fledgling collection of English and American literature. Brad had recommended Peter, and there was a lengthy job interview, but the two men did not hit it off, as Jonathan had explained to Brad, and the matter was dropped.

"Are you free for lunch?" Peter asked Brad.

"Not really. I'm expecting Jonathan Avery in the shop in a few minutes. He's already invited me to join him."

"I won't stay, then. Wouldn't want to embarrass you."

"You're not an embarrassment, Peter."

"Well, Avery and I aren't exactly chummy, and I wouldn't want to cause any friction between you." Peter hesitated a minute. "You and Avery are fairly close, aren't you?"

"I would say so," Brad answered. "Why do you ask?"

"Have you ever taken the time to look at his collection?"

"He's bought a good deal of it through the shop," Brad answered warily.

"But did you ever really take the time to go through the collection, book by book?"

"Just to make 'want' lists on authors Jonathan wanted to complete in first editions."

"Never to look at books Avery bought from other dealers?"

"Peter, what are you driving at?"

"I don't know whether you're aware of it or not, but I've been doing some research with the collection."

"And?"

"Well, I've been finding some peculiar things and I just wanted to know if anyone else had seen them too."

"What do you mean, 'peculiar'?"

"Nothing I want to talk about now. We don't have the time, for one thing." Peter held up the book of aphorisms. "Did you notice that these plates are by Theodore de Bry? You didn't mention them in your description."

"Peter!"

"It's too late to raise the price. It's mine."

"Peter, what about Jonathan's collection?"

"Can you send a bill to me at the library?" Peter asked, already halfway down the stairs.

"What about Jonathan's library?"

"Some other time. I promise." Peter turned around. "Enjoy your lunch."

"Let Mrs. Johnson copy our code off of the book before you leave," Brad called after him. As he returned to his desk, he glanced into the Rare Book Room and saw Jebediah dusting the top edges of Jonathan's books, seemingly lost in his work.

# Chapter

## 4

Joseph Sabatino stood by the pay phone next to the Atlantic
Terrace Motel in Montauk, Long Island. The beach, in off-season,
was empty, and as Joey looked out over the sand dunes in front
of him, he could not see even a fisherman for two miles in either
direction. There was just Joey, and the sounds of the surf, the wind,
and the gulls. He looked at his watch and waited for the second hand
to sweep around one more time and read two o'clock, exactly. Then he
picked up the telephone and dialed the number he had been given the
day before. He heard a tone and entered his credit-card number. A
mechanical voice thanked him.

The credit card was a gift from a man Joey knew from Las Vegas. It
belonged to the man's wholesale food business. "Use it for business
calls," the man had told Joey. "They'll be harder to trace." Joey had
thanked him and had used the card number ever since for all his
long-distance calls, business and personal. No one had ever questioned
him about it.

The telephone rang twice. "You're sure you got a safe line?"

"Jesus," Joey said in disgust.

"Okay. I'll patch you through. Remember, don't use any names."

Joey hated all the new high-tech equipment his bosses had started to use, and he hated the high-tech people who went along with it. ("Only thing they respect is their goddamned machines. College boys. Huh.") Joey liked the old days when if you had a problem and needed to talk to someone, you sat down across a table from the man, eyeball to eyeball, and settled the matter then and there. Respect, Joey thought. They showed respect then.

"I understand you had a problem delivering the merchandise," said a voice from the telephone. It was a slightly garbled transmission, but Joey recognized the voice clearly.

"Yes, sir."

"I was told that a man hit you and it was he who took the merchandise."

"Yes."

"Question: If he knocked you unconscious, how are you sure that he was the one to take the package?"

"When I got back to my seat, it was gone. The fella sitting next to me said he saw the nigger take it. I don't think he lied."

"The people who did this, how many of them were there?"

"Three."

"Did you recognize anyone?"

"I never seen them before."

"Could you identify any of them if you saw them again?"

"The nigger, definitely. You don't forget someone who zaps you."

"And the others?"

"The skinny one in the front holding the big piece, I can make him. The broad I'm not too sure of. She was all covered up like."

"These people. Did they just take money, or did they take watches and jewelry?"

Joey paused to think. "The girl took one watch I can remember. Yeah. I think they pretty much took what they could get."

"Are you sure of that?"

"Yeah. I'm sure."

34

"Good. I'll have people check on the usual outlets for that sort of merchandise. Perhaps we'll get lucky and our package will be among the goods."

"I hope so."

"If not, we may be able to come up with the name of the salesman at least."

"What do you want me to do?" Joey asked.

"Go home. Call the laundry each morning at ten and ask if your shirts are ready. We'll let you know if we find the package."

"Anything else?"

"By the way, how is your head?"

Joey smiled. "All right, I guess."

"It was good you were able to get out of the bus before the police arrived and that you could call us. That was good thinking."

"Thanks."

"Now, remember. Ten A.M. every day."

"Call the laundry and ask for my shirts."

"Right."

# Chapter

# 5

Anthony Patronsky came into the bookshop first and looked around. He was a neat, nondescript man in a light gray suit, white shirt, and dark striped tie. A casual observer wouldn't be able to pick him out of a crowd easily, unless he happened to look into his eyes. They moved constantly in short darting glances, taking in everything they saw. Patronsky had scanned the bookshop and was apparently satisfied with the scene, because he held the door open for Jonathan Avery and another man. The other man was shorter and balding, but he was dressed almost exactly like Anthony Patronsky. His name was Felix. There was a chauffeur, Joel, waiting for them outside in Jonathan Avery's limousine. Privately Jonathan referred to the trio as Larry, Moe, and Curly.

Jonathan smiled and said hello to Mrs. Johnson as he passed. Then he went directly up the stairs to Brad's office without waiting to be announced. His bodyguards stood in the shop looking at books near the base of the staircase. Jonathan had acquired the trio after the FBI uncovered a kidnapping plot against him. They had stumbled on the information when they raided what turned out to be the headquarters of a worldwide terrorist group outside of Asbury Park, New Jersey.

"I'm not worried about terrorist groups per se, especially ones with headquarters in Asbury Park, but the fact that the FBI in all their penurious wisdom saw fit to offer me agents to guard my person twenty-four hours a day—that scared the living hell out of me," he'd admitted to Brad.

The addition of three full-time shadows to Jonathan's household had had little effect on his life-style. He had been living a retiring existence since, as Jonathan so aptly phrased it, "I became disgustingly wealthy from computers in the mid-sixties."

"Hello," he called out now at the top of the stairs. "Where are my Anthony Powells?" He greeted Brad with a "Good to see you" and a gigantic bear hug that lifted the bookseller off his feet.

Brad led Avery into the Rare Book Room, where the volumes destined for him sat on the library table in the center of the room. Anthony Powell's important twelve-novel roman à clef, *A Dance to the Music of Time*, follows the book's main character from his childhood, just before the First World War, through the 1960s. All the characters were based on real-life artists and socialites in England. Brad had found a spectacular set of the novels that a close friend of Powell had once owned. The owner had had the books rebound and interleaved with blank pages and there had written notes about the real people and incidents on which Powell's fictional world was based. The author himself, probably over several late-night brandies, had thoroughly annotated the set in his own hand, adding ribald comments and libelous gossip that was not to be found in the printed text.

"Ahhhh," Jonathan hooted. "This is marvelous, Brad." He pointed to a page in the book. "This incident with Widmerpool actually happened to Hubert, Fiona's uncle. Look here, Powell even mentions the old goat in this note."

Brad watched Jonathan alternately giggle and roar as he paged through the set. This is what Brad liked most about selling books. There weren't too many professions he could think of where you could make someone as happy as Jonathan was at that moment.

Jonathan stood by the table for some time examining his new purchase. He wore a baggy Brooks Brothers suit, one of twelve he had bought with his first fortune when he was still in college. He still wore one of them daily. Jonathan was completely absorbed in the books, like a child at play. It was hard to watch his zest for life without admiration.

Brad often wondered if this excitement spilled over into Avery's work at NASA. He had never been able to get a clear picture of what Jonathan did from the computer experts or bureaucratic types that he occasionally met at Avery's estate. They were a close-mouthed lot—a prerequisite for the job, no doubt. The nearest he ever came had been at a dinner party, when an overweight executive sitting next to him volunteered that he was "damned glad Avery's working on our side. Man's a national resource like the Grand Canyon. He's the only person I know who even stands a chance of getting old Reagan's Star Wars program off the ground." That said, the man sat back in his chair, and didn't speak another word for the rest of the meal.

When Jonathan was completing his freshman year at MIT, he had asked his father for a loan of twenty thousand dollars to start a company that would manufacture a computer device he had invented. "Simply, the gizmo let one computer talk to another, and we had programming worked out so that we could translate from one manufacturer's machine to another's. By the end of the summer we had worked out most of the design glitches, and then IBM came along and offered me seven and a half million dollars for the company—patents and all. This was still the nineteen sixties, mind you. We were very advanced."

Jonathan had accepted the offer. "All IBM wanted was to tuck the patents away someplace for safekeeping. A guy at NASA who has a mind for such things told me that IBM saved over three hundred million just in keeping the device off the market so that their competitors could be frozen out of the game. He asked if that bothered me. I told him not at all. I went back and spent my entire sophomore year inventing new gizmos and selling them to the IBM boys."

Jonathan had left school early that year with a personal fortune just shy of thirty million dollars and never again worried about lacking enough money for anything he wanted to do.

Jonathan usually didn't talk about his past, his work for the government, his personal life with Fiona. He kept all of these parts of his life in their own little nooks and crannies. Even though Brad was one of Jonathan's closest friends, their relationship was confined almost exclusively to the world of books. Brad felt singularly honored on those rare occasions when Jonathan did reminisce.

"I was born the day after Pearl Harbor, back in 1941," Jonathan once told him. "It was one hell of a day for our family. My grandfather, Samuel Avery—I never told you about him, did I? Anyway, Samuel Avery started celebrating early that morning. The fact that my mother was in labor with me, his first grandson, was purely incidental. Samuel was celebrating the beginning of the war."

Brad and Jonathan had been drinking cognac that evening by the side of Jonathan's pool, and the story was interrupted by staccato slaps as Jonathan killed mosquitoes on his arms and neck. "My grandfather, you see, had nursed his small manufacturing company—mostly electrical switches and ball bearings—through ten long years of the Depression. Now, with the United States formally declaring war, he rightly saw that he was on the verge of making magnificent profits from what surely was to be an unprecedented war effort on our part. Unfortunately for Grandfather, he suffered a massive stroke halfway through his second bottle of champagne. At least that's the story the family told. My father, however, was in his cups one night and *he* said that when he rushed into Grandfather's office—the old man was sitting behind his desk, gasping for air—he saw Grandfather's secretary buttoning up her blouse. It hardly matters how the old boy really did celebrate. The fact was that it was just too much for him.

"It must have been quite a scene: Grandfather lying on the couch, knowing he was dying, knowing his company was on the brink of making a fortune, looking up at my father, a man he thought of as a ne'er-do-well and a bum. He grabbed Father's shoulders and pulled him closer so that he could speak. Then, in a whisper that only my father could hear, he said, 'Goddamn putz. I work hard for twenty-five years and now I have to leave my business to you. Life isn't fair.' My father said that first he could do nothing but stare at Grandfather, aghast. Then he started to laugh. Those were Grandfather's last words. The old man lapsed into a coma and died the next day.

"Everyone wanted to know what Grandfather had told my father, but he wouldn't say, just muttered something about him revealing 'the meaning of life.' I've got to give Father credit, though. He buckled under and ran the business all through the war years. He probably would have made grandfather proud of him after all, but on the day the Japanese surrendered, that very day, Dad sold the whole business, lock, stock, and barrel, and went out and bought a hotel. That's what he always wanted to do, and he did it. He had lived out my grandfather's dreams, and from that moment on, he started to live out his own."

"Jebediah, would you wrap Mr. Avery's books and take them out to his car?" Brad said.

"It's somewhere in the parking lot behind the shop," Jonathan added, "and please tell Joel that I'll be back to the car within the hour."

Brad and Jonathan walked across the brick patio to Rusterman's Restaurant. Anthony Patronsky led the way and Felix followed.

Both Parker's Rare Books and Rusterman's were located on Duke of Gloucester Street, in the center of a four-block shopping area called Merchants' Square. The square was set between the colonial village and the College of William and Mary, so that tourists could walk to it without getting into their cars and losing the eighteenth-century experience of Williamsburg itself. The Colonial Williamsburg Foundation owned and operated the complex. The shops and restaurants were, in the main, upscale and conservative.

"Mr. Avery," the hostess at the restaurant said, smiling at Jonathan.

"Hullo, Margaret. We can find our way, if that's okay." Jonathan led his party through the various dining rooms and into the kitchen.

Antoine, the chef, looked up at them and managed a half-smile. He was in the middle of demonstrating the finer points of adding ingredients to a sauce, and it was difficult to abandon the scowl he had adopted for the two assistants who stood nervously at his side. Jonathan led Brad to a table in the corner. It was where the chefs ate. It had a simple butcher-block top, on which a waiter had arranged a vase of flowers and two place settings. Anthony Patronsky and Felix took seats at another table on the far side of the room, where they had a better view of the swinging doors to the dining room. Aside from the staff, no one was allowed to eat in the kitchen but Jonathan and his occasional guest.

"God, I love eating here," Jonathan said, looking around at the activity in the kitchen. "It reminds me of my father's hotel."

The chef walked over to the table after he had finished his demonstration.

"Antoine, I am famished," said Jonathan.

"What do you prefer: steak, chicken, seafood, veal?"

"How about seafood?"

"Oysters? They're very good today. You like shrimp, don't you?"

"Shrimp is fine."

"Oysters and shrimp in a nice light sauce, a touch of garlic, wine, butter, all served over a bed of squash fettucini."

"Sounds great."

"Brad?"

"It sounds good to me too."

"Anything first?" Antoine asked Jonathan.

"A little salad." Jonathan looked at Brad, who nodded. "Two, then."

"Wine with your meal?"

"Do you have any of the Clos du Val Chardonnay left?"

"Good choice. I think we can find you a bottle."

"Please take care of Moe and Curly for me," Jonathan added, nodding toward the two bodyguards at the other table.

"It's already been done."

Jonathan and Antoine talked about seafood and the problem of finding and keeping a reliable wholesaler for scallops.

"Fiona tells me you're coming out Wednesday to put the final touches on the banquet menu," Jonathan said.

"Fiona's pretty much decided on everything," said Antoine. "On Wednesday, we'll just go over the details one more time." He went back to place their orders for lunch.

"Are you coming to the opening of the library with Lady Samantha?" Jonathan asked Brad.

"Sam and I wouldn't miss it for the world."

"Fiona's going crazy over the arrangements."

"Well, it's not every day you have the governor of Virginia coming to your house to accept a research library as a gift for the state."

"With all the bother, I'm beginning to wonder if I didn't make a mistake offering it in the first place."

"That's just last-minute jitters. We've had this conversation before, as I recall."

"You're probably right, and if I am going to do it, now is the time."

"It will be fine."

"I guess, but up until now the collection, the building, it's all been mine. After Friday it will belong to the state."

"You've still managed to keep control through the board of directors. No one will do anything you don't want done."

A waiter came to their table and served the wine and salad.

"Fiona's sent for two of the staff from the London house to help organize things for the dinner after the ceremonies," Jonathan said.

"I'm impressed."

"You're supposed to be. I think she wants to show us Americans what we've missed by breaking away from the mother country two hundred years ago."

"Antoine's doing the cooking, I take it."

"Nothing but the best. Fiona's right there. Damn the expense, full speed ahead."

* * *

Over coffee Jonathan asked, "Brad, do you have the time to stop over at the library this afternoon?"

"I'd love to, but I really can't. I have to go out and see Greta Riesling."

"Carl's wife?"

"Widow. Carl just died."

"Died? How?"

"You're the second person to ask that, and I'm embarrassed to say that I don't know."

"Good grief, I just spoke to Carl a few days ago."

"I didn't know you knew him."

"He would sell me the occasional book, that's all. I do buy some books from other dealers, you know."

"I was just surprised, because when I think of Carl, I think of low-cost, scholarly books."

"These were rather nice, actually. He quoted books from time to time through the mail, and we talked on the telephone. We never really met, but you can develop fast relationships over the telephone with some bookdealers, as you no doubt are aware. Why are you going out, if I may ask?"

"Greta wants me to make an offer on Carl's books."

"If you see anything there for me, call. I'm still interested in buying, even though I am giving away the library."

"I will."

"Carl had some wonderful things. Two weeks ago I bought a completely unrecorded Herman Melville item from him. Something Melville had printed when he worked at the *Brooklyn Eagle*. A little paperback with the sermon from *Moby Dick* issued as a separate book. I can't remember the exact dates, but this was published eleven years or so before the novel came out."

"Unbelievable."

"You see why I'm so interested. Carl never sold me anything that good before, but some of the other books he came up with were special in their own right."

"I'll keep my eyes open."

"Do that," Jonathan said, and signaled the waiter for the check.

# Chapter
# 6

"How was lunch with Jonathan?" Samantha asked as they were driving out to the Rieslings'.

"Fine. We ate in Rusterman's kitchen. Jonathan says it reminds him of his childhood. Did you know he grew up living in a hotel?"

"Fiona told me. His father owned it, didn't he?"

"That's right."

"He's a monk now, you know."

"Who?"

"Jonathan's father. He started some sort of monastic order on property he owned in Colorado. Fiona says he spends his time writing religious poetry."

"I never heard that before."

"I'm surprised. I thought you two were close."

"Jonathan likes to keep his life compartmentalized. What with his government work and all, there's a lot I don't know about Jonathan Avery. He's a very private person."

"You two met when he was divorcing his first wife, didn't you?"

"Yes. That was a nasty scene. *National Enquirer* articles and everything."

"She ran off with an Argentinian polo player, didn't she? Fiona told me."

"Correct."

"What was she like?"

"I never met her, but I'd say 'wild' would be a fitting adjective. Jonathan still thinks of her as one of the few true nymphomaniacs he ever met. How did he put it? 'Having sex with Tzara offered a cornucopia of possibilities most men never even consider.'"

"She must have been a real treat."

"The CIA thought so. They asked me to come down and see how Jonathan was bearing up under the ordeal."

"What did you report?"

"That he was doing fine, thank you very much."

"When did you discover you both collected books?"

"That first day, over lunch," Brad said. "We became friends. I used to come down to Jonathan's estate with Phyllis and the kids about once a month for the weekend."

As Brad said this, he could sense the change in Samantha. She felt that he had not yet worked through his feeling of loss and grief at the deaths of his family. He didn't accept this—if Samantha had asked him to rate his life and emotional prowess at that moment, he would have given himself high marks for throwing himself back into his work, not allowing himself to feel self-pity, and having the courage to begin a new relationship with her. It was Samantha who sensed the problem, if only subconsciously, and she stiffened when the subject of Brad's past life was mentioned.

"Enough about Jonathan," Brad said. "How did your trip go? I never did have a chance to ask."

"Probably because you really don't want to know."

"That's not true. I'm just not rooting for you to get a job that will have you living in New York for the next three years."

"Monday through Friday. I still would be back on weekends."

"Whoopee."

48

"Brad, this is the most important eighteenth-century reconstruction project to come along in years. I'd like you to be happy for me if the firm gets it."

"I know."

For Samantha, their relationship took her breath away—partly out of the joy of finding someone to share her life with again after a devastating divorce, but mostly out of overwhelming fear. Being with Brad had awakened emotions in her that she had not felt since she was twenty, emotions she had never expected to feel again. Along with the giddiness and joy came a certain vulnerability and self-doubt that washed over her from time to time like a wave, causing momentary panic before it ebbed. She had built a life of her own after her first marriage and wasn't eager to compromise her hard-earned independence and share her being one more time with someone else, even Brad. It was during a particularly uneasy period, six months before, that she had decided to end their relationship. She told Brad she wanted marriage, knowing it was a commitment Brad was not prepared to make. But a week later he surprised her and proposed.

They had talked for a long while that evening and finally agreed to wait. Then she was offered the possibility of a job in New York. "It's not easy having a love affair in the eighties," Samantha admitted.

Now they drove along in silence until Samantha said, "The curators liked our presentation, but the board of directors still has to give final approval, so let's not worry about New York until they make a decision. Okay?"

"When's that?"

"Two weeks at least."

Brad hesitated. "Christ, Sam. I don't . . ."

"I know. Just let it be."

They turned off Route 5, onto a narrower paved road. "By the way," Samantha said, "Fiona called. She wants us to come out tomorrow night for an informal dinner."

"What did you tell her?"

"Yes, but I can call her and cancel if you like. I think all she wants is someone to hold her hand with the banquet coming so soon."

As they drove around a curve, Brad could see flashing lights from the two police cars parked in the small area next to the two-room concrete block structure that served as Carl Riesling's office. Greta was standing in the doorway talking to one of the officers and another man in a rumpled suit.

Greta wore a plain housedress. She still showed signs of having once been an attractive woman. At fifty, her brunette hair had turned to dull gray. Her high cheekbones, which framed a pretty face in old photographs, were now gaunt, creating harsh angles. It was as if she had let out a huge sigh and her entire body had sagged, drooping on her the frame of her skeleton. She stopped talking when she saw Brad and Samantha getting out of the car, and came toward them.

"It is all right," she said. "The police are just leaving." She was carrying a glass in her hand. As she got closer, Brad could smell gin.

"Greta, what is going on here?"

"The police are investigating Carl's accident," Greta said.

"What accident?" Samantha asked.

Greta looked at Samantha with a confused expression.

"Greta, this is Samantha Frye," Brad said. "She's a friend."

The man Greta had been talking to when they drove up, the one in the rumpled suit, walked toward them. "Mrs. Riesling, if you'll sign this statement, we'll be on our way." He looked at Brad. "I don't believe we've met. I'm Tom Egan."

"Aren't you running for police chief?" Samantha asked.

"Yes. A substitution after Chief Hanson had his heart attack last month."

"From the newspapers, it sounds like you're in the middle of a political donnybrook."

"A lot of politicians wanted to appoint their own candidate, but Chief Hanson wanted me, so I figure it's my job to stay in the race, for him, if for nothing else."

"What's happened here?" Brad asked, pointing to the cars and Carl Riesling's office.

"I'm sorry. I just assumed you knew," Tom Egan said. "You do know that Carl Riesling is dead?"

"Yes. But why the police?"

"Mr. Riesling died in his office last night. Apparently he was sitting at his desk when the bookcase behind him collapsed and fell on top of him."

"I told him," Greta said as if she'd suddenly woke up from a sound sleep. "I told him that mess would kill him some day. He thought the books were his friends, but I knew they would kill him."

Samantha reached over and touched Greta's shoulder. "Let's go up to the house and put on a pot of coffee."

"But I want Brad Parker to look at Carl's books and buy them."

"He'll do that while we're making coffee."

Greta looked down blankly at the clipboard Tom Egan had handed her, trying to remember what she was supposed to do with it.

"I'll get you to sign this in the morning," Egan said, and took it from her. Greta started walking unsteadily toward her house, which stood immediately behind the office.

Brad looked at Samantha. "Will you be okay?"

"I'm going to try to get her to bed. She's exhausted."

Brad went over to Tom Egan, who was watching a second police car drive away. "I'm glad you and Miss Frye showed up. I was getting concerned about leaving Mrs. Riesling alone."

"We'll stay here for a while."

"The way she's been knocking back the gin this afternoon, I don't suspect that she'll be needing company for much longer."

"Who found the body?"

"She did. She said she woke up just before seven and got concerned when she found that her husband hadn't been to bed. So she walked down to the office here and found him dead behind his desk with that big bookcase on top of him."

"And she called the police."

"The emergency squad, actually. They called us when they arrived."

"Any idea when Carl died?"

"The medical examiner will pin it down for us, but I suspect sometime late last night. He had been dead for several hours when I got here. That's for sure." Tom Egan gave a short shiver.

"The unmistakable odor of death."

"Exactly. Most people never get to smell it, thank god."

"My experience was in 'Nam."

"You were in the CIA too, weren't you?"

"Administration. The dead bodies there are metaphorical."

"We have some of those in local politics, too."

"What was Carl doing in the office so late?"

"Mrs. Riesling said he liked to work at night. He left shortly after dinner, she said. Told her he had an appointment to meet a customer. Mrs. Riesling walked down the next morning thinking he just fell asleep at his desk. Wasn't concerned until she saw the bookcase."

"Does she know who the customer was?"

"No. She never asked."

Brad and Tom walked into the building. It was ten degrees cooler inside than it was out in the sun. A musty odor permeated the air in the first room they entered. It was a terrible jumble of boxes and books. The back wall, except for the spaces created by three windows, was lined from floor to ceiling with bookshelves. In front of the bookcases, stacked in makeshift pyramids, were odd-sized boxes filled with books, some arranged neatly, some collapsed and askew. In front of the boxes were piles of loose volumes. Carl Riesling, like most booksellers, enjoyed buying books more than selling them. The boxes and loose volumes in this room were the leftovers from collections bought over the years—bones in an elephant's graveyard. Brad stopped and tried to take in the scene. He prided himself at being able to guess how many books were in a library, or shelved against a wall. One look at this mountain and Brad knew he was beaten.

Silently Tom Egan had walked into the other room, where Carl Riesling had died, and waited for Brad. Someone had propped the two fatal sections of bookcase back up against the wall. They were open bookshelves, unpainted, hammered together from one-by-twelve-inch planks of number-two pine by Carl himself. The books that had cascaded down when the shelves tore loose from the wall were mostly in piles along the edges of the floor.

Brad put his hand under one of the shelves and tried to lift the unit off the ground. The shelving was eleven feet high and fifteen feet in length. It didn't respond to his tug.

"Heavy mothers," Tom Egan allowed. "Doubly so with books on them. Mr. Riesling had them bolted into the cinderblock."

Brad looked up at the wall and saw four sturdy angle irons still attached to it and another hole where one of the supports had come loose.

"The way we figure it is that the wood just got dry and splintered against the weight."

"My God."

"The good thing about it was that he never knew what hit him. The medical examiner told me he died of a sharp blow to his spinal column at the base of the skull. Broke his neck. The man probably died instantly."

Brad just stared at the shelving and at the ceiling.

"I think he must have heard it give way, though," Tom said.

"Why's that?"

"The look on his face. Frightened." Tom made a gesture in an attempt to describe Carl Riesling's final expression, something he found impossible to put into words.

"What a terrible thing to happen."

"Sure was." Tom Egan hesitated. "Carl Riesling wasn't from around here, was he?"

"No. He was born somewhere in Germany."

"Why did he settle in Williamsburg?"

"As I understand, he came to work for Colonial Williamsburg as their resident printer in the historical village."

"I saw he had some printing equipment over there in the corner."

"They're his own. Nineteenth-century steel presses. CW hired him to work with their eighteenth-century ones."

"I heard some rumor once that when he left, it wasn't exactly a pleasant parting of the ways."

"All I know was that there was some kind of argument. It was a major item of gossip at the time, and I'm sure someone will remember the story. I wasn't in town then. All I could tell you would be secondhand hearsay."

"But he stayed on and started a book business." Tom Egan looked around at the seedy, ill-lit clutter. "I wouldn't think that anyone could run a business out here in the woods."

"Carl sold books by mail. He sent lists of books he had for sale to people, and then he would mail them the books they ordered."

"Can you make a living that way?"

"Carl did. That's the wonderful thing about the antiquarian book business, there are as many different ways to sell books as there are bookdealers. It's an iconoclastic trade."

"Yep." Tom Egan hesitated again. "You have any idea who his customer was last night?"

"No. I really don't know much about Carl's clientele. They're more readers than collectors."

"Don't your customers read?"

Brad laughed. "Yes, but they're concerned about what edition a book is and how well it has weathered the years. I guess it's the difference between a person who buys an antique chair and someone who just wants something to sit on."

"In other words, your customers are richer."

"That's another way of putting it, but we have a great many middle-class customers, too. In fact the truly rich are probably less apt to spend their money on rare books than on other collectibles."

"Why's that?" Tom asked, seemingly genuinely interested.

"It takes a lot more knowledge and study than, say, painting or antiques, and books are less likely to impress people than a nice piece of furniture or a dazzling picture or print hanging on the wall."

Tom pointed his finger at Brad, hesitated, and then said, "But you did say that Mr. Riesling did most of his business by mail?"

"Yes."

"Then wouldn't it be unusual for a customer to call on him?"

"Yes and no. Under normal circumstances, yes. But it could have been that another book dealer came into town, or one of Carl's mail-order customers. Even people who sell books exclusively by mail can't avoid meeting some of their customers one time or another."

"I suppose."

Samantha came to the door. "She's asleep," she said, and looked around the room. "Brad, if you didn't have a shop where people came every day, would you let your apartment look like this?"

"I hope not."

"Is that Carl's desk? Where he died?"

"Yes, ma'am," Tom Egan said.

"It's eerie."

"What's the glass beaker used for, over there near the printing press?" Tom asked.

"I don't know."

"Looks like part of a chemistry set."

"I haven't a clue."

Tom looked at his watch. "If you folks don't mind, I'd like to lock up now."

"Could I have a few more minutes?" Brad asked. "Tomorrow I have to talk to Greta about buying her books, and I'd like to get a better idea of what's here."

Tom looked around at the books. "Well, I guess I could let you lock up, you being friends of Mrs. Riesling and all."

"Are your people through with the room?"

"Yep. Move anything you want." Tom Egan made his good-byes, said Thanks, and left.

"Good luck with your campaign," Samantha called after him. "Are we going to be long?" she asked Brad.

"No. It's going to be impossible to come up with a price. I just want to poke around a bit." Brad began systematically looking through the shelves, running his fingertips along the spines of the books as a means to focus his attention and not miss anything. Occasionally, seemingly at random, he would stop and pick a book from a shelf, look at the title page, and riffle through the leaves before replacing it. "How was Greta?" he asked.

"Feeling no pain, but I suspect that she's going to be in for one hell of a hangover tomorrow."

"Undoubtedly," Brad replied, still working.

"You would have been proud of me, by the way. I became a bona-fide detective up there."

"What did you find out?"

"For one thing, Greta and Carl had a very unhappy marriage."

Brad looked at Samantha over his glasses. "Oh, really?"

"She told me that she had been going to leave Carl."

"Why? Was Carl fooling around on the side?"

"No. She said he was a thief and that if there was one thing she couldn't do, it was live with a thief."

"She said that Carl was a thief?"

"Yes."

"Did she give you any details?" Brad asked, still running his fingers over the spines of books.

"I was about to ask, but she passed out on the couch and started to snore."

"I hate to be the one to tell you this, but one of the chief attributes of a great detective is perseverance."

"I think by that time gin had a closer place in her heart than our newly formed girlish camaraderie."

Brad had been through half of the wall of books when he saw a volume lying behind some others on a shelf by his left shoulder. "That's interesting."

"What is?"

"A book called *A Sermon for Sailors* by Herman Melville."

"Never heard of it."

"Neither did I before lunch today. Carl apparently sold a copy to Jonathan. Jonathan told me it was the only copy he had ever seen, and now here's another."

"Maybe Carl found two copies at the same place."

"Stranger things have happened. Do you think Greta would mind if I took it back with me to show Jonathan? If it's the same book, it could be worth a considerable amount of money."

"My dear, this evening Greta wouldn't care if she were being raped by the entire Russian army."

"I'll leave a note on the shelf telling her I have it," said Brad. He wrote it and continued looking at the books. After a few more shelves he sighed. "I'm ready to leave."

"Do you think you'll want to buy all this?"

"Probably. There are enough good titles here, a first English edition of Jefferson's *Notes on Virginia*, a shelf of salable Mark Twain firsts— really a lot better than I thought. And Carl's reference library is pretty decent too."

"What's all this printing equipment in the corner?" Samantha asked.

"What you have your hand on is a mimeograph machine. Carl printed his own catalogs and sales lists. Behind you is an old Albion printing press. Those cabinets beside it are filled with type— Here, I'll get the lights."

Brad stopped to take one last look at the bookcases leaning against the wall, the splintered wood, and the bolts jutting out from the cinderblocks, and he shook his head. "God, you never know. Everything just falling down after all those years."

"You booksellers work in a very dangerous profession. It really turns a girl on."

"We antiquarian booksellers have to deal with groupies like you every day. I'll see if I can satisfy some of those carnal lusts tonight."

"Think you're up to the task?"

"I can see I have my work cut out for me," Brad said, locking the door.

"You bet your buns, bunkie."

# Chapter

# 7

Jebediah came back to the bookshop after eating a quick dinner at McDonald's. He hadn't yet achieved the new, grander style of living he had promised himself. He needed leisure time as well as money to indulge the gourmet lurking in his stomach. It was his first day back, and he still had several orders to finish wrapping. As usual when he was away, the work did pile up. After all, he said to himself, I'm the only one who gets things done around here.

He had asked Brad for a part-time packing clerk and was told the business "just can't afford it now, but maybe in a few months." That was four months ago.

"Cheap bastard," Jebediah said out loud. "Look at this shop. The man must be making a fortune, and he won't even hire a part-time packer on a regular basis."

Fleder looked up at him from her corner of the wrapping table. "And," he said in a louder voice, "how many bookstore managers have to baby-sit a goddamn cat?" With that, he abruptly threw a rubber eraser at Fleder; it hit a calendar on the wall, a full foot off its mark. The cat continued licking her fur and preening indifferently. Theirs was a cold war of vaguely concealed loathing and mistrust.

Jebediah finished counting the packages he had wrapped and checked them against the United Parcel forms. It had taken him an extra two hours to get caught up, and he resented having to give the business this time. Sitting back, he took out his pipe and worked it until it started drawing easily. Fleder approached him and angled her head under his hand to be petted. To Fleder, even enemies had their use.

"If I didn't have to get this work done tonight, I could have gone out and bought a new Smith and Wesson," he said to the cat. "Now I'm scheduled to work for the rest of the week. I won't be able to go till next Monday." He took a long, slow puff on the pipe. "Maybe I'll ask them to let me try one of those automatic pistols at the shop. Wonder what it would feel like?"

He reached down into his jeans pocket for the cigarette case, the one Deborah had given him from the robbery. It was his good luck piece, a promise of future success. Then he heard that familiar voice, softly calling to him from inside his head. Sometimes it was the voice, other times he heard music, or a sound like the whirring of a gigantic engine. Even though he had not said anything or even moved perceptibly, Fleder noticed the change in him and slouched away, off the wrapping table.

The voice began to get louder, as it always did, repeating nasty things, things Jebediah didn't want to hear. He could feel the pressure building inside his head, like a balloon that a carnival clown kept pumping more air into. "Got to think of something else," Jebediah told himself. "Like the cigarette case. Got to concentrate on the scrollwork." As he did, the voice began calling his name in a softer tone and the balloon in his head shrank. It was working. Over the years, Jebediah had learned to control the voice.

It wasn't like before. It wasn't as bad now as the time in Philadelphia when he was sitting at that bar and the man called him a queer. He still remembered the bar, a time-stained joint near Twelfth Street and Chestnut. He remembered the man making his remark and then repeating it again and again to the assortment of tramps, businessmen, and outpatients who made up the clientele in midafternoon. Jebediah remembered that it wasn't crowded, just ten or twelve people sitting around. He remembered the pressure building, building. Then the bottle. Jebediah could still see the beer bottle at night when he lay in his bed before going to sleep. He remembered picking it up, smashing it on the brass bar rail, and then grinding it into the stunned man's face. He remembered the surprise, the exquisite cathartic moment of recognition and shock that registered on the man before he, Jebediah, obliterated those features forever. Suddenly, quickly, it was over: the deed, the pressure, the voice in his head. Then he had turned and walked out of the bar. No one had stopped him. He thought he remembered two people going over to the man with no face, but that could have been in his recurring dream. Jebediah had merely walked away, undisturbed, both in his dream and in reality. Of that he was certain.

The telephone ring brought him back from that memory. "Probably your owner," he said to Fleder, who crouched in the far corner of the room. Jebediah put the cigarette case on the edge of the wrapping table and went to answer it.

It was a wrong number.

As Jebediah walked back, he saw Fleder swipe at the pretty cigarette case, which gleamed in the light, and watched the case fall to the floor. The catch opened, and four cigarettes fell out.

"Damn cat."

Fleder now returned to the corner of the wrapping table, having satisfactorily killed another enemy.

Jebediah reached down to pick up the victim. "How could anyone smoke Salems?" he said. He broke them in half and threw them into the wastebasket. Still holding the case, he noticed that the inside lining had been jarred loose. He was just about to snap it back into place when he spotted something glistening near the seam. He got the dentist's tool he used for regluing books and wedged it into the seam. The inner lining popped out, and now he could see a small strip of film inside.

"What have we here, Fleder?"

Jebediah held the film up to the light, but he couldn't make out the tiny markings on it.

"Microfilm?"

Fleder looked at him quizzically.

"Well, we'll have to see about it tomorrow morning." He carefully put the film in between two of the firm's calling cards and placed them in his wallet. Then he snapped the cigarette case closed again and shoved it back into his pocket. "Come on, Fleder. It's time to call it a night."

# Chapter
## 8

**B**rad was tired. He watched the steam rising from his coffee mug and thought about youthful stamina. He would rather have been home sleeping next to Samantha, but instead he was talking on the telephone with an insistent Greta Riesling. His only consolation was that he was certain Greta was in far worse shape for a sustained argument than he was.

"I cannot wait a week for you to make an offer on the books," he heard Greta say. "I am leaving for Germany, for Hamburg, tomorrow. I go there to stay with my sister for a while. I must empty the building for the realtor by then."

"I'm happy for you that you have somewhere to go," Brad said, "but, Greta, be reasonable. Carl left those books in a complete mess. I don't think I could even just physically look at all of them by Friday, let alone make you an intelligent offer."

"But you could give me some idea."

"Greta, none of those books are even priced. There's too much work to be done. What you ask is impossible."

"Then what are we to do?"

Brad leaned back in his chair and put his feet up on the desk. "I can do this, Greta. I can send two men over today to start packing the books. Once that's done, I can take them to my warehouse. My guess is that we could have them out of Carl's office by, say, late tomorrow afternoon. That would give me some time to look them over. I can come up with a price for you in three weeks and cable you at your sister's."

"You will buy them, then?"

"From the few minutes I spent there yesterday, yes, I think so."

"I want a fair price."

"If you don't like my offer, you can always have someone else come in and give you another one."

"Carl told me I should trust you. I guess I have no choice."

"Jesus, Greta, dealing with me can't be that desperate."

"Oh, I don't mean—" Greta sounded flustered. "My English. Please, I know you will be fair."

"How is your cash situation? I could let you have a down payment if you need it."

"That should be no problem," Greta said.

"Carl's insurance?" Brad asked.

"No. Carl did not believe in insurance," Greta replied. "I am to collect some money on one of Carl's business arrangements."

Fleder jumped into Brad's lap. "Then it's settled," he said. "I'll send the young man who works for me, Jebediah Stuart, along with a helper. They'll start packing the books this afternoon. I'll also send you a letter so that you have something in writing about our agreement." Brad added, "Oh, I did take one book with me last night. I didn't think you'd mind. I wanted to do some research on it."

"You and Carl. Always looking up your books in other books, finding out what they are, what price to charge. You both remind me of two little schoolboys. I hope you can make this business pay better than Carl did—but don't start making your fortune with my books."

They said their good-byes, and Brad hung up the telephone. Jebediah was standing silently in the doorway with his omnipresent pipe. Brad wondered how long he had been there. Jebediah never seemed to enter a room; he would just appear. Brad attributed it to something vaguely sinister in the young man's nature, but Samantha reminded Brad of how strongly he concentrated on what he was doing. Brad glanced at the clock. It was nine forty-five.

"Sorry I'm late again," Jebediah said. "I had to go to the library this morning."

"Yesterday it was the bank. This isn't the first time we've had this conversation," Brad went on sharply. "I need you here before we open, to clean the shop and take care of the mail. If you want a few minutes during the day, Mrs. Johnson will cover for you."

Jebediah still stood there with his air of dilettantish indifference.

"If you really feel that way, why don't you just fire him?" Samantha had once asked Brad after hearing him rant on the subject. Brad wasn't able to give her an answer. He merely mumbled something about how he didn't like change.

"It's your problem, and you'll solve it in your own time, I guess," Samantha had said. "If you have a toothache, sooner or later the pain will get bad enough to force you to go to the dentist."

Right now was not the time for such strong medicine, however. Brad was in no mood for confrontation. "We're going to buy Carl Riesling's bookshop."

Jebediah raised his eyebrow in a mock salute. "The stock only, or his reference library too?"

"Everything."

"That's great. Carl had a tremendous reference collection."

"You've seen it?"

"Many times. Carl was teaching me to print."

"I didn't know that."

"I told you about wanting to start a private press."

"I didn't connect that with Carl."

"He was helpful. I still feel it could be a profitable venture if I can keep my editions small enough and create instant collectibles."

Jebediah puffed on his pipe and reflected. "And it would give me a grand excuse to meet the poets, themselves."

"I told Greta Riesling that you would be out this afternoon to start packing the books."

"I can't pack everything myself."

"Call Louis Mellon; perhaps he can help you part-time for a couple of days."

"On this short a notice?"

"Try."

"What about the shop?"

"Mrs. Johnson can handle it."

Jebediah stood there, pouting around his pipestem.

"What's wrong?"

"Packing books is an unpleasant job."

"It's going to be even more unpleasant if you have to do it yourself. Go and call Louis, then let me know what happens."

Jebediah went down to the shop. Mrs. Johnson wasn't at work yet, and the place was quiet. The cat sat in her spot on the corner of the wrapping table watching Jebediah make his call. Once he had an assurance of someone to work with him, his anger subsided. "Quite a find you made last night, Fleder," he said, walking over to her and petting her head. "Your little discovery gave me a lot to think about."

Jebediah had been the first person in Swem Library at the college when its doors opened that morning. He went directly to the microfiche reader in the corner of the reference room and gently took the piece of microfilm from his wallet, placing it between the two glass plates in the front of the machine. He pushed the plates forward until the microfilm was directly under the lens. The reader didn't quite project the film up to the size of a page, but the figures were large enough to read. He took out his pencil and the small pocket notebook he carried everywhere and wrote down the first two lines:

66

| 12/6/82 | $10,000 | Cash | Peter Axom | Gunston appointment |
| 5/1/83 | $35,000 | 9P467J995 | Peter Axom | Carmine contract |

Jebediah didn't read a newspaper on a regular basis, and he didn't make a concerted effort to keep abreast of current events. ("Look, the Arabs hate the Jews, and we don't like the Russians," he once said. "Why read a paper when you know what the headlines will be before you begin?") But it didn't take a master of political trivia to recognize the name of Senator Peter Axom, Chairman of the Armed Services Committee, and further down the column, Al Pender, another senator, although Jebediah couldn't remember his committee or the state he represented, if he had ever known.

"Gunston appointment?" Jebediah said out loud. "Harvey Gunston." Jebediah went to the Periodical Reference Index and looked up the name in the 1982 volume. Just from the reference notes, Jebediah remembered that Gunston was a special "watchdog" from the Office of Management and Budget, "'appointed by Peter Axom'—I'll be damned—'to oversee Pentagon contracts.'" Jebediah reached for the 1983 volume and looked up "Carmine." "'Carmine Industries'—there it was. 'Multimillion-dollar Defense Department electronics contract.'" Jebediah replaced the book. "Jesus," he almost shouted. A brunette in a neat plaid skirt and a white blouse, sitting at the next table, glared at him in silent indignation.

He ignored her and went back to the microfilm reader, reinserted the film, and started mentally adding the sums of money in the second column. He stopped three-quarters of the way down the list, when he reached two million.

They have to be payoffs, he thought, and the next column indicates how they were made. Jebediah guessed that the letters and numbers were Swiss bank accounts.

He replaced the microfilm in his wallet and set off across campus to the bookshop. No wonder the fat man Napoleon hit was so anxious to hide this, he thought, remembering the motel room and Deborah finding the man's wallet. Christ, she told us what his name was. He walked faster, puffing on his pipe, concentrating on the scene at the motel. A student or two, customers at the bookshop, said hello in passing, but Jebediah was lost in his own world. "Think," he said out loud. The image was so clear, Deborah sitting in her lotus position, the smell of Napoleon's beer. "It was Italian, an Italian name." It was someplace in his mind, but it hadn't surfaced by the time he reached Parker's, and then, of course, he had words with Brad Parker.

"How long will you be gone?" Mrs. Johnson asked.

"Mr. Parker thinks about two days. I haven't seen the books myself yet, so I really don't know. At least Louis is meeting me out there this afternoon to help pack."

"What about Fleder? Mr. Parker knows I don't want to be left alone with that cat."

"You'll have to remind him," Jebediah said. He was putting some packing tape into a box when it came to him. "Sab—Sabatino. Carl? No, Joseph. Joseph Sabatino."

"What?"

"Nothing. I was just remembering a name."

"I thought I was the only one who forgot names," Mrs. Johnson said, walking into the shipping room.

Jebediah went over to the telephone book and looked up the area code for northeastern Pennsylvania. It was worth a try. "Information for Altamont, Pennsylvania," he said to the operator. "The number for Mr. Joseph Sabatino. I don't have an address." He waited until he heard several clicking sounds. Then a metallic voice gave him a telephone number.

"Bingo," Jebediah said, writing the number in his pocket notebook.

Peter Eastrovich stuck his head into Brad's office. "Everybody was busy downstairs, so I took the liberty of coming up."

"Come in. I was going to fix myself another cup of coffee. Would you like one?"

"Yes, I would, really."

Brad went over to his Mister Coffee machine on the filing cabinet in the corner of the office. "Black?"

"You have a good memory."

"For books and coffee only, I'm afraid. If the business ever goes belly-up, maybe I can get a job as a waiter."

"I was downstairs and saw Jebediah bringing out empty boxes. Did you buy a library?"

"It's not finalized yet, but I think we're getting Carl Riesling's stock and reference books. I guess you've heard by now that Carl died."

"Someone mentioned it," said Peter. "An accident or something, wasn't it?"

"The bookcase behind his desk collapsed and fell on him. What a freak thing to happen."

"For each man is killed by the thing he loves."

"It's too early to misquote Oscar Wilde to me."

"Ah, a literate bookseller. I didn't even know booksellers could read."

"One of my customers read it to me."

The intercom bleeped. "Jonathan Avery for you on line one," Mrs. Johnson said. Peter moved as if to get up.

"Stay," Brad said to him, and then into the telephone, "Jonathan, how are you? Thanks for calling back." Brad reached for the Melville pamphlet he had taken from the Rieslings'. "Remember yesterday at lunch, you mentioned buying a Melville pamphlet from Carl? Well, I was out there in the afternoon poking around, and I think I found another copy of it."

Jonathan said something in reply.

"The title on the copy I found is *A Sermon for Sailors*, New York, Printed for the Author. Right, eighteen thirty-five."

Peter Eastrovich sat transfixed, looking at the pamphlet.

"Sure. I thought you might like to see it. How about if I bring it out tomorrow night? Your wife invited Sam and me for dinner, in case she didn't tell you." Brad paused to listen to something Jonathan was saying. "Right. See you then."

"May I take a look at that?" Peter asked when Brad was finished.

Brad handed him the Melville pamphlet.

"Where did you find this?"

"Stuck in back of a shelf in Carl Riesling's office. According to Jonathan, it's unrecorded. Not even the Melville scholars have heard about it."

"Carl found two copies?" Peter asked, still examining the pamphlet.

"Apparently. If it's really the same thing. I'm going to take it out to Jonathan's tomorrow and compare it to his."

"Would you sell it to me at the library?" Peter asked.

"First, it's not mine to sell. I haven't bought the books from Greta yet. And you heard my conversation with Jonathan."

"Yes, but if it is identical and Jonathan already has a copy, it wouldn't seem right for him to own the only other known copy too."

"A point well taken."

"Then you'll keep me in mind?"

"I will."

"If the price is within reason, I'd like to buy it for my own research."

"What is this research you keep alluding to?"

"At the Avery Library. I've been working on it for the past year."

"The way you and Jonathan feel about each other, doesn't that get dicey at times?"

"Jonathan might not like me personally, but he made a public offer of opening his collection to all serious scholars, and now he can't back down without causing an incident."

"Yes, but you must feel uncomfortable."

"I'm not making it my problem. This project means too much to me. Anyway, the reality is that I'm out there every day, working. Jonathan's not around all that much. He's just a rich dilettante."

"A dilettante doesn't spend ten years building a research library, Peter."

"He had people like you to do that for him."

"He directed it, and, don't forget, he was the one who paid for it."

"I never said he didn't have money."

"But don't you find it amazing that a person with all that money would even care? He could have spent his life clipping coupons. I really admire Jonathan for sticking with it."

"You're right," Peter said without conviction. He got up from his chair. "But don't forget me on *A Sermon for Sailors*."

"If this copy is the same as Jonathan's, you have right of first refusal. That is, if Greta accepts my offer and it's mine to sell in the first place."

"Fair enough."

Brad walked Peter to the steps. "You know, you never did tell me what this research project is you've been working on."

"A good scholar never says until he's finished."

"Suit yourself."

"This is one I'm going to play close to the vest. I need it. Let's face it, my career here is at a dead end. When I finish this project, I could get a book out of it that will make the powers that be sit up and take notice."

"Well, I hope you get what you want."

"Thanks. I hope so too."

At the bottom of the steps Peter paused to talk with Jebediah. "I'll keep my eyes open," Brad heard Jebediah say. Brad shrugged his shoulders and went back into his office.

# Chapter
# 9

Joseph Sabatino sat at his kitchen table wearing an old-fashioned looped undershirt, boxer shorts, and black knee-length socks. He was having toast and coffee he had prepared himself. His sister, Anna, who lived downstairs, usually did most of the cooking, but she had gone shopping with her five-year-old daughter before Joey was out of bed.

The red telephone in the corner of the kitchen rang. Joey looked at his watch. It was five past ten. Business, he thought. Joey had warned Anna about the telephone when she moved in with her two children. "One rule of the house: Never answer my telephone."

"What if it wakes Anita?"

"Stuff cotton in her ears. You listen to me, and don't interfere."

"Some brother."

"You don't like it? Go back and live with your husband." Joey remembered the remark because it had brought on a flood of tears and crying. Anna had just walked away from her husband and their marriage, taking with her a considerable legacy of doubt and fear. Crying, especially Anna's crying, had always had a disquieting effect on Joey, a fact not unnoticed by Anna herself. "Hey, stop," he had said pleadingly. "You're better off without the prick. I don't want to see you cry."

Joey picked up the receiver on the second ring.

"Michael Scarponzi?" a voice asked.

"You got the wrong number," Joey replied and hung up.

Joey went to his bedroom and put on the white shirt and suit he had left draped over the door the previous night. He thought about choosing a tie but decided against it. The caller on the telephone had in effect told Joey to go to the shopping mall on Church Street and wait for a second call there. The name was a code. If the man had said, "Mark Johnson," the second call would have been made to a phone booth at the Holiday Inn, just up the road. In all there were eight different names for eight locations. Joey hated the system, but he did as he was told.

At the shopping mall, there were three pay phones on the far right of the main entrance. A woman was talking on the one in the corner. Joey looked at his watch. He had five minutes. He walked to a place he imagined to be just on the edge of the woman's line of vision and patiently folded his arms across his belly. The woman looked back at him. Her hair was in curlers, which were only partially hidden by a paisley scarf.

"These other phones ain't being used," she said to Joey, covering the mouthpiece with her hand as she spoke.

"I wanta wait for your phone," Joey replied.

"No, Ruth," she said into the telephone, projecting an air of disgust. "Just some man standing behind me."

Joey stared at her, meeting her eyes when she turned around to look.

"What are you, some kind of pervert?"

Joey stood there, enigmatic, a half-smile on his face.

"Some people belong in a mental institution," the woman said loudly. Then Joey watched her complexion pale as she looked back and realized that Joey, in all probability, had just come from exactly that type of place. "Ruth, I'll call you back," she said hurriedly, hung up, and quickly walked away.

74

Joey stood in front of the pay phone, answering it on the first ring.

"Was somebody using the telephone?" the voice said.

"An old broad."

"You weren't followed when you left the house, were you?" Joey recognized the voice as belonging to Teddy Simon. He was one of the new breed of smart college men. "I got a name and address of someone who pawned jewelry from the bus," Teddy continued. "Didn't find your cigarette case in what he pawned."

"At least you got a name and address," Joey said, reaching for a pen and the back of a crumpled envelope on which to write the information. "Go ahead."

"I'm to give you the information when I see you in the city."

"What is this? Give it to me now, and the layout too, so I know how many men to bring."

"No men, Joey. Just you."

"Hey, this is my problem, my responsibility. I take care of my own."

"They don't want you to go on this one."

"What 'they'? You give me *agita* on this, I'll make a few calls and give you more heat than you ever seen."

"It's nothing personal, Joey. It's bigger than that now. It's between families. The decision was made at the top. They want me to handle what happens in New York; they want you along to ID the man from the bus."

"Which one is it, the faggot or the nigger?"

"The black man," Teddy said. "The one who hit you."

It was an insult, a lack of respect, not being allowed to see this through himself, but the thought of seeing the man from the bus again brought color to Joey's cheeks. "So where do we meet?"

Teddy gave him instructions. "And remember, I give you my word, after we talk with him and get the cigarette case, he's yours. A present."

Back in the apartment, Joey was ready to take a shower when he heard his sister bringing Anita back from the stores. "Anna," he called, "I'm going to New York for a couple of days." He stood at the top of the stairs in his underwear and kneesocks.

"Hey, whatta you standing there in your underwear for? My daughter's here, for Christ's sake."

"Hi, Uncle Joey," the little girl said.

"Go," her mother ordered.

"What are you doing, raising the kid to be a fucking nun?"

"And watch your language, for Christ's sake."

"Ah, *fungul*," Joey replied, holding his testicles in his left hand. Just then his red telephone rang.

"You're a disgusting pig. You know that?" Anna yelled from the bottom of the steps. "A pig."

By then Joey had the telephone in his hand. He heard what sounded like a coin being inserted in a pay phone. Then, there was silence at both ends.

"Joseph Sabatino?"

Joey didn't recognize the voice. "What?"

"I have something of yours. You might be interested in buying it back."

Joey was still trying to place the nervous, weedy voice.

"Something you lost on the bus to Atlantic City a couple of days ago."

There was a long pause. "Yeah, go on," Joey said, conjuring up a mental picture of Jebediah standing in the front of the bus with his Smith and Wesson.

"The price is two hundred thousand. Nonnegotiable."

"I don't have that kind of money," Joey replied automatically.

"But you know people who do."

"Maybe I do, maybe not. If I have friends like that, how do I get in touch with you?"

"I'll call you," the voice said. "Today's Tuesday. We'll talk on Thursday. I have your number."

Joey remembered the line might be tapped. "Is this a joke?"

"I don't think Senator Axom or Senator Pender would think so."

"What's this 'senator' shit?"

With that the line went dead.

"Fucking lunatic," Joey said into the receiver just in case someone was listening.

It was certainly an unexpected turn of events, and Joey sat at the kitchen table contemplating it. In the end, he decided that the best thing he could do was to meet Teddy in New York at six, tell him about the call, and let him make the decision. "He wants to be boss, let him." Then he showered and dressed for the trip.

# Chapter
# 10

It was just after five when Samantha brought an indoor picnic in an elegant straw basket to Brad's apartment. The basket was one of her favorite possessions from the past. It conjured up many fine memories for her. Her late father-in-law had given it to her during the early, good years of her marriage. He had been a gentle and kind man, with an innate sadness that went deep within him. Purchasing the basket, the best one sold by Abercrombie and Fitch, had been an extravagance for him at the time. It was an elegant piece, with straps to hold its custom-made glassware, china, and silver—all the essentials of an upper-middle-class picnic. When Samantha had heard the news of her father-in-law's death years before, she had taken the basket from her closet and had a picnic, alone, in his honor.

Now everything was spread out over a blanket in the middle of Brad's living room floor. "And we begin with goose-liver pâté with just a hint of orange flavor, flown in especially for the occasion by the elegant Samantha Frye and her catering service, pandering to the whims of middle-aged bachelors."

"Bachelors—plural?"

"You presumed to think you were the first?"

"But I thought—you're so virginal and withdrawn."

"Withdraw yourself to the kitchen and uncork the wine while I fix the salad."

Brad reached into the refrigerator and took out a bottle of Pouilly Montrâchet that he had put there to chill only fifteen minutes before. He didn't like white wines so cold that you couldn't taste them.

"What about the Sauternes for later?" Samantha asked.

"It's being chilled."

"Good."

"Are you trying to get me drunk?" Brad asked her.

"That's supposed to be my line." Samantha arranged the salad on two plates. "You know what tonight is, don't you?"

"Tuesday?"

"No, silly, it's our anniversary."

"Anniversary of what?"

"Anniversary of the first time we slept together. Don't you remember?"

"I remember it very well. It was the date that threw me."

"Well, here we are, one year later. Whoda thunk it?"

They ate the cold salad with the julienne duck on top.

"Picnics have been the happiest times in my life," Samantha said.

They looked quietly at each other and at the fire crackling in the fireplace. Fleder lay on the corner of the blanket nearest the hearth, sated by the better half of a can of people tuna wisely given to her before dinner began. After the salad they sat together, their backs resting against the side of the couch, watching the fire slowly die. They never did get to the bottle of Sauternes or to the chocolate mousse Samantha had made for dessert.

Their lovemaking later was slow and gentle, without the hungry passion of the night before. Shortly after eleven, Samantha left.

"I have a half-unpacked suitcase and several thirsty plants at home waiting for me, and I have to be in the office early tomorrow. You won't have to get up that early, and I'd start feeling sorry for myself if I had to see you still sleeping in bed when I left in the morning."

Brad put on a pair of slacks and a sweater and walked her to her car. He felt like a teenager walking his date home, one of the splendid moments of déjà vu he had learned to appreciate on reaching midlife. They didn't say much. Brad just watched as she drove away.

Back in the apartment, he washed the dishes and fitted them back into their proper places in the picnic basket. The night air had an invigorating effect, which didn't last long after the work was done. He ate a bowl of cereal, leaving the residue of sweetened milk on the counter for Fleder, as was their custom. Then he showered and climbed into bed with the Melville pamphlet he had taken from the Rieslings'. Brad read himself to sleep every night. Sometimes he would read for three or four hours, well into the morning, but he didn't feel that this was going to be one of those nights. Halfway into the third page, he put the pamphlet down on his night table, took off his glasses, and turned out the light.

It was a tinkle of glass. Brad lay there listening. "Fleder?" He moved his foot toward the left, where Fleder usually slept next to him on the bed. There was no Fleder. The warm, floating sensation of sleep rippled over him again. Warm like a blanket. Then he heard a scraping sound in the living room, like cups or books being moved along the table. Brad didn't know what it was, and nothing he could think of made any sense. He was almost awake now, thinking of Fleder. "Damned cat." He turned on the reading light by his bed and groped for his glasses. There would be no sleep until he found out what was happening.

"Fleder, you're a pain in the ass," he grumbled as he padded down the hall in his Jockey shorts.

He was reaching for the light switch when he became aware of someone else in the living room, behind him, to his left. He didn't actually hear anything. It was just an awareness, maybe a sense of warmth, smell—he was never actually able to sort through these sensations. His only remembrance was that as he started to turn around to face whoever it was, he saw a white light in the middle of the dark room and heard a muffled noise, like waves, throb in his ears. Swallow, he said to himself. Swallow and the noise will go away. That was what his mother used to tell him. And he could see his mother now. "Swallow," she kept saying. "Brad, if you swallow, your ears will pop." She said it again and again, like a record stuck between grooves. She was shaking him now. But why was his mother shaking him? Brad's mother lived in Massachusetts in a nursing home, and he . . .

He tried to focus his eyes on his mother, but she was blurry. Not so out of focus, though, that he couldn't see now that it wasn't his mother after all. It was a man, albeit a blurry man.

"Harry, I think he's coming to," the blurry man said, and then he repeated his name: "Mr. Parker? Mr. Parker?"

The man was ill defined—like a Matisse. "Glasses," Brad muttered. "Do you know where my glasses are?"

"Here, Mike." The man called Harry handed a pair of glasses to the blurry man who was holding Brad in a sitting position, and Brad took them from him. The right earpiece was bent up at a forty-five-degree angle like Dizzy Gillespie's trumpet, but Brad was able to ease it back into relative normalcy. He put his glasses on with pain. It made the world a little clearer, but just barely.

The next two hours, as Brad remembered them, were not a coherent whole. Harry and Mike, two Williamsburg policemen, tried to look after him like friends tending to a drunk at the end of a bender. One of them, Brad forgot which, went to the kitchen and came back with a plastic bag filled with ice. This he applied directly to the back of Brad's head. They said they would wait and take him to the emergency room at the hospital, and were patient as Brad stumbled around. In order to help, they began a litany of clothes as Brad tried to dress himself for the trip.

"Good, you got your pants on now."

"Socks?" Harry said, in a tone used in talking to four-year-olds.

"No socks," Brad replied.

Brad saw what he thought was a look of disappointment on their faces.

"Shoes?" Harry said tentatively.

"Shoes," Brad repeated.

As time went by, Brad began to feel the pain more, which made the hospital that much more uncomfortable. A young nurse slowly cleaned off the blood from what had become a large lump near the back of his skull. X-rays had already been taken, and were waiting for the doctor who would examine them.

"We don't feel tired now, do we?" a middle-aged nurse asked for what must have been the fifth time as she breezed past them. Brad had already identified her as the person in charge.

"Could I have two aspirin?" he asked.

"We'll have to wait for the doctor to prescribe them," she said cheerfully. "We'll just have to be patient."

"Uh," Brad growled, at the pain and at the nurse.

"Not drowsy, are we?"

"If you're trying to aggravate me just to keep me awake, you're succeeding," Brad replied.

The nurse stiffened and left him sitting on the edge of the bed while the younger nurse finished her cleaning. The bed was surrounded on all four sides by white curtains. When the younger nurse left, Harry poked his head through one of the openings.

"How's it coming?"

"Okay, I guess."

"You sure are lucky to be alive."

"What happened? I don't even know what happened."

"You were hit over the head."

"That much I'd figured out."

"Did you see who did it?"

"See who hit me?"

"Yes sir. As near as we can tell, someone broke into your apartment, and that person must have hit you with something."

"I remember hearing noises in the living room. I thought it was my cat."

"Not unless your cat's name is Mike Tyson."

"Why would anyone want to break into my apartment? I don't have anything worth stealing."

"A thief might not know that."

"Uh," Brad said, feeling the pain in his head more sharply when he talked. "How did you two happen along? Did someone call you?"

"Not about your getting hit over the head. We got a call from Colonial Williamsburg security around midnight that your store had been broken into. They'd tried calling you at home, but there was no answer."

"My store?"

"Yeah, and it was a slow night for us, so we volunteered to drive past your house and tell you. We were going out for coffee anyway."

"My store, Parker's Rare Books?"

"It was broken into."

"You said that." Brad didn't know if it was he or the policeman. "Do you know any details?"

"Someone came in through the skylight. The first floor doesn't seem to have been touched. Just the second."

"Was anything taken?"

"That's what the Williamsburg security people wanted to ask you. It was sure a mess up there."

"I want to go to the shop now. Can you drive me?"

"Well . . ."

With that a slender young man came into the room wearing a white medical gown and a stethoscope dangling from his neck. He had curly blond hair and a suntanned face. He introduced himself in a thick Southern accent as Dr. Eric Hamilton. His cheerful manner couldn't hide the exhaustion in his voice. Thirty years old, Brad thought, and already burnt out. Brad watched him as he paused to read the information on Brad's chart. Dr. Eric Hamilton's expression changed from casualness to one of concern.

"You're a very lucky man, Mr. Parker," the doctor said gravely.

"Why is that?" Brad asked.

"Your X-rays show no skull fracture, but of course we'll want to keep you here for a day or two for observation—concussions, that sort of thing."

"Doctor, I just found out that my store was broken into tonight. The police have volunteered to drive me there."

"That would be impossible."

"Why is that?" Brad asked.

"You've had a serious blow to the head. You need to stay here for observation."

"If I start convulsing, I'll give you a call."

"I just can't allow you to walk out that door."

"Are you going to pay my hospital bill?"

"You have insurance."

"Who is going to force me to sign the forms?"

In the end Brad agreed to have his head bandaged to at least ensure a clean wound. The hospital released him after he signed his insurance forms, and Brad was also able to negotiate two extrastrength Tylenol tablets—at a dollar eighty-nine apiece.

"You're a real pistol when you get mad," Harry told Brad, chuckling, when they were back in the squad car.

"I just hate hospitals, is all."

"By the way, when we left your apartment, I put your cat in the bathroom," Harry said. "The window on the downstairs door was broken. I didn't want to take a chance on the cat getting out."

"Fleder?"

"Is that the cat's name?"

"Yes. That's who I thought I heard out in the living room."

"The cat was just lying there on your chest when we came up the steps. When Mike and I were trying to bring you around, it kept rubbing against my leg. I guess it wanted me to feed it or something."

"That's my Fleder."

"Kind of made me glad I have a dog."

"Watch cats aren't what they're cracked up to be."

# Chapter

# 11

Joey drove to New York City in his Cadillac Seville. Ever since he first could afford one and for the past twenty years, Joey had bought a new Cadillac each fall when the next year's models were announced. It was always a Cadillac, and it was always white.

"I was crazy about Cadillacs," Joey told anyone who would listen. "When I was a kid I knew everybody in town who owned one and could tell two blocks away whose car it was. You got to remember, in the late thirties and early forties there weren't all that many around."

Joey talked about his Cadillacs with all the fervor of an Old Testament prophet. It was his only passion. "I was ten and playing third base in a pickup game at the playground. Freddy Scanton was at bat when out of the corner of my eye I saw this brand-new, shiny white Cadillac turn the corner. I never seen a white Caddy before.

"Then what does Freddy do but hit a line drive right at me. Hit me square on the forehead. Christ, the damned thing knocked me out. When I came to, it was like that car was etched in my brain. I knew then and there I wanted one of my own, and I didn't stop until I got one."

Driving into New York was fairly easy. The heavy traffic was heading out of the city in the other direction. Briefly, Joey found himself bumper-to-bumper near the George Washington Bridge with the commuters who worked in New Jersey and lived in New York, but it broke up nicely on the bridge itself. It was shortly before six when he found a parking space on one of the side streets west of Seventh Avenue in Greenwich Village, and six o'clock exactly when he walked into the Madrid Restaurant.

The place was dark. It was early and the crowd was thin, ten or so people congregated around the bar up front. Waiters were setting tables and straightening up. Finally Joey saw Teddy Simon sitting at a booth in the rear.

"Joey," Teddy yelled, and motioned for him to come back and join him. "Hey, Joey. You gotta try these sausages. They're fantastic."

Teddy Simon was born Theodore Simoneste. His name was changed for him when he was four and his father moved the family out of the city and into the suburbs, where they began to assimilate. Teddy was trim and tanned and wore a navy pinstriped suit. He could have passed for a stockbroker.

"You got a place we can talk?" Joey asked, still standing in the aisle by the booth. "I think we got problems."

"This is a good place for talk," Teddy said, motioning for Joey to sit opposite him in the booth. "Now, why do you look so down, and what are all these problems we have?"

Joey told him about his telephone conversation and the caller's demands.

"Two hundred thousand. What were you carrying with you on the bus?"

"A cigarette case. I don't know what was in it. I was just the delivery boy. It wasn't my place to ask."

"Jesus."

"What do we do?"

"First, I want you to tell me again about the call. Word for word. All you can remember."

88

Joey repeated his story.

"And the man mentioned Senators Axom and Pender?"

"Yeah."

Teddy was silently mulling over Joey's story.

"What do you think it means?"

"I don't know, and I don't want to guess." Teddy walked over to the pay telephone by the men's room and dialed a number. "Mr. Jackson," he said into the phone, taking his gold Cross pen and leather notebook from his jacket pocket. "Do you have a number where he can be reached?" He wrote something down on his notepad and returned to the table.

"Let's take a walk," he said to Joey, throwing down a twenty-dollar bill next to a half-eaten plate of grilled Spanish sausages.

The two of them walked down to Sheridan Square and then south on Seventh Avenue until the road doglegged slightly and became Varick Street. A few blocks later Teddy led Joey into a cavernous building with the words "BAR—RESTAURANT" printed in large letters behind a looping tube of neon that no longer lit. The lower half of the windows along the street had been painted over with white paint. Inside, the room had too many fluorescent lights hanging from the ceiling; they provided more light than the sun did on a hot August day at the beach. To the right was a thirty-foot, mahogany-stained bar separated from rows of tables and chairs by a cheaply constructed plywood partition. The place originally had been a lunchroom and watering hole for the printing and manufacturing companies that used to be centered in the neighborhood. Truckers would stop outside before heading through the Holland Tunnel to New Jersey and points west. Now, with the old buildings being converted to artists' lofts and chic apartments for the upwardly mobile, BAR—RESTAURANT had become a local anachronism and an eyesore, frequented by street people and other kindred lost souls too old to be Grateful Deadheads. Joey was surprised Teddy knew it existed.

They ordered two beers at the bar and took them over to a telephone cubicle against the wall. Teddy dialed a number and told the person on the other end the details of the call Joey had received. Joey didn't know who Teddy was talking to, but from the tone of his voice and the care he was taking in phrasing his words, Joey guessed it was someone important. Joey listened to Teddy's end of the conversation for fifteen minutes, sipping on his beer. He noticed that Teddy never touched his glass.

"I think we should still go ahead with tonight," Teddy finally said. "If we can talk with this man, we can put pressure on him and his partner to stop all this nonsense and give back the merchandise."

Teddy paused for a second and winked at Joey to let him know that things would be all right. "I agree with you," he said into the phone. "Even if we just find out the name of this man's partner, we'll be ahead of the game."

The conversation went on for another five minutes. "Yes, sir. I will get another two men for tonight, and we'll be careful." He paused. "Yes, I'll arrange to bring him there so that you can talk to him yourself. No problem."

With that Teddy hung up the telephone. "Everything stands as planned. It looks like you're going to get a chance to meet your buddy from the bus tonight," he said. "But you heard the conversation. We have to be real careful to keep the man healthy and alive."

"Sure."

"We're just going to introduce ourselves and ask him to take a ride and meet a friend of ours."

"I heard that," said Joey.

"But don't worry. What I said to you this morning still holds. When we're finished talking, the man is yours."

"Good." Joey smiled. He was beginning to like Teddy Simon more and more.

# Chapter
# 12

E rnest Hyman unlocked the door to his new Dodge van, parked at a meter in front of 22 Jones Street in Greenwich Village. He was showing Miss Candy Pritchard, a girl he had just met that evening in Margolin's Pub, the custom interior work he had done on the van. Ernest noticed a tingling sensation in his skin and was aware that his heart was now racing as fast as his mind. Ernest was a young nineteen, and this was the closest he had been to getting laid. His overwhelming concern at the moment was that he keep from hyperventilating.

"Get in, Candy. We can lay down and listen to tapes."

Ernest had installed quadraphonic sound above a heated waterbed, the van's focal point, which was reflected in the newly installed, silver Art Deco walls and ceiling.

Candy climbed in and rolled her lithe frame back and forth on the bed. "Wow," she said, gazing at her reflection in the ceiling. A careful sampling of pharmaceutical products had heightened her awareness of such things, producing the noticeable side effect of limiting her ability to express it.

"That fur rug on the bed's really warm next to your skin," Ernest suggested, trying as best he could to keep any hint of a leer from oozing into his voice.

"Neat," said Candy, rubbing her face on a corner of the fur. Then Ernest's heart began to pound as he watched Candy pull her T-shirt over her head and slip off her jeans. All the hours he had worked to pay for the van, over a splattering grill at the Teaneck, New Jersey, McDonald's, were suddenly justified. He quickly climbed into the back and closed the door behind him.

Just as the door closed, a large black man turned the corner and started walking up Jones Street in the general direction of the van. Napoleon Robespierre Jones was whistling as he walked. He held a six-pack of Schlitz malt liquor under his left arm as he fumbled for the keys to the outer door of his apartment. He lived at 22 Jones Street and took a certain amount of pride in living on a street with the same name as his. "Jones from Jones Street."

That evening Napoleon had watched a heavyweight fight on cable television at the Fourth Street Café. He had won fifty dollars on it from a man sitting next to him.

Napoleon unlocked the front door to the apartment building and walked up the steps to the second floor, where he lived. He was about to open his own apartment door when he noticed that a piece of Scotch tape was dangling loose from the upper jamb. It was a little trick he had learned from Bernie Babcock in the Teamsters Union. "You just put a piece of Scotch tape on the outside of the door, on the top where nobody looks. You put one end on the door, the other on the doorjamb, and you check this before you ever walk in the room. If it's not there or not still stuck in both places, someone's been in your place—or maybe is still there."

"You're a crazy old man to do stuff like that," Napoleon had said.

"Depends on what business you're in. If you're a shoe clerk, it's crazy, but we're not in the shoe business, are we? You listen and do as I tell you."

Napoleon had listened. He stood there hesitating by the door for a second, and then decided to go back down the stairs. As he turned away from the door he saw the head and shoulders of a big white man in an overcoat who was coming up the stairs. He had never seen the man before, but the stranger stared directly at Napoleon as he approached, taking the steps two at a time. Napoleon now noticed that there was a gun in his hand, and he regretted that his own was rolled up in a sweater in his bottom dresser drawer. He turned to run down the hall away from the man on the steps, and he heard the man say "Hey!" behind him. Then Napoleon sensed movement everywhere. The doorknob to his apartment began to turn, and he could hear footsteps coming down the staircase from the floor above. Napoleon ran straight down the hall, away from the steps, and flung himself through the closed window there, splintering the wood and shattering the glass panes. Outside the window was a landing for the fire escape, with Jones Street twenty-five feet below.

Napoleon got to his feet, realizing that climbing down the ladder at the far end of the landing would take too much time. He glanced down at the street. A van was parked directly in front of the building. He took two steps and with an athletic move jumped up on the railing of the fire escape. Using that as a springboard, he dove off, keeping his eyes glued to the top of the van, his target, which he hoped beyond hope, would cushion the fall.

"Shiii— " Napoleon never completed the cry, arriving directly in the middle of the van's roof in a spread-eagle belly flop. His momentum rolled him off the roof and onto the street, where he landed on all fours, instinctively keeping his legs and arms moving until he was standing. On reaching the corner, he broke into a dead run.

He heard voices behind him from the apartment building, then a gunshot. A bullet hit something close to him as he ran, still clutching his six-pack of Schlitz like a football. "No shooting," someone screamed. A car engine started and tires squealed from a parking space, but by then Napoleon was running down Morton Street, across Seventh Avenue.

Napoleon knew he had to make some decision and he knew he had to make it soon. His initial burst of adrenalin had evaporated, and he was gasping for breath. That wasn't crucial for the moment. If he kept running they would catch up with him anyway. He had to find someplace to hide. Bernie Babcock had given him some advice once. "You got to hide up high. It's like that trick I taught you with the tape and the door. Nobody ever looks up. It has to do with bad posture and people's sacroiliacs."

Napoleon looked for a fire escape to climb, but then he thought about all the people living in apartments who might see him because they were looking down. If anyone saw a black man climbing a fire escape in this neighborhood, Napoleon knew, they would automatically call the police. If there was anything he didn't want to do that evening, it was sit down and try to explain to the police what had happened when he wasn't sure himself.

So in three strides, Napoleon rejected Bernie Babcock's advice. And anyway, Napoleon thought to himself, breathing deeply, what did Bernie know? Napoleon had met him shortly after Bernie came out of Attica after doing six years of a fifteen-year sentence. I think—breath—the cops caught him—breath—on a fire escape—breath—after a robbery, he remembered.

Napoleon came to a corner. He looked down at his left arm and saw he was still carrying a dripping six-pack of Schlitz. He tossed it into the darkened side entry of a building. There was a line of parked cars down the street to the right. A white panel truck with "Smith Florist" printed on its side sat midway between the corner and a fireplug. Napoleon ran to it and rolled underneath. The panel truck had sufficient clearance for Napoleon's bulk, and there were cars both in front and in back to help hide him. Napoleon wasn't certain how they would come after him. All he knew was that they would. He crawled directly under the center of the truck, so that he had an equal chance not to be seen from the sidewalk or from a passing car.

It took Napoleon what seemed like fifteen minutes to control his breathing. He was too old for this. He made a promise to himself that if he got out of this alive, he was going to go to the gym and work himself back into shape. He could feel the bruises now from his fall, and the moisture seeping up at him from the ground. Despite the cold, Napoleon knew he was drenched in sweat. He tried to wipe some from his forehead, but it didn't help.

A large, white car with Pennsylvania plates drove by slowly. It would drive past four more times throughout the night, before dawn.

Meanwhile, in front of 22 Jones Street, there was noisy confusion as neighbors and passersby came out to see what had happened. Napoleon's leap onto the van had been so sudden and violent that the impact had popped its windshield from the rubber molding and bounced it onto the parked car in front. The impact had also sprung the van's rear doors irrevocably open.

When the big bang actually occurred, Ernest and Candy were experiencing a moment of their own. "I screamed hysterically," Ernest later told a psychiatrist. "I swear to God, I thought it was her father, or a bunch of religious fanatics."

Candy, in her drug-induced fog, merely thought the thud and Ernest's screaming were part of some intense orgasm that she had previously missed during her brief but active sexual life. Sensing that her evening was over, she calmly dressed herself, ignoring the people outside who were now peering into the van at her and Ernest. When she finished, she hopped out between the open rear doors. Several people asked if she was all right, but, having been taught never to speak to strangers, she silently walked past them toward Sheridan Square, where she hailed a taxi going south on Seventh Avenue.

It wasn't as easy for Ernest, who had barely stopped screaming and put on his trousers before the police arrived. Not knowing what had happened, and with a natural sensitivity about his own activities, he spent three hours under repeated questioning before the police finally let him go, after he promised that he would have the van towed from the parking space within twenty-four hours.

Ernest's local paper, the *Bergen Evening Record*, picked up on the story, earning him the nickname "Buster Hymen," an embarrassment that followed him through college and into graduate school.

Meanwhile Joey, Teddy, and Teddy's men were methodically combing the streets of Greenwich Village and Soho, trying to find Napoleon and salvage what was turning out to be a very bad situation.

The sun, beginning to rise over the horizon, mixed its golden-yellow rays with the bluish-white glare of the streetlights. The white car with the Pennsylvania license plates hadn't passed for an hour and a half when Napoleon decided, finally, to move. "It's time," he grunted as he rolled out from underneath the panel truck. His entire body ached, and he hoped he didn't have any internal bleeding.

Napoleon brushed some of the dirt from his slacks and leather jacket. As he did that, his fingers ran across heavy scuffmarks around his elbows. "Four hundred and forty bucks, brand-new. Shit," he said.

His first few steps were stiff and tentative, but as he walked, he regained his normal rhythm and some of the stiffness and pain evaporated. Napoleon charted a zigzag course across lower Manhattan until he finally got to the Bowery. There were street people there, starting their day, and after last night, that was the world in which Napoleon felt most safe and at home. The threat of death followed by a night of cold and fear had had an unsettling effect on him. This was where he wanted to be for now, but he was confident that after he made a call or two and got whatever it was resolved, everything would be fine again.

Lying underneath the van had certainly focused his attention. Napoleon had run through a laundry list of his sins, things he'd done that might have led people to want to kill him, but the list became meaningless when he considered the number of people who had come for him. "One on the steps, another one in the room, one on the third floor, somebody else shooting at me in the street, and somebody started that car." There was no one he knew who would have gone to that amount of trouble.

As the night wore on, Napoleon began to concentrate on people he knew in the Teamsters or people with connections to organized crime. He remembered his friend Max. It takes a certain amount of professionalism, he thought, to assemble a small army like the one around the apartment. People who could do that were major-league trouble, trouble that had to be faced head on. If anyone knew who they were or could find out for him, it would be Max.

At seven o'clock Napoleon found a pay telephone that worked in the back of a diner off Houston Street. He called Max, whom he had worked with for several years when he started providing muscle for the union. He had once known Max's last name, but had forgotten it. It was one of those Latvian names that no one could spell and your tongue got a hernia trying to pronounce. To Napoleon he was just Max, and Napoleon had memorized Max's home telephone number soon after a frustrating encounter with an information operator. He hadn't called Max in years and hoped he was still alive.

"Hello."

"Max, is that you?" Napoleon asked.

"Max," a tired voice repeated.

"Napoleon Jones, Max. Remember me?"

"It is quarter to seven. I don't remember anyone who would call Max at quarter to seven."

"My watch says seven o'clock."

"You're a lucky boy. Max's watch doesn't talk. When your watch says, 'Hey, it's nine o'clock,' then you call Max back. Okay?" With that Max hung up.

Napoleon reached deep in his pocket and came up with another quarter. He put it in the slot and redialed. When the phone stopped ringing Napoleon quickly said, "Max, don't hang up. This is my last quarter."

"Why do you want to use your last quarter to irritate me?"

"You told me once if I got a problem, I should call, and right now I got one of the biggest problems of my life." Napoleon told Max about what had happened the night before.

"You sure it's not police?"

"Nobody identified themselves."

"It could have been FBI."

"Trust me. These guys weren't FBI."

Max listened quietly, occasionally stopping to ask for a detail. "You said you spent the night under a car."

"It was a panel truck."

"Truck, schmuck. You have any ideas under there about who would want to kill you?"

"No. I told you. I never messed with people who can put on that much heat."

"Oh, you're a real choirboy."

"It's got to be some kind of a mistake."

"Seven professional men, maybe more. That's a pretty big mistake."

"I called you, Max, because I figured you might be able to get the word out and find out what it's all about."

"What kind of contacts you think Max has?"

"Used to be pretty good ones."

"Awright, I'll make a few calls for you. I probably find out that you stuck your dick someplace it shouldn't have been. That's what I think."

"I hope that's all it is."

"So, if you're right about how pretty good my contacts are and I find these bad guys, what do you want Max to tell them?"

"Tell them I don't know what I've done, but I want to make things right."

"Okay. How do I get in touch with you?"

"I think it'll be safer for both of us if I call you."

"You know my number."

"How long are you going to need?"

"Call me when your watch talks to you again and says, 'Napoleon Jones. It's twelve o'clock.' Hah, talking watches."

"I'll call you then," said Napoleon. "And thanks, man."

"I don't want thanks. If Max makes a contact, Max gives you a bill. You'll owe me. That's why Max is in this country. He likes free enterprise."

"I understand."

"It's like you have credit card account with me."

"Understood."

When they finished, Napoleon walked uptown toward Forty-second Street. He thought for a few minutes about getting some sleep at one of the twenty-four-hour movie theaters there. At Twenty-seventh Street he considered that someone might have them staked out. First place I'd look if I was looking for me, he thought.

He continued walking in the same direction, however, and ended in a Chock-Full-of-Nuts coffee shop off Forty-second between Fifth Avenue and the Avenue of the Americas. He ordered a regular coffee and two whole-wheat doughnuts. When he finished, he ordered the same thing again. The lunch counter where he sat looked out on the street. Across Forty-second Street was the New York Public Library. Napoleon had been there once with Jebediah, and remembered enough about it to know it was safe as a church. After he paid the cashier with his last twenty-dollar bill, he walked over and waited on a bench near the building entrance until the library opened at ten o'clock.

Once inside, he walked straight up the stairs to the main reading room. It had impressed him when he was there with Jebediah, with its ornate decorations, high ceilings, and long tables. He remembered thinking that this was how he imagined a royal palace would look, and here it was in the middle of New York City. Napoleon walked through the main reading room and into a smaller area where they kept their genealogical books.

Jebediah had taken him to this room during his visit. "We're descended from French royalty on my mother's side," Jebediah had said.

"My mama would have been impressed with that, but me, I already knew there must have been a queen in your background somewhere."

There were five people sitting there when Napoleon arrived alone. They were all elderly and white.

Napoleon pulled a large, leatherbound book from one of the shelves and took it over to a small unoccupied desk. He pulled out a chair and sat down, making a screeching sound with the chair. In a knee-jerk reaction, all the other readers in the room raised their heads slightly and stared at him.

"Just looking for my roots," he said to them in a low voice, and sat back in his chair until it tilted weightless on the two back legs. He continued sitting there, rocking back and forth, until it was almost noon. Then he walked back through the building, retracing his steps until he found a bank of telephones he had seen on his way in.

"Max?" he said into the receiver after making the call.

"Choirboy," Max replied.

"You find out anything?"

"It took three calls, but Max knows who came after you last night."

"Who?" Napoleon said, with a mixture of relief and fear.

"The man said you would know."

"Well, damn, I don't."

"That's what Max tells him. Then he tells Max to set up a meeting, but not to use names."

"What kind of shit is that?"

"Powerful shit. He did not tell me what you did, but you have made a big enemy, Napoleon Jones."

"What is it, Teamsters? The Mafia?"

"I can't say."

"Well, fuck him."

"When you called this morning, you told Max to find this person and to tell him you want to make things right. He wants to talk to you and do that. Now you say 'fuck him.' I don't understand that."

Napoleon was silent, looking at the wall of the telephone booth, trying to collect his thoughts. "Where does he want this talk?" he finally said.

"You know where the zoo is in Central Park?"

"No."

"You go in the Park at Fifty-ninth and Fifth Avenue. It's near there. Ask. There are benches in front of the entrance. Three-thirty. Don't be late."

"You going to pick me up in a taxi?" Napoleon asked.

"If you want, but for this I charge you extra."

"It's a joke, an old song, but I would like you to be there."

"Okay," Max said. "The man I called said you should bring along what you took from him. He said he would not be blackmailed."

"What? I never blackmailed anybody in my life."

"I know, you're a choirboy. I just repeat what the man said to me."

"He's crazy."

"I'll tell him if you want, but it's better you talk together at three-thirty."

"Right."

"One more thing. I think you have a chance to get yourself out of this. If they wanted to kill you, you'd be dead now. The man I called really wants to talk. Be smart, don't fuck it up. Believe Max, this man is as strong as the pope. You won't be alive if you play it cute."

"Right. See you at three-thirty," Napoleon said. The connection went dead.

# Chapter

# 13

One of Colonial Williamsburg's security guards was standing in front of Parker's Rare Books when Brad arrived with the two policemen. The guard had a decidedly military bent, standing at parade rest in his freshly pressed uniform, his eyes focused on an imaginary spot directly in front of him. It was early Wednesday morning, and dawn was beginning to turn back the darkness everywhere but inside Brad's head.

"Looks like it hurts," the guard said to Brad as he held the door open for him.

"Mr. Parker," said another guard, one of two more standing inside the shop. "The chief's upstairs. He wanted to see you when you came in."

"I'll be a minute," Brad said, pointing to the bathroom at the far side of the wrapping area.

"I'll tell him you came in," the guard said, the New England twang in his voice blending with the static on the two-way radio fastened to his belt.

Brad walked directly ahead, turned on the bathroom light, and shut the door behind him. The first thing he did was to reach for the bottle of Excedrin and take two tablets with a large gulp of water. The way the pain in his head throbbed, he figured that the pills would be about as much help as someone's handing a handkerchief to a naked lady. Still, old habits die hard. The CIA taught their agents their concept of pain—that it was something to rise above or learn to accept philosophically. Pain was never to be used as an excuse, or as a reason for failure. It was an idea Brad felt worked better in theory than in actuality.

He looked into the mirror at himself, and for a second he had to turn away. The bandage, the glasses slightly askew—he began to take an inventory and finally decided that things could be worse. A few gentle bends made his glasses sit straight on his nose again, but there was little he could do to improve the red eyes behind them. He reached for the electric razor he kept on a nearby shelf and shaved the stubble from his face, going rather gingerly around a red scrape on his cheekbone, the result of having bumped against something when he fell. With shaving out of the way, he brushed his teeth. Looking squarely into the mirror for a second time, he decided he would survive and that it was time to rejoin the world.

The glass from the shattered skylight lay over the stairs and the hallway of the second floor. Scattered on the carpet, intermingled with the shards of glass, were most of Brad's reference library as well as the volumes from the quote shelf.

"Bastards," Brad said under his breath.

He walked carefully up the steps, trying not to disturb the books or the debris. Still there were the inevitable crunching sounds from the glass as he made his way into his office.

"Ah, Mr. Parker," said a man Brad assumed was the chief. He was standing in the office directing another man on the roof who was trying to arrange a temporary plywood cover over the broken skylight. "Be with you in a second," he said to Brad, and then spoke some unintelligible words into the two-way radio he held in his hand.

If anything, Brad's office was an even greater disaster than the hall. Someone had taken all the files from the cabinets and thrown the papers in a pile at the center of the room. The drawers from Brad's desk were on top of the pile, lying facedown, along with two drawers of index cards—his entire mailing list.

"How's your head?" the chief asked.

"About what you would expect."

"Nasty-looking."

"So is this office," Brad replied.

"Yeah, it sure surprised our guard when he came up to take a look around. You can imagine; the downstairs wasn't even touched."

"What made your guard want to come into the bookshop in the first place?"

"Oh, the glass and the broken slate shingles on the walkway outside. The stuff must have slid down the roof and landed on the path. The guard noticed it when he made his rounds. Took out his flashlight and saw that the skylight was broken. Then he called us on this new radio system we have."

Brad looked around the room at the papers and books, wondering how long it would take him to put everything back together again.

"We figure that if the thief didn't hear the talk on the radio, he would have torn into the downstairs the same way. Probably looking for money to buy drugs. All these addicts . . ."

"Wait. You mean that the thief was still here when your guard called?"

"Yeah. Didn't I tell you?"

"Did your guard see the thief?"

"Yeah, he saw him running out of the back door while he was waiting for us to bring him the key. I asked him why he didn't try the back door first. He said he didn't think of it."

"Did he give you a description?"

"He just saw him for a split second through the window. The thief was gone by the time Howard ran around back. He couldn't even say for certain whether it was a man or a woman. Whoever it was just took off across the parking lot."

"And your guard obviously didn't catch him."

"Poor old Howard, always kidding about himself being built more for comfort than for speed."

Brad looked at the door to the Rare Book Room. It was hanging open, and the doorframe was splintered in the general vicinity of where the lock should have been.

"We figure that the thief probably used that crowbar in the corner to force the lock," the chief continued. "We might be able to trace it if it was bought around here recently."

"Don't bother. It's mine. We use it to open crates."

"You get many wooden crates?"

"Occasionally."

"Well, we asked someone to come over from the Police Department to dust for fingerprints first thing in the morning."

"Who did you call, Tom Egan?"

"You know Tom?"

"We just met."

"Well, it probably won't be him. He'll send one of his men to do that. Don't forget to call me when he comes. I want to make sure he doesn't ruin any of your books, dusting them wrong, that sort of thing."

"Thanks." Brad squeezed by the chief's ample stomach and went into the Rare Book Room. There were books scattered on the floor and on the top of the library table. Brad was glad he never locked the bookcases. If he had, undoubtedly they would have been shattered like the door.

"The police will probably ask you for a list of what was stolen."

"I'm sure."

"My advice is to take some time getting that list together," the chief said, lighting a cigar. "You don't want to forget anything with those insurance boys. I know a few shop owners, wouldn't mention names, who added a few choice items to the list of stolen property when their stores were robbed. It's all part of the game. You turn a little adversity to the good, within reason of course, and nobody's going to say anything." He stood there poised with his cigar, rather proud of having delivered his sermon.

"When did your guard report finding the glass outside?"

"Oh, my men have the exact time logged back at the guard's center, but it must have been around eleven-thirty. At least that's when the center called me at home. Just turned off the television and was going up to bed. I told them to get the emergency keys and go in the shop and see what had happened."

"Eleven-thirty?"

"Approximately. After we saw the mess, we reported the burglary to the police and tried to call you. I guess that was around one o'clock. We didn't know if we had dialed an old telephone number or what, when you didn't answer. One of our guards said he thought he'd heard that you'd moved. That's when the police sent some people around to see if you were home."

Two new guards Brad hadn't seen before came from downstairs with a report. All the security and maintenance people scurrying around reminded Brad of an ant colony.

"I don't think there's anything more we can do tonight," the chief said, breaking away from the others. He walked over to Brad and shook his hand like an old-time evangelist greeting the faithful after a service. They went downstairs together, where the chief stopped for ten minutes to discuss Tom Egan and the upcoming election. "You're not a personal friend of Sam Ellington's, are you?"

"Sam who?" Brad replied, half-listening.

"The man running against Tom. Spends his vacations going to boot camps run by those ex-Green Berets. Supposed to teach survival. He thinks he's a tough cookie, but he's headed for a lot of trouble if he starts beating up on people in front of tourists. This town wouldn't be anything without tourists."

Finally the chief was quiet, run down like a battery-operated toy, and Brad was able to say good-night diplomatically and close the door.

The silence of the bookshop at night had been Brad's solace ever since the shop had opened, but he had never appreciated the solitude more than at that moment. He decided that he didn't want to see his office again, at least not just yet, and walked back to the bathroom, where he swallowed two more Excedrin. The lights were off in the shop, and Brad made a pot of coffee in the wrapping area by the dim light of the bathroom. This was Mrs. Johnson's domain, a fact she vigorously reaffirmed whenever Brad entered, but he felt that even Mrs. Johnson would have understood had she been there. With the coffee and water measured and in their respective places, Brad sat behind the counter with his feet resting on the top of the desk, listening in the near-darkness to the coffee pot perk and gurgle.

The primary thought that kept flickering through his mind was how thankful he was that Samantha had gone home last night. He wanted to call her now, to be with her, but it was very early still and he had to use the chance to think while he was alone. Everything had happened so fast and was so unexpected that Brad hadn't had time to react to it—not that he would have done anything differently, even if he had had the opportunity.

Brad didn't know if it was human nature, in times of trouble, to "do something"—anything—or whether this was a learned response American culture firmly encouraged. When he worked for the Company, he had found that with his agents it bordered on a visceral reaction, as automatic as a leg jerking to the tap of a doctor's mallet. Brad knew that people were vulnerable when they were surprised, and that vulnerable people were not in the best position to act and take calculated risks. Blind, instinctive rage was fine for a prizefighter, but it was potentially a deadly habit for anyone in what was then Brad's world. Brad had learned, in his work, to be a patient man. He had tried to teach this quality to others, but found that patience, like most virtues, was rare.

"Why do you say that you are alone and people don't like you?" a psychiatrist had once asked him.

"Because it's true."

"Why do you think these people you work with don't like you?"

"I don't know."

"Come, now, Mr. Marks, you must have some idea?" he had said, sitting back and waiting for Brad's reply.

The psychiatrist knew him by this other name—Marks. Brad realized that if the Company became aware he had privately sought professional help, he would have been shelved, or perhaps even fired. Instability was a sign of weakness, and weakness was not to be tolerated.

"They don't know what I'm thinking."

"Why don't you share it with them?"

"I can't."

"Certainly you can," the psychiatrist said. "The question is, why won't you?"

Brad never did explain. Fear of security leaks, fear of ridicule, fear of censure? He merely said, "Fear."

"This fear is what is isolating you," the psychiatrist said.

"Terribly," Brad agreed.

His work, the life he had chosen, was one aspect of his isolation, one that he could deal with in his own manner, but his marriage had become a distant, long-term habit, a series of meaningless encounters and nights too often spent sleeping in the den in front of a flickering television screen. That was why he had secretly gone to the doctor for help, and, over time, the sessions began to work. At least Brad had felt that he and Phyllis were coming closer. Then there was the accident.

Brad was trained not to accept accidents and coincidences blithely, and the questions lingered: Did Phyllis drive off the road on purpose? Did her death and the death of his children have anything to do with his work for the Company? He went back several times to see the psychiatrist about this, but he never did ask these questions—questions like those about the Kennedys' assassinations, that he knew no one ever could answer truthfully. In the end Brad had accepted that his family was dead and that the answers to the questions didn't really matter. He had decided to leave the Company no matter what the answers might be.

Brad poured a cup of coffee for himself and searched through the drawer beneath the coffee maker for Mrs. Johnson's sugar water. His father once said that a man was a fool to drink before he was forty and a fool not to drink after that. Brad poured a generous tot from Mrs. Johnson's bottle into his cup.

With the coffee in hand, Brad opened the small safe under the wrapping table and removed his stack of inventory cards. Each of his more expensive books, those in the Rare Book Room and in the locked cabinets that dotted the shop, had its own three-by-five index card, which Brad filed by the author's name. Beside the author's name, the card held the book's title, price, and the amount that Brad had originally paid for it. He kept the cards in a fireproof safe for the insurance company. This was the first time he'd used them.

The sound of walking up the stairs over the pieces of broken glass reminded Brad of the scrunch of walking on very hard snow. It was a sound he hadn't thought of since he was a boy.

Brad started picking up the books that were scattered on the floor in the Rare Book Room. He wanted to make a pile of damaged books that would have to be sent to the bookbinder for repair. The others he put back on the shelves. It was a simple enough task, but with his headache it was one that took all of his concentration. When he was a little more than halfway around the room, he decided to let Mrs. Johnson and Jebediah do the actual inventory and find out what was missing. He was tired and needed some sleep.

Mrs. Johnson's Irish coffee seemed to have helped his spirits, and he was also pleased that there were only three books in the pile that needed work by the bookbinder, and those only minor repairs. At eight o'clock Brad began calling people.

He started by asked Mrs. Johnson if she could come to work early and did the same with Jebediah. From the pile of papers on the floor of his office he dug out his address book and found the number for a carpenter he had once used. A new door and frame were ordered and promises made to install them before evening. He left Samantha for last.

"I'm at the shop."

"Is something wrong?"

"It was broken into last night." Brad didn't mention his head or the incident at the apartment.

"What was stolen?"

"I don't know yet. Not much, from the look of things. Whoever broke in really messed up the Rare Book Room and my office. I've been here all night."

"Why didn't you call?"

"I wanted to, but—" Brad left the statement dangling.

"You should have, you know."

"I know."

"Do you want me to come over and help?"

"No. I called Mrs. Johnson and Jebediah. I'm exhausted. I'm going to go home and take a nap. Let them sort everything out."

"Ah, the privileges of management." Samantha paused. "Will we be able to go to the Averys' tonight?"

"I forgot about them."

"I can cancel."

"No, don't. I'll be all right."

Mrs. Johnson arrived a half hour later. "What happened to you?" she asked.

Brad looked bewildered. A second cup of her coffee and sugar water had mellowed his outlook to the point where he had forgotten about his head.

"That bandage on your head?"

"Oh. Someone broke in—"

"You were at the shop last night?"

"No, at home."

"I'm confused."

Brad had just finished explaining when Jebediah came in.

"What happened to you?" he asked. "That bandage on your head?"

Brad left instructions on how he wanted the inventory done and asked Jebediah to sort through the pile of papers in the middle of his office and try to put the mailing list back in order.

"What about the Rieslings? I'm supposed to meet Louis out there in a few minutes."

"I'm sure he'll call when you don't show up. Can he work out there alone?"

"I suppose," Jebediah said, tamping down the tobacco for his first pipe of the day.

"I'll let you decide. The inventory and the mailing list here are top priorities, though. Understood?"

"Sure."

"Won't you be here?" Mrs. Johnson asked.

"No. I've been up all night. Put a sign downstairs that we're closed for the day. That way you won't be bothered going back and forth to the shop. It's going to take both of you to do this."

"What's going to happen with Carl's printing equipment?" Jebediah asked.

"I don't know. Why?"

"I'm interested in buying it if the question arises."

"A sudden influx of money?" Brad asked.

"I have some set aside," Jebediah said in a defensive fluster, "but I was counting on getting a bargain. It'll be hard to dispose of that equipment quickly. I thought I might be doing you a favor in return."

"I'll check into it," Brad said.

Jebediah stood where he was.

"Later," Brad added, arching his eyebrows, and Jebediah left.

*  *  *

Brad called for a taxi and it arrived in five minutes. He sat quietly in the back, glad he had decided to leave.

At the apartment he taped a piece of cardboard over the missing pane of glass in the downstairs door as a temporary solution. He put the tape and knife away before he released Fleder from her prison in the bathroom. She gave him a churlish growl when he opened the door, and walked past him toward her food dish with her tail held perpendicular, not waiting to be petted.

Inside the bathtub Brad found the remnants of the cat's toilet. He removed what he could and then scrubbed the entire tub before drawing water for his bath. As the cat got older, she didn't use her litterbox on occasion, usually when she was displeased, making emphatic statements about whatever mistreatment she thought she was getting. Despite three litterboxes strategically placed in the apartment, praise in good times, scolding in bad—nothing seemed to work.

As he was unbuttoning his shirt, the doorbell rang. Brad walked down the steps and saw two Williamsburg policemen standing on the steps.

"Mr. Brad Parker?" the taller officer said.

"Yes."

"Your people at the bookstore told us you were home. Detective Egan asked if you would mind coming with us."

"As a matter of fact, I do. I've been up all night, and—"

"Detective Egan was very insistent."

"Can't it wait?"

The two policemen stood outside the door, implacable mutes.

"Christ, let's get it over with then. I just have to turn off the water upstairs."

Brad rode in the back of the police car. He had assumed that they were driving to the police station, but when the car went past the town, he asked, "Where are we going?"

"To the Rieslings'."

113

As they rounded the bend before the house, Brad noticed several police cars in the driveway. Tom Egan was standing in the entrance to the office talking with a man carrying a camera. When he saw Brad in the police car he broke away from what he was doing and came over to them. There was a quickness and purpose in his walk. Brad had to wait until Egan opened his door from the outside.

"What happened to you?" Tom Egan asked. "That bandage on your head?"

"I thought that's why you wanted to see me," Brad replied. "My shop was broken into last night."

"When did this happen?"

"About eleven-thirty."

"You work long hours."

"No, I wasn't at the shop at the time."

"Then what happened to your head?"

"Someone broke into my apartment later that evening and—"

"Wait a minute." Before Tom Egan could ask the next question, he saw a white station wagon pull into the driveway with the call letters WMSB boldly printed on its side. "This will have to wait, but don't get lost. I'll be right back." With that he walked over to the television crew and left Brad standing in the parking lot by himself.

Next to the door Brad saw Louis Mellon, the college student who had been hired to help Jebediah pack. He was just outside the door to the building, leaning against the cinderblock wall.

"Louis," Brad said. "What's going on here?"

"I was waiting for Jebediah, just putting books into boxes like he'd told me to do when a squad car pulled up and three policemen came in. They asked me who I was and what I was doing here. I told them. One of the men said that I couldn't pack up any more books, that Mr. Riesling's office was now considered a murder scene. So I stopped and got ready to go. Then another cop comes over and tells me I can't leave. Then he took my keys for the place and I've been waiting here ever since."

Brad and Louis stood by the door watching Tom Egan being interviewed by the TV people at the far end of the parking lot. They couldn't hear what was being said, but Egan's gestures looked agitated and defensive. Brad guessed that things were not going well for him.

When Tom finished, he came over to join Brad and Louis. "Who are you?" he asked Louis.

"His name is Louis Mellon," Brad answered. "I hired him to help Jebediah pack up Carl's stock and move it to my warehouse."

"So you bought the books already."

"I'm having them boxed up so that I can look at them and make an offer."

"If they're not yours, why are you moving them?"

"Mrs. Riesling wanted them out of here to help the real-estate people sell the property."

"The grieving widow isn't wasting any time, is she? And while we're on the subject, do you know where she is?"

"She told me that she was going to visit her sister. Why?"

"The autopsy report came back. The cause of death turns out to be due to something a little more specific than a mere blow to the base of the skull. The coroner found bruise marks on the skin in the shape of letters." Tom Egan reached into his jacket pocket. "It seems like Riesling was hit with this." Tom was holding a composing stick filled with individual pieces of type. "We found it in the printing area after the coroner called. There are traces of blood on it, hair, the works. There's no doubt that this was the murder weapon."

"What about the bookcase that fell on him?"

"My guess is that whoever killed Mr. Riesling sat him behind his desk after he killed him and then tipped the bookcase over on top of him to make his death look like an accident. It seems the killer used a crowbar to pry the shelving loose. We have the crowbar and marks on the wall that support this theory."

"Any fingerprints?"

"Clean." Tom glanced over at Louis. "Why are you still hanging around?" he asked him.

"The policeman told me to."

"You can leave any time you like." Tom turned back to Brad. "Do you happen to have an address or telephone number for Mrs. Riesling's sister?"

"Back in the office. Probably in the pile of papers the thieves dumped in the middle of the floor." Brad hesitated. "You're not going to like this but Greta's sister lives in West Germany."

"You mean Mrs. Riesling left the country?"

"I don't know what plane she was taking, but . . ."

"Her husband's not even buried yet and she takes a plane to Europe?"

"She's not your typical mourner."

"Not even cold in the ground . . ."

Tom Egan sputtered for a few more minutes and then calmed down enough to get details from Brad about the occurrences the night before. Then he stopped as if an idea had suddenly surfaced from the deep recesses of his mind. "You know anything about what Mr. Riesling printed?" he asked.

"Not really."

"There's a lot of printing equipment in there, all apparently in working order."

"I do know he was teaching my shop manager, Jebediah Stuart, how to print."

"Why?"

"Jebediah has aspirations of publishing small editions of poetry for collectors."

"No, I meant why would a curmudgeon like Carl Riesling agree to teach someone about printing? It's not in character."

"Common interests make for strange relationships."

Tom Egan shook his head. He arranged for Brad to be driven back to his apartment. There, Brad ate a bowl of cereal, careful to leave the remainder of the milk for Fleder. It was after one o'clock. He set the alarm for four and collapsed across the unmade bed still wearing his clothes.

# Chapter
# 14

Napoleon got up from his bench in the Central Park Zoo at exactly three-thirty, as the animals on the clock by the seal pond began doing the same circular dance they did every half-hour. Napoleon knew the dance well. He had seen each performance since he arrived at the zoo shortly after his last telephone call to Max. He was glad the clock was there. His watch had been working erratically since his leap to the top of the van, and by being able to see the animal clock he didn't have to bring attention to himself by asking passersby what time it was.

Napoleon remembered being with Max once on Teamsters business. They had arranged a contract negotiation for two o'clock at a hotel on the West Side. They waited outside until they saw the company's negotiator coming toward the entrance. Then Max left the car with Napoleon and a large, hairy man Napoleon knew only as "Mongo." Max pushed the company man into a vacant parking lot and talked to him for several minutes while Napoleon and Mongo watched. Then, at the meeting in the hotel, Napoleon sat on a side chair and saw the company grant the Teamsters all the major points in the disagreement. Napoleon never asked Max what was said in the parking lot, but today of all days he didn't want to be put in the same position.

As he walked out of the zoo, Napoleon saw Max sitting on a bench by the entrance. The sun was shining, but Max sat there in his long gray overcoat and knit cap, looking like an immigrant just off the boat. He hadn't changed in all the years here, resistant to the seduction of American culture. He still wore heavy coats out of habit, because "in Latvia, you never know when it gets cold, choirboy," he'd once told him. He also carried two Hershey chocolate bars in his coat at all times and kept the cabinets in his small apartment stocked with canned goods. Max did not feel insecure, just well prepared for life's adversities, like a boy scout. He was trim and hard, working out three days a week in a gymnasium in Brooklyn. He looked to be forty years old, but was probably sixty.

"Hey, Max," Napoleon said, sitting beside him on the bench. "Thanks for coming, man."

Max looked straight ahead. "Fifteen minutes late."

"Your watch is crazy. The clock in the zoo says three-thirty."

"Must be peachy, talking clocks."

"Max, you're one crazy dude."

"Max must be a crazy dude to sit here on bench with you." He looked down at his watch again, still talking straight ahead, not looking at Napoleon. "You bring what the people want from you?"

"I told you, I don't know what your friend's talking about."

"I guess we both find out pretty soon."

With that a trim man in a gray sharkskin suit, Italian leather shoes, and a silk paisley tie walked up to them. Max stood.

The trim man looked at Napoleon. "Come on."

Napoleon remained on the bench, stretched his left arm over the back of the seat where Max had been, to project a casual look. "We'll talk here," he said.

"The car's double-parked on Fifth."

"What car?"

"The car that's going to take you to meet the person who wants to talk to you."

"You tell the man we talk in the park."

"Mr. Calvado doesn't talk in parks," the thin man replied.

"If this Calvado wants to talk with me, he'll come to the park." The name, Calvado, meant nothing to Napoleon.

"As I understand it, you're the one who wants to talk to him." Napoleon glanced over at Max. "What do you think?"

"Max arranges the meeting. That's all."

"Now I'm asking you for advice."

Max turned and looked directly at Napoleon for the first time. "Choirboy, you want to live, you got no choice."

Napoleon sat there for a few seconds with a ponderous look on his face.

"Well, what's it going to be?" the thin man asked.

Napoleon's smile returned. "I do believe it seems like a nice day for a ride," he said and walked with the man and Max to a black Cadillac stretch limo that was double-parked on Fifth Avenue.

The thin man held the back door of the Cadillac open for Max and Napoleon.

"Say, my man, what's your name?"

The thin man shut the door slightly to prevent Napoleon from getting into the car. He waited until Napoleon looked over at his face, and their eyes met. "My name is Ted," he said slowly, "and we're going to get along a lot better if you remember two things. First, I am not 'your man'; and second, we're never going to be friends. So just get in the car and keep quiet." He opened the door wider, allowing him to pass.

Napoleon still grinned, but the grin now seemed artificial, like a plaster tableau on the wall of a second-rate public building.

There was no one else in the car except for the driver, a stocky blond with a flattop. Teddy sat in the front, leaving the back for Max and Napoleon. There was a glass panel between the front and back seats. Napoleon looked around at the small television set, desk, and refrigerator. "Nice set of wheels," he said to no one in particular.

The driver spoke into a microphone and his voice came from a small speaker in the door. "Go ahead and help yourselves," he said. "There's a complete bar underneath the desktop. It flips up from the front." Napoleon lifted the top, and Max kicked his foot. Napoleon put it down again and sat back in his seat. Nobody spoke.

The car drove down to Sixtieth Street, veered right, and made the turn in front of the Plaza Hotel going west on Fifty-ninth. They drove up Broadway from Columbus Circle. The driver was very careful and smooth and made none of the urgent stops and starts you felt in a taxicab. At Seventy-ninth Street they made a left turn and then turned again onto the north ramp of the West Side Highway.

Napoleon watched the well-muscled neck of the driver and his firm chinline. "You still fight in the ring?" he asked, trying to make conversation. The driver either couldn't hear him or just ignored the remark.

They took the exit for the George Washington Bridge. "Max, looks like we're going to New Jersey," Napoleon said. He remembered the stories about how the families took their enemies to Jersey and dumped their bodies in the marshes there, but he knew that Max was right: that they wanted to talk to him, or he would have been dead already. The thought that they needed him gave him confidence. His mind was loose and clear. He even wondered if there might be a way to turn a profit from all this.

They followed the signs for the Palisades Parkway and wound their way onto it, only to leave at Exit 1: Palisades Avenue, Englewood. They kept going straight after the exit and drove halfway down the hill toward the main business district. Then the driver put on his right-turn signal and smoothly pulled onto a narrow, two-lane road. There were expensive houses on either side of them. As they drove for three blocks, away from the traffic of Palisades Avenue, the expensive houses gave way to "estates." Soon the driver slowed and put on his turn signal again. There, on their right, was a ten-foot brick wall, painted white. The driver pulled into a paved driveway and stopped in front of two iron gates that broke the solidity of the long brick wall.

The driver turned slightly to Max and Napoleon and said into his microphone, "This house used to belong to Gloria Swanson."

They waited. Suddenly the gates began to open, as if by magic, and the car slowly drove onto the estate. Napoleon looked back and saw the gates close behind the car. There was no one in sight.

The main house was in front of them. It was a brick Tudor with leaded windows and a gray slate roof. The walls were dark and foreboding, reminding Napoleon of houses in late-night horror films. He thought they would stop at the main entrance, but they just drove past. He had started to open his door, but the inside handle seemed disconnected, like those in the back seat of a police car. After they passed by the front of the house, the driver swung the car to the right, onto a narrower driveway. This led directly to a ramp that descended into a concrete underground garage.

As they drove in, Napoleon heard the whirring noise of a motor and saw an overhead door close behind them. The garage was cold and barren with cinderblock walls and thick concrete pillars spanning the unadorned floor and ceiling. The lock to the back doors clicked, and Napoleon got out as the driver turned off the engine. The garage was fairly large and could accommodate twelve cars. As Napoleon looked around he saw a BMW 450 SL, a mid-engine Porsche, a black van, and a late-model white Cadillac. What impressed Napoleon most was that the garage even had its own gas pump.

"You carrying a piece?" Teddy asked Napoleon.

"No," Napoleon replied.

"Knife?"

Napoleon shook his head.

Another man, silent, dressed in black slacks and a matching turtleneck sweater, stepped out of the shadows and motioned them into a smaller room. The room was lit by a bare lightbulb dangling over a sturdy wooden table. The table was dented and stained with oil.

"Empty your pockets on the table," the other man said. He had an accent, but Napoleon didn't know what it was. Both Max and

Napoleon walked to the table and put the contents of their pockets on top. Max even took off his overcoat, probably, Napoleon thought, to show good faith. Max had always said that gestures were important.

Ted came into the room with an electronic scanner similar to ones Napoleon had seen people use at airports. He held it in his left hand and swung it in an imaginary arc six inches from Max's body. He repeated the movement with Napoleon.

"Okay?" the quiet man asked.

Ted nodded.

Napoleon heard a click, then a whirr of another electric motor. This time, instead of closing a door, it was moving the entire far wall of the small room they were in, floor to ceiling, along metal tracks. On the other side of the wall was a much larger room, carpeted in a thick, light beige pile that covered the floor. The furnishings in the room were Art Deco. Immediately inside, no more than a foot from where the wall used to be, was a long, inlaid table that held a frosted glass sculpture of a naked woman.

"Etling," a man said. He was seated at a bar on the far right of the room. "I saw you looking at the molded glass sculpture. It was made by the Etling Company in France sometime during the nineteen twenties. It was probably the work of Lucille Sevil, but I have no proof of that, just that it reminds you of her style, doesn't it?" He paused, and seemed to wait for some form of confirmation from Napoleon or Max.

Napoleon looked around the room. It was dimly lit and filled with art.

"Gentlemen, please come in and make yourselves at home," the man said. He seemed to be in his early fifties, fit, with neatly trimmed gray hair and moustache. He wore a quilted maroon dressing jacket with a black suede collar in a sophisticated style favored by tailors in Paris. "Welcome to our humble bomb shelter, built by a paranoid former owner. We, of course, have done the decorating. What do you think?"

"Nice," was all Napoleon could say. The opening they'd entered through closed as they spoke.

"We can sit in the corner over there and chat," the man continued. "But first, would either of you gentlemen like something to drink?"

"Water," said Max.

"A little Chivas on the rocks," Napoleon added in a more expansive mood.

"Ah, a lover of scotch," their host said. "We do have Chivas, but I might recommend a single malt scotch that isn't available in this country through liquor stores. It's quite good. The distiller only sells entire barrels to his customers. He ages and bottles the scotch exclusively for them. My particular scotch is twenty-five years old. When I was a young man, I purchased several barrels for my old age. It was an audacious purchase for a man in my profession, but I have outlived the expectations of my rivals. Unfortunately fate played an ironic trick: In the interim I developed a bleeding ulcer, and my only pleasure now is in offering my scotch to others and watching their enjoyment. So, Napoleon Robespierre Jones, what is your decision?"

"Your scotch will be fine."

"I would recommend drinking it neat."

Napoleon nodded his head slightly in agreement.

The host turned to the man behind the bar. "Jeffrey, could you serve our drinks over by the couch?" he said, and led Max and Napoleon to the far side of the room. Napoleon glanced behind the bar and saw an Uzi leaning against a shelf near Jeffrey's right leg.

The sitting area had three high-backed library chairs with their backs to the room and a red-leather Chesterfield couch facing the chairs. Separating them was a low black coffee table that seemed to have been carved from a single piece of rock. The host angled himself toward the library chair in the center and directed Max and Napoleon to the couch. As Napoleon sat down, he saw that there was another person already sitting in the chair to the left of their host. He sat quietly, holding a drink in his hand. Napoleon thought he had seen him before, but he didn't remember where.

"Joseph," the host said, "is this the gentleman?"

"That's the nigger," Joey replied.

The room focused on Napoleon, who raised himself to the front edge of his seat. "I remember you," he said, his eyes fixed on Joseph Sabatino's smirking face.

"Feels a little different now that my side has the guns, doesn't it?"

"There's no reason to get upset, Mr. Jones," the host interrupted, "but now you must have some idea why you were invited here to talk."

Napoleon sat on the edge of the couch, transfixed. If he had been able to scan the room, he would have seen Teddy and Jeffrey with their guns in hand at their sides, both positioned on the far side of the room with an unobstructed view of Napoleon. All movement in the room stopped.

"So all this has to do with the bus robbery," Napoleon said, staring at Joey with a puzzled look on his face.

"That's what we want to discuss."

For some reason, Napoleon felt relieved. Perhaps it was because the great mystery of why people were trying to kill him was now answered. Perhaps it was because in his mind the robbery, serious as it was, fell into a class of crime with embezzlement and tax fraud—three to five years, but certainly nothing to kill someone over. His body relaxed, and Napoleon sat back on the couch, his ready smile once again in place.

Jeffrey brought the drinks. "Theodore," the man said, rolling his *r*'s, won't you join us?"

"Yes sir, Mr. Calvado." Teddy returned his revolver to its holster and sat in the empty seat on Calvado's right.

Calvado began. "Mr. Jones, first let me apologize for our bungled attempt to have this talk with you last evening. We had no intention of forcing you to make that death-defying leap to the street."

"No problem. Just want to straighten out this disagreement."

"That's very wise of you."

Napoleon looked directly at Joey. "Man, I'm sorry I hit you. I didn't know who you were."

"Unfortunate things sometimes happen during the course of business. All we are looking for is the return of the cigarette case."

"The cigarette case?"

"The one you took from Mr. Sabatino on the bus."

"Shit. We gave that to Jebediah."

"Your partner in the robbery?"

"Yeah."

"Well, Mr. Sabatino claims that this Jebediah called him on the telephone on Tuesday morning and offered to sell the cigarette case back to him for two hundred thousand dollars."

"What?" asked Napoleon, looking at Joey. "Is this jive?"

"I can assure you, Mr. Jones, this is quite serious."

"Jebediah did what?"

"Your friend is attempting to blackmail us for two hundred thousand dollars."

"Mister, you got to believe, I don't know nothing about this."

"Whether you do or not is immaterial."

Napoleon stared at him.

"I don't care if you knew what your friend was doing. We are not people who pay blackmail. What we are interested in from you is help to persuade this Jebediah to return the cigarette case to us."

"What makes it worth two hundred thousand?" Napoleon asked.

"It contained some information your friend found inside. That's all you need to know. Jebediah thought two hundred thousand was a suitable price for it, but as I said, we do not pay blackmail."

"If I help you, what's in it for me?"

"Your life, for one thing," Calvado said. "For another, possibly a job in our organization, if that would suit you. I would rather not think that I had to buy your help, however. I would rather you gave it to us freely as an act of good faith. Such faith is often rewarded."

"If I help, no more men with guns in my apartment."

"None. Our sole purpose is to have our property returned. For that we would be grateful." Napoleon glanced at Joey Sabatino. From the look on Joey's face Napoleon knew that Calvado spoke for himself, not for the entire group.

"Okay, you got my help."

"Where is your friend?"

"Williamsburg."

"Williamsburg?"

"Williamsburg, Virginia. Jebediah works down there."

"All right, tomorrow morning you can fly to Williamsburg with Theodore and Joseph to talk to this Jebediah fellow." Calvado glanced over at Sabatino. "I forgot, Joseph, you don't like to fly."

"No, sir."

"If you prefer to drive, you can meet Theodore and Mr. Jones at the airport in Williamsburg at noon Thursday."

"I'll help you," Napoleon said. "But when I talk to Jebediah, I want to talk to him alone."

"No way!" Joey blurted.

"Why do you ask this?" said Calvado, raising his hand to quiet Joey.

"Jebediah is a skittish fag. If he sees me walk up to him with all this muscle, not telling what he'll do."

"Joseph, do you still object?"

"I don't trust this nigger. I don't like it."

"It seems reasonable to me. Theodore, what do you think?"

"I'd let him see his friend alone, but I'd want to be within sight of him when he does it."

"Is this agreeable with you, Mr. Jones?"

"Fine."

"Joseph?"

"I still don't trust him."

"It's my ass if I fail, brother," Napoleon said sharply, "and from what I've seen of you I ain't so sure you wouldn't spook him crazy."

"I think we can allow Mr. Jones a chance to talk to his friend alone," said Calvado, "under your distant but watchful eye. Any other points to consider?" Calvado looked at his watch. The meeting was over.

"Mr. Jones," Calvado added, "please be our guest tonight. You'll fly to Williamsburg tomorrow in our private plane." It was a statement, not a request. "If you'll trust Theodore with your keys, he'll go by your apartment and pack your suitcase."

Napoleon and Max hugged each other before Max left to be driven back to the city.

"Take care of yourself, choirboy."

They embraced again like two Roman centurions on the eve of battle.

Napoleon was led up a passage to the main house and was shown to his room and told that dinner would be served to him there. It came on a rolling cart: roast beef, baked potato, and green beans. There were three bottles of Beck's beer on the cart along with a bottle of Calvado's personal scotch and an ice bucket. Napoleon ate, showered, and went to bed. He had a restless but heavy sleep. He dreamed of being asked questions about the robbery. He remembered telling someone about Deborah, about Jebediah, about how he felt having sex with white women. Then he sensed the light being turned off and someone telling him not to remember the questions, or his answers, or the night. He was still in a drowsy sleep when a man poked him and told him breakfast was served. There was another cart in his room then, and it was morning. He showered again and drank three cups of coffee. He tried the door to his room, but it was locked. Outside his window, in the walled garden below, were three guard dogs, Alsatians. He dressed slowly and tried to shake the dusty dreams from his consciousness. It should be Thursday morning, he thought, but he was not sure.

# Chapter

# 15

Wednesday, 4:00 P.M.

The alarm rang just as Brad Parker was opening another box. It was a dream he had had many times before. Someone has given him a present, which he unwraps only to find a box. Inside the box is another box; inside that, another; and that is how the dream goes, with each successive box the same size as the one before. Brad experiences the same mixture of frustration and hope with each opening. This was the first time in three years he could remember having the dream.

Brad woke up covered with perspiration and had to force himself to get up and slouch toward the bathroom. He ran fresh bathwater for himself and, while the tub filled, went over to the mirror above the sink and began cutting away the bandage. Fleder watched him from her perch atop the toilet tank.

He spent a half-hour in the bathtub, letting some of the water drain out and adding hot water to the bath at frequent intervals. He lay in the tub with his eyes closed, his neck resting on another improvised icepack made from a green plastic garbage bag.

After the bath, he shampooed his hair gingerly and cleaned most of the dried, clotted blood from around his wound. Dressed and fortified with a large scotch, he drove to the bookshop and arrived at five-thirty.

Brad was happy to see that the shards of glass had been removed from the steps and the books at the top of the staircase were back on their shelves. Inside his office Mrs. Johnson sat behind Brad's desk with what looked like a glass of bourbon in her hand. From the color of the liquid, Brad guessed she was drinking it neat. He heard Jebediah in the Rare Book Room, still arranging books.

"You certainly can time your entrance," Mrs. Johnson said. "We just finished."

Jebediah came to the door looking pale and sweaty. Physical work was not a part of his preferred life-style. "We finished the inventory," he said, "and as you can see, the books are back on the shelves in order. The papers from your desk and the files are stacked on the floor of the closet. I'm afraid you're going to have to deal with those yourself."

"How much was stolen?"

"Not a book."

"Nothing?"

"All present and accounted for," Mrs. Johnson said, raising her glass in Brad's direction.

"We have a book for every inventory card except for Jefferson's *Notes on Virginia,* but we sold that to Dr. Ferrar. We just forgot to pull the card."

"Are you sure everything's here?"

"Unless the person who broke into the shop stole a book and its inventory card too."

"Did you find any more books that needed repair?"

"Two more. Minor damage. We had a careful thief," Jebediah said.

"We had no thief at all," Mrs. Johnson corrected.

Brad asked Jebediah to tell the police what the inventory results were.

"Speaking of the police," Mrs. Johnson said, "did they get in touch with you? Two policemen came in the shop shortly after you left."

"Yes."

"A police officer came to the shop this afternoon and asked me about Carl Riesling teaching me to print," Jebediah added.

"How did it go?"

"Fine, I guess. We talked about private presses and printing poetry. I don't think he understood any of it. All he seemed interested in was how Mr. Riesling and I got along." Jebediah looked puzzled. "You don't suppose they think I had anything to do with Carl's death, do you?"

"They're probably just being thorough, touching all the bases."

Brad's remark seemed to unknot the tension in Jebediah's brow.

"You look a lot better than you did this morning," Mrs. Johnson said to Brad.

"You never see a model with bandages in *Gentleman's Quarterly*."

Samantha got into the car and reached over to kiss Brad.

"Ouch."

"Your head."

"It's just tender. I didn't mean to yell."

"There's a lump on it the size of a golf ball." Samantha looked down at her hand. "I think it's still bleeding a little."

"It'll be okay."

"My God, what happened?"

Brad went through the entire story about investigating sounds in his living room, his trip to the emergency room, and finding out that his store had been burglarized. "Actually it wasn't a burglary, because nothing was taken."

"Come again?"

"Jebediah and Mrs. Johnson did a complete inventory today, and nothing was missing."

"That's crazy."

"If someone broke into the bookshop and didn't find what they were looking for, you have to wonder if that same person might have thought I took whatever it was home with me to the apartment."

"It doesn't make sense."

"No, and what's more insane is that now the police think Carl Riesling was murdered."

"Oh, my God. Why?"

"The autopsy report. It appears that what killed him was a blow to the back of his head with a composing stick. You know," Brad said, moving his hands to simulate the process, "one of those things a printer uses to set type. According to the coroner, you can see marks from the letters embedded in Carl's skin."

"Then what about the bookcases?"

"Probably tipped over afterwards to make people think it was an accident."

"Good God."

"Things get curiouser and curiouser."

She reached over and gently touched the lump on Brad's head. "Do you think you should be going out tonight?"

"I'll be fine."

Brad turned onto an unmarked street. After a quarter of a mile there was a small sign: "Private road." The road divided shortly after that and there was another small sign with an arrow pointing to the left. Brad kept to the right. A half mile farther there was a gate between two stone pillars. In front of the gate, on the driver's side, was an intercom system. Brad leaned out of the car and pressed a red button.

"Yes?"

"Brad Parker and Samantha Frye."

"Drive in, Mr. Parker," the voice from the speaker said. Jonathan once told Brad that he had wanted to install a plastic clown face over the speaker system, like the ones in Jack-in-the-Box restaurants, but Fiona wouldn't let him. "My dear, there are some things that just aren't done, even in America," she was reported to have said.

Inside the gate the road forked again. They kept to the right. The road to the left led to the Jonathan Avery Research Library. There was a public entrance off the main highway, but this was Jonathan's private entrance, the road leading directly to the wing where he had built his office.

The drive to the house was another mile and a half of winding road. There were deer grazing on the property, looking up with only mild interest as the car passed. The house itself was less than half a mile from the gate, but Jonathan had wanted a winding road that would give the visitor more time to leave the modern world behind.

The Avery house itself had been built by Addison Mizner in the 1920s. With its stucco walls and tiled roofs set on different levels, it had most of the elements of Mizner's better-known Florida homes. He had set the house on the top of a gentle hill where it caught the last rays of the sun at twilight like a solitary actor alone in a bright spotlight against a darkening stage.

Jonathan Avery greeted them as they parked their car in front of the house.

"Where's the Melville?" he asked.

"Oh, Jesus. I forgot to bring it."

"What a memory."

"Be kind to him, Jonathan," Samantha said. "His store was broken into last night and he was hit on the head."

"What is this?"

"Samantha has a flair for the melodramatic," Brad said. "Let's go inside. I'll tell the story to you and your wife so I won't have to repeat it more than once."

"I must warn you, if you are really hurt Fiona will insist you go up to New York to see her new doctor. You know how she gets."

"Nonsense. I'm fine."

"You don't have to convince me. It's the lady of the house you have to worry about."

They walked through the entryway and a large, ornately furnished reception room that the Averys used for formal entertaining. Beyond, toward the patio, was Jonathan and Fiona's private apartment. "You own a fifteen-thousand-square-foot house and you end up living in an apartment at the rear," Jonathan had once said. "I feel like the gardener, but Fiona was raised in one of the great English country homes and that's the way she's used to living, so there you have it."

Fiona sat in the middle of her informal living room. It was brightly colored, and everywhere you looked you saw chintz and potted plants—the Laura Ashley look gone wild. Fiona Avery was a slender woman in her late thirties with naturally red hair in an outlandish shade that made her look like Maggie Smith in one of Lucille Ball's secondhand wigs. She was elegant rather than beautiful, more stylish than sensual.

"We both must hear Brad's story," Jonathan said, and they all listened as Brad told about the break-in at the shop and the intruder in his apartment. When he finished, Fiona asked, "Do doctors allow their patients to drink when they've received a bump on the head?"

"I don't see why not," Brad answered.

"Isn't modern medicine wonderful?" Fiona replied, "and that, Jonathan, in case you're too dense to recognize it, is your cue for fixing drinks. We're servantless tonight."

Jonathan went to a large globe sitting in the corner of the room and raised the northern hemisphere with his left hand to reveal a fully stocked bar underneath. "Will martinis do, or have you succumbed to the California habit of white wine like most of our friends?"

"Martinis," said Brad and Samantha simultaneously.

The conversations paired, with Fiona and Samantha talking about the library dedication and the party to follow, while the men talked about books.

"We're going to go down to the library if you keep talking this nonsense," Jonathan said.

"You were going to go down to the library in any event," Fiona replied. "You certainly don't need to blame us. Anyway, social events don't just happen, they're planned."

"Then you plan it, right down to the silver."

"You haven't been listening. We're eating with gold."

Jonathan looked at Brad. "Gold-plated knives and forks! Can you believe it?"

"We're giving away a research library, darling, and we're going to do it with grace and style."

"Let's get away from this silliness," Jonathan said to Brad.

"Go," Fiona said, "but don't be long. You're going to have to put the steaks on in an hour, Jonathan."

They drove down from the house in a Jeep Jonathan used around the estate. The Jeep was equipped with a homing device that was monitored in the room the FBI agents used and was tied into a security system for the estate itself.

"I didn't want to talk to you about this in front of the women," Jonathan said, "but what kind of a situation are you involved in—with the break-ins and all?"

"I don't understand it myself."

Jonathan raised an eyebrow.

"Really."

"If you're in danger, you and Sam are welcome to stay here. The way Larry, Moe, and Curly have things set up, you would be hard pressed to get a mosquito bite in here."

"Thanks, but I think I'd do better settling back into my routine. That way I might be able to see some connection that would make sense out of this. I didn't want to tell Fiona, but Carl Riesling's death wasn't an accident."

"Murder?"

Brad explained about the autopsy.

"Bad things are happening. From the sound of it, you could easily have joined Carl."

"I very well might have."

"Well," said Jonathan, "the offer to stay here still stands."

"I appreciate it."

Jonathan pulled the Jeep into a parking space behind the library. He let them in through a plain metal door that led directly to his office.

Jonathan's room was large, twenty-five by thirty feet, set at a forty-five-degree angle from the library itself. Three of the walls were antique brick. The fourth, to the right of the entrance door, was a large glass window, floor to ceiling, that overlooked the sculpture garden extending along the rear of the library, on Jonathan's side of the property. The library cut through the ten-foot fence that surrounded the estate, allowing visitors to enter the building without giving them direct access to Jonathan's private world. Its location had been a Solomon-like compromise between Jonathan and the FBI. The agency had insisted that no outsider be given permission to enter the estate, while Jonathan was equally adamant that he be able to visit the library without having to go outside the wall to do so.

"This is a beautiful room," Brad said, looking around.

"I spend a lot of time here when I'm in Virginia."

"You have that wistful look in your eye."

"I don't know if I'm ready to give the library over to the state," Jonathan said, and then saw the surprise on Brad's face. "Oh, I don't mean that I'm not going to go through with all of this. It's just that sometimes I wish I wasn't so impetuous. I was having trouble getting a librarian I liked and I wanted to find a way to open the collection up to the public. Then the chancellor at William and Mary suggested I could eat my cake and have it too."

"Which made sense."

"Logically."

"Jonathan, you got exactly what you wanted. This building. A professional staff paid for by the state. Now scholars will still be able to use the library and see what you've created."

"Yes, but to do it, I've lost control."

"You still control the board of directors."

"No, you don't understand. I've built this collection. I helped design this building. Now other people are going to share in that, and it won't be mine anymore.

"You know what's given me the most pleasure? I love buying books, finding special items or buying entire collections to add to my own, but I get the greatest pleasure just sitting here with the books themselves."

"I feel the same way in the bookshop at night."

"Then you know. It's just me and the books, just sitting here staring at the spines, remembering where I bought that one, or when I first read this book over here. I don't even have to take a book down from the shelf, or even handle it. Do you understand?"

"I think so."

"They've become part of my life. I've never experienced a feeling of peace like I've had here, and now I'm frightened. I don't know whether I'll ever feel that again. I'm scared that it's going to be like meeting an ex-wife after a divorce. You feel some of the old ties, but you realize that she's sharing her love with others. It's not just between the two of you anymore."

"But you wanted scholars to use your collection. You said that from the start."

"Yes, but I didn't think it through to the emotional level."

Jonathan got up from his desk and opened the door to the main reading room. Everything was dark and quiet except for a few dim safety lights. He stood in the doorway, looking out; after a minute or two he shut the door. "The reveries of an old fart," he said to Brad.

Brad couldn't think of anything to say.

"Here," Jonathan said, breaking the silence.

"What's this?"

"A Xerox copy of the Melville pamphlet. Is it the same as the one you found?"

"It certainly looks like it."

"Well, if it is, you've got yourself a rare book."

"How rare?"

"Damned rare. I thought I had the only known copy. I even wrote to Florey at Yale, the Melville man. He'd never heard of it either. In fact, he's coming down in two weeks to take a look at it."

"When I get home, I'll check your Xerox against my copy."

"If there's even the slightest difference, I'll want to buy it," Jonathan said. "And if it's the same, I'll probably want it anyway."

"If it's an exact duplicate, I've already promised Peter Eastrovich the right of first refusal."

"Eastrovich?" Jonathan's voice rose. "What the hell does he want with it?"

"He said he wanted it for his research."

"Research. The bastard's come to the library every day for months. I've asked the staff to find out what kind of research project he's working on. He won't tell them. It's all hush-hush and mysterious."

"I didn't mean to bring up a sore subject."

"Oh, hell. Offer him the book. Just put a price on it that will knock his socks off. It's worth it, and if he doesn't think so, I'll buy it."

"It's a tempting, mercenary thought."

"Good. I'll hold you to it."

"Jonathan, there's no sense getting excited about this now. The book's not mine to sell. It belongs to Greta Riesling."

"But it will be yours."

"Not necessarily. Buying books from widows can be a tricky business."

"Well, if you can sell it to me, I'd like to own it. It's nice being the only person in the world to own something."

"Jonathan, you've become a bibliomaniac."

"I didn't say my book collecting was ennobling. I just said I wanted to be the only one to own a copy of this Melville pamphlet, and I'm willing to pay serious money for the privilege. That's all." While he was talking, Jonathan began turning off the lights. "In any case, it's time to get back to the girls. Did I ever fix you one of my steaks?"

"I don't remember."

"You would have. I coat both sides with Dijon mustard and pepper."

"Really?"

"It's wonderful. The mustard burns off, and all you're left with is the zesty taste. You'll see." Jonathan was about to shut the door when he remembered the Xerox of the Melville pamphlet. "Here," he said, going back for it. "Don't forget this. In fact I'm going to put it on the seat of your car for you."

"Pptttuu."

Fleder's tail flicked across Samantha's nose and mouth. She woke and looked down to see Fleder's spreading haunches firmly planted just below her neck.

"Off," Samantha said.

The cat pretended not to hear, and Samantha had to pick Fleder up and put her on the floor.

"Brad, that cat has got to sleep somewhere else." As she spoke, Samantha reached over to Brad and found empty blankets. With that Samantha opened her eyes and realized that she was alone in the bedroom with Fleder.

"Brad?" She heard noises in the living room. Samantha looked at the clock. It was three-thirty. She put on Brad's robe and walked toward the sounds, calling to him again.

"In here."

"Brad, it's three-thirty in the morning. What are you doing?"

"Looking for a book that's not here."

"It's too early for riddles."

"The Melville pamphlet."

"The copy Jonathan gave you?" Samantha asked, remembering that it was on the dining room table.

"No, the copy I took from Carl's. It's gone."

"Where did you have it last?"

"It was next to the bed last night, before I was hit on the head. I remember reading it before I fell asleep."

"Then what are you doing out here?"

"Making sure." Brad looked up from the bookcase at Samantha standing there in his partially closed robe. "I couldn't sleep so I thought I would compare the two copies, only the one I had wasn't where I remembered putting it. I just wanted to check all the possible places that it could be before I . . . and now I've woken you up. I'm sorry."

"Fleder woke me up, not you, but now that we're both awake, let's go into the bedroom and make a thorough search. It might have slipped behind the night table."

It took ten minutes, but they looked everywhere. The pamphlet wasn't there.

"You think that whoever hit you took the book?"

"It would appear that way."

"My God."

"What?"

"Not that many people knew you had it."

"That occurred to me too. But I did tell Greta, and God knows who else she might have told. Would you be a dear and put on a pot of coffee for me?"

"Coffee isn't good for you."

"At this time of morning it isn't bad. If you do that, I'll fix eggs and bacon."

"Speaking of bad for you."

"Or toast, sans butter, if you prefer."

Samantha chose the toast. After they ate, Brad sat in his library chair, his eyes half-closed and his fingertips steepled in front of him like a monk's in prayer, lost in meditation.

Samantha made a few attempts at conversation, but finally went back to the bedroom unnoticed. Brad sat in his chair until daybreak, with Fleder dozing on his lap. At some point he drifted off to sleep. He was opening another box and for the first time in a long while he was looking forward to opening the next.

# Chapter 16

"A Tom Egan called this morning," Mrs. Johnson said as Brad walked through the door with Fleder in her carrying case. "He said he was with the police department and wanted you to call him first thing when you came in."

Brad opened the cage door for Fleder, who bounded to her perch in the window. "If he calls back, tell him I haven't come to work yet."

"You want me to lie to the police for you?"

"Why not? It's as American as insider stock trading."

As he walked up the stairs to his office he heard Mrs. Johnson, in a loud stage whisper, mutter, "Men!"

Brad sat down at his desk and reached for his address book. He looked up a number and dialed it, glancing at the clock. It was nine-thirty.

"Madeleine, is Peter in his office?" he asked. "This is Brad Parker."

"Surprisingly, he is. He was here before me today," Madeleine said, "but he's away from his desk just now."

"What does his schedule look like for this morning? I really have to talk with him."

Brad heard a rustle of paper in the background. "His schedule is as empty as a church on Monday as far as I know, but something's afoot. The secretary is the last to know."

"Do me a favor. When he comes back, tell him I need to see him and I'll be right over. In fact, I'm leaving the shop now."

Jebediah was looking through a stack of mail by the counter when Brad rushed by him. "Watch the shop for a few hours, will you?" he asked. "I'll be at the library."

"Don't pay any attention to him," Mrs. Johnson shouted from the packing room. "He hasn't come to work yet."

Jebediah looked confused.

"Ask her," Brad told him. "She'll explain." And with that, he was out the door.

It was a beautiful autumn day, warm but without the oppressive humidity of the summer months. The Virginia summer with its unrelenting string of ninety-degree, ninety-percent humidity days drove Brad inside to air conditioning. He lived for the spring and fall, but walking across campus this morning he was oblivious to the weather. He walked with the grim, determined stride of a lethargic, middle-aged man who has just been told by his doctor that he has to take long walks for exercise.

The library building was set on a slope, and its entrance was on its third level, which coincided with the top of a gentle hill. The entrance was reached by crossing a short bridge. Below the bridge were long reflecting pools that ran along the front of the building, giving the appearance of a moat.

Special Collections was on the second level. "Poignantly suspended between the front doors and the watery abyss below," as Peter Eastrovich had described it once too often. Aside from graduate students working on theses and the odd undergraduate scholar, most students were unaware of the department's existence. The books shelved there ran the gamut from early Virginiana to collections of first editions and manuscripts of modern authors. The collections grew randomly with new gifts in new subject areas. There was even the world's largest collection of books about the dog, given to the university by a man named Howard Chapin in honor of his cocker spaniel, and another collection, also the world's largest, of paintings hidden on the fore-edges of books.

When Brad walked into the Rare Book Reading Room through the open wrought-iron gates, there was an otherworldly quietude. An elderly man sat at one of the long reading tables looking through Civil War manuscripts, and the only other occupant, an unkempt graduate student, was encamped in a corner surrounded by piles of books on the table in front of him and others standing upright on a library cart by his side. The reception desk was unattended. Brad turned left and knocked on a door labeled "Private."

Madeleine sat at a desk in her office enveloped in a cloud of smoke, a gray, oval English cigarette dangling from her lips. Imported cigarettes were her sole luxury and vice. Otherwise she lived alone on a poverty-level wage. Madeleine virtually ran the department during the long periods of desultory depression that Peter drifted into from time to time. For her efforts Peter had nicknamed her "keeper of the kingdom" or, alternately, "chief screw."

"He's just returned from the crapper," Madeleine said to Brad as he walked over to her desk. "He told me to tell people on the telephone that he had just stepped away for a few minutes, but he didn't tell me what to say if someone walked in."

"He must be trying for a more dignified image."

"Oh, you've seen him today?"

"No. Why?"

"Peter is the frog turned prince. You'll see. He's back in his office."

Brad walked through the reading room to a door in the rear corner, and knocked. If a person's office reflected his political status in an organization, Peter was, politically, on a par with the cleaning woman. His office was small, perhaps ten feet square, made smaller by the intrusion of several gray metal bookcases that jutted out from the walls. In addition to the shelving, someone had managed to find room for an ugly gray metal desk, a matching credenza, and a typing table. In front of the desk were two ancient wooden chairs, probably purchased with a WPA grant in the 1930s.

"Hello," Peter said cheerfully, "Madeleine said you were coming over. What brings you to our little corner of the world?"

Brad saw what Madeleine had meant. Peter, who had made unpressed shirts and khaki slacks into a personal uniform after his divorce, now stood in his office dressed in a new navy-blue suit, white shirt, and striped rep tie. His hair, which was usually combed and cut with the same attention given his clothes, appeared neatly groomed. Brad wanted to look at Peter's hands to see if he had gotten a manicure, but he didn't have the opportunity.

"Nice outfit," Brad said.

"Thank you," Peter answered in a gracious manner, with a slight hesitation implying that he'd rather his new suit wouldn't be considered out of the ordinary.

"What's the occasion?"

"Does there have to be an occasion to dress well?"

"No."

"But you didn't come over to see my new suit," Peter said abruptly. "Or did you?"

"No. I need some information."

"I can't give you much time. I'm rather busy now."

"This won't take long."

"Five minutes," Peter said, looking perfunctorily at his watch.

"It's about the Avery Library."

Peter's body visibly stiffened and his face turned red. "Goddamm it," he exploded. "Who told you?"

"Told me what?"

"Don't play dumb with me."

"Peter, I don't have the vaguest idea what you're talking about."

"You expect me to believe that you just happened over here to talk about the Avery Library just before the television crew arrives? Who sent you? Did Jonathan Avery hear about it and ask you to come over and try to talk me out of it?"

"Peter, nobody sent me."

"Oh, of course," Peter shot back sardonically.

"Not 'of course.' Just ask yourself, Peter, have I ever lied to you or treated you unfairly?"

Peter's face was flushed. He began taking deep breaths while staring intently at Brad's eyes. After a while he began breathing normally. "All right," he said warily, "just what do you want to know?"

"For the past several months, you've been dropping hints that there's something not exactly right about Jonathan's collection. I haven't pressed you on this, but now something's happened and I need to know exactly what it is you think is wrong."

"Tune in to the news at noon and find out," Peter said with a smirk.

"If you're going to tell the world at noon, what harm would there be in telling me now?"

Peter Eastrovich walked over to the narrow window in his office and looked out. His eyes were following a student walking across campus, but his mind seemed a light year away. When the student turned a corner and passed out of view, Peter was still gazing at the path where he had been. Finally he abruptly turned back to Brad. "Fine," he said, "but I'm on a tight schedule. Follow me."

Peter walked out of his office and Brad followed. As Brad passed the door to Madeleine's office, he saw her imitate Peter's new found pomp and circumstance with a silly grimace. Brad smiled at her and nodded in agreement.

When Brad finally caught up with Peter, he was already in the stack area, where he was putting books on an empty library cart.

"Here," he pointed to the cart. "You can help. I'm looking for octavos and quartos with nice shiney morocco spines. Find some and put them on the cart. I'm going to need about twenty feet of leather."

"You sound like an interior decorator."

"The television crew is coming here to film me for an interview, and I want to be able to give them a suitable background."

"Oh, my."

"Laugh if you want, but image is very important in today's world."

"I'm not discounting the value of image, Peter. It just is a little amusing to hear this coming from you."

"Don't help if you don't want to."

"No offense, but let's just say that you've always been more interested in scholarship than politics."

"Well, if I was, it was my mistake."

"Look, Peter, it's important for me to find out what you suspect is wrong with Jonathan's library."

"As I said, that's the reason for the news conference."

"I don't know anything about a television news interview. What I came over to find out was why your eyes lit up when you saw the Melville pamphlet lying on my desk the other day."

"First things first." As Peter spoke, he walked over and shut the door that separated the stack area from Madeleine's office and the reading room beyond. "You've probably thought I turned into a crazy man during the past three months. I know I made a lot of veiled comments to you about the Avery Library. That was childish. But here I was, sitting on a very important story, dying to tell somebody about it, but not being able to say anything until I was completely sure I was right.

"I wanted to tell you all along, but you sold books to Avery, and I couldn't take the chance of word getting back to him. He would have stopped me from doing the rest of my research if he'd found out, and, God, I needed to get the chance to complete that."

Peter sat down on a stool next to the library cart. "It's no secret that Avery and I never got along. Some of it's been my fault, granted. That incident at the president's house when Avery and I almost got into a fistfight, that should never have happened. I was drunk and I was having some bad times with Joan and the divorce. I should have just gone home, but it happened and I regret it."

"What's your point?" Brad asked.

"Simply this. I had to be sure of my facts, all of them, before I said anything. I know damn well that people will say I just have a vendetta against Avery, but now I've got the proof and no serious scholar is going to doubt me."

"Go on."

"It all started when you introduced me to Avery, back when he had just built the library and was looking for a librarian. I went over there several times to familiarize myself with his collection. As you know, it's a very fine one. You sold him a good number of books yourself.

"Anyway, I started to look at the collection in depth, picking out individual authors and seeing how complete Avery's holdings were. When you do that enough, with any collection, you start seeing patterns, not just that some titles are missing, but you get a sense of the condition of the books, if there are presentation copies, manuscript material, secondary books, biographies—that sort of thing.

"I spent a lot of time looking over the holdings before Avery decided not to hire me. Little by little, scrutinizing the collection as closely as I did, I became aware of just how many unique books were in it."

"What do you mean, 'unique' books?"

"Unique-unique books. Books that don't exist anywhere else—not in the British Museum, not at the Library of Congress, not at Harvard, not at the Beinecke. Books for which there are no other known copies. That kind of unique book."

"So?"

"Every great collector finds his share of rare books, and Avery is a great collector, you've got to give him that, no matter how I try to discount him at times. He has deep pockets, and he's been avidly collecting books for fifteen years. You'd expect that he would buy a few really desirable one-of-a-kind items. But studying his library, then, and going back as I have been doing for the past year, I started to get a clearer idea of just how many unique books he had.

"And not only in quantity but in quality. An early book written by

Hemingway—a short story he had printed for friends when he was an ambulance driver during World War One. Another book, poetry by F. Scott Fitzgerald that Scott had printed at his own expense in Tryon, North Carolina, for Zelda's birthday when she was staying in the mental hospital in Asheville. These are not trivial pieces of ephemera we're talking about here. These are major finds, books by important authors, books that English professors would give up sex just to have the chance to write about."

"What are you trying to say—that Jonathan's lucky?"

"Lucky? Lucky is finding one, even two, books like this in a lifetime. Avery is rich and knows a good many rare-book dealers who would give him first crack at this type of material. I could stretch luck to allow Avery five, even six, such finds, but going through his card catalog as I did, I found twenty-nine definite examples of unique books, and there are probably more. Those are only the ones I could positively identify. Twenty-nine unique books, books of considerable scholarly merit. That's not luck. That's a miracle."

Peter paused to see if the importance of what he was saying had sunk into Brad's consciousness. "And it's not just quantity. I want to stress that. The Hemingway book, there's a perfect example. It's a short story. He uses the plot later on as part of *The Sun Also Rises,* but there's no crisp prose in this version. It's like reading Dickens or Willkie Collins. When did Hemingway develop his writing style? It's the type of question a young English professor could build a career speculating over."

"Peter, I might be dense, but I still don't see your point."

"My point is that Hemingway scholars have been at work since the nineteen twenties, and no one has even heard a whisper of this story. There's nothing in letters from Hemingway or from Hemingway's friends even hinting that the story was ever published. Now Jonathan Avery comes along and magically a copy appears. What conclusions would you draw?"

"I don't know, Peter. Why don't you tell me?"

"I will. Now that I've done my homework with the collection, I can." Peter paused a moment for effect. "The books that I've been talking about, the unique books, they're all forgeries, all twenty-nine of them—thirty if you include the Herman Melville pamphlet, *A Sermon for Sailors,* that was on your desk that day. There's another copy just like it in the Avery Library. That's why I was so interested in looking at it—and why I still want to buy it, by the way."

"You're saying it's a forgery?"

"A very interesting one. Here's a book, supposedly published in eighteen forty, the year after Melville shipped out as a cabin boy on a boat bound for Liverpool and a full eleven years before *Moby Dick* was published. If Melville really wrote *A Sermon for Sailors* then, it would mean that he was carrying around the idea for his whale book for at least twelve years."

"Why do you say it's a forgery? Just because no one was aware of it before?"

"No. It's much more than that. There's the matter of the paper it's printed on, the type the printer used. It's technical and I don't have time to go into it just now, but I'm right. Trust me on that."

"I still don't see what all the fuss is about. All you're saying is that Jonathan was duped and bought a few forgeries."

"That's one possible conclusion, but there's more to this," Peter said. "Come back to my office. I want to show you something."

Back in his office Peter unlocked his desk drawer and pulled out a file folder. "There are my notes for the book. I have them duplicated at home, and I have left another set with a friend just in case Avery should try to steal them."

"Peter, what is this book you're talking about?"

"I've written a book on the forgeries. I've been writing it for over a year. In fact I've just got the galley proofs from the publisher the other day. It should be out in another two months."

"You found a publisher? I would have thought a potential libel suit would have frightened anyone away."

"He checked into my research, and he believes me. So do his lawyers."

"I'm impressed."

"But this is what I wanted to show you." Peter handed Brad a sheet of paper. "It's a Xerox copy of Jonathan's catalog card for the Hemingway book. Notice on the lower lefthand corner of the card how Avery has written a neat code. The letters tell how much he paid for the book—this one was a hundred fifty dollars—and the numbers that follow are the month and year the book was purchased. The final letters, after the date, are a code for the dealer or auction house that sold Avery the book."

"And you cracked the code."

"With the help of Avery's secretary. She thought I knew what it was already, and blurted it out one day. Anyway, the interesting point is that all the books on my list of forgeries were purchased from three dealers, all fairly local, and would you like to guess who the most prominent dealer on the list is?"

"It's not me, is it?"

"No, you're not on the list at all. The principal dealer is Carl Riesling."

"Carl?"

"Yes, but it gets better," Peter said. "The other book businesses were in Norfolk and Gloucester, local businesses, but I had never heard of either of them. Both businesses had post office boxes for addresses, and neither one was listed in the telephone directory. I even tried the information operator for new listings."

"Odd."

"I've never heard of an antiquarian bookdealer without a telephone before, myself."

"So naturally you checked into the matter."

"Naturally. First I wrote. I asked to be put on their mailing list if they issued catalogs."

"And?"

"No response. So I did a little detective work on my own. Don't ask me how, because it wasn't strictly legal, but I got photostats of the applications for the two post office boxes." Peter smiled like the Cheshire cat.

"Who signed them, Peter?"

Peter Eastrovich paused. "Greta Riesling, and the cherry on top of the sundae is that the books on my list of forgeries are the only books the three firms sold to the Avery Library. I had to go through the entire card catalog to come up with that fact, but it was worth the effort."

"Have you told any of this to the police?"

"Why should I?"

"It very well might have something to do with Carl Riesling's murder."

"Murder? I thought it was an accident."

"The autopsy proved different."

Peter sat on the edge of his desk, obviously stunned. "Murder?"

"What you've told me could be important."

"The police watch television. They'll find out in due course. It's not like I'm trying to keep it a secret."

"Why not tell them now?"

"And have them steal my interview? This is my career we're talking about here. I'll handle the publicity and the police in my own way."

"Was waiting until the day before Jonathan gave his library to the state part of your plan?"

"It can't hurt."

"Obviously you think Jonathan had something to do with creating the forgeries?"

"Oh, yes."

"But I assume you don't have any hard evidence."

"Not directly, no. I can tell you, however, that the total amount the Avery Library paid for the thirty books was less than two thousand dollars. If Carl and Greta were in the forgery business to make money, they were clearly not going about it in the right way. It would have cost them more than that to print the books."

"They might have sold other copies."

"It's possible, but I did check these titles against all the major university libraries in the country that would buy this kind of book. They didn't purchase copies, and they would have been the end market for them, even if Carl had sold them to dealers first."

"And that leaves Jonathan."

"It's a logical conclusion. You knew Carl. Do you think he was clever enough to think of this himself?"

"Probably not."

"Yes, I think Jonathan had something to do with the forgeries. I think he was the author of the whole plot. I think he paid Greta and Carl Riesling to print the books and sell them to the Library."

"But why would he do that?"

"I'm no psychiatrist, but possessive people, collectors, get an abnormal pride in having the only copy of—whatever. In Avery's case, having unique books raised the caliber of his library from just another very good reference collection to the next plateau. You know Avery. The man's an egomaniac. Everything he does, he wants it to be the best. Am I wrong?"

Brad stood silently by Peter's desk.

"Who knows why? Maybe because he doesn't have a formal education, he wanted to play a joke on the academic world, show that he was smarter than the star scholars. One thing I do know: Jonathan Avery is the type of person who wouldn't hesitate to bend the rules to get anything he really wanted."

Peter took the paper he had given Brad and returned it to his file folder, which he put back into the desk.

"And now, if you'll excuse me," Peter said. "I have a television interview to prepare for."

# Chapter
# 17

Napoleon Robespierre Jones stood on Duke of Gloucester Street looking into a shop window. The books on display there outlined the history of early color printing, a subject that especially appealed to Brad Parker, the shop's owner, who had spent several days assembling the exhibit. Napoleon didn't notice the books, however. He looked past them, focusing his attention inside to where Jebediah was waiting on a customer. Out of the corner of his eye Napoleon noticed something move near the top of the window. He looked up quickly and saw a cat staring down at him. Involuntarily he jumped back a step, so quickly that his movement surprised Fleder, who leaped from the window and ran across the shop and up the stairs on the far side, to the safety of Brad's office.

Jebediah had just given change to a blue-haired lady and was putting brown wrapping paper over a print when Napoleon entered. There was a tinkle from the bell on the front door, but Jebediah was concentrating on his wrapping and didn't look up.

"You sell picture books of people doing strange things with each other?" Napoleon asked in his best mellow, cultured voice.

Jebediah's head jerked toward him, the blood drained from his face.

The customer seemed to pay no attention to the remark, continuing to drop her change into a worn leather purse. When Jebediah handed her the print, she gathered up her other packages and walked demurely out of the shop, giving Napoleon a naughty wink.

"Nah," Napoleon continued after she left, "this doesn't look like one of them bookshops. This store has real class."

"Napoleon? What are you doing here? I thought we . . ."

"You and me, Jebediah, we got to have a talk," Napoleon said.

"I get off at five-thirty."

"We gotta talk before five-thirty."

"I don't know if I can."

"What's wrong with right now?"

"I'm watching the shop."

Napoleon glanced toward the wrapping room, where Mrs. Johnson was humming to herself.

"I guess I could ask Mrs. Johnson to fill in for me."

"Good. You got a place here we could go?"

Jebediah pointed to the steps. "Upstairs, I guess." Then he went back to speak to Mrs. Johnson.

With that taken care of, Jebediah led Napoleon up the stairs to Brad's office. As Jebediah turned to face his visitor, he saw, much too late to do anything about it, Napoleon's right shoulder dip. His punch embedded itself into Jebediah's stomach, lifting his entire body six inches off the floor. With his left arm, Napoleon reached around Jebediah's back to keep him from stumbling across the room and making noise. The impact of the punch violently expelled all the air from Jebediah's lungs with the speed and force of a cork exploding from a bottle of champagne. Jebediah's face twisted as he noisily sucked air back into his body. Napoleon still supported his limp frame as he quietly closed the door to the office with his right hand. He looked at Jebediah and hoped that Jeb wouldn't throw up all over him and the rug.

"That was for almost getting me killed, mother—" Napoleon said.

Jebediah gasped.

"And this is for messing with people on your own without asking me."

Napoleon brought his knee up sharply into Jebediah's groin and then let his body quietly slump to the floor.

Fleder watched the scene indifferently from her food dish in the corner of the room. She continued eating as Jebediah lay on the floor, wheezing and coughing, his body folded into a fetal position. Jebediah's eyes were wild, but there was no thought behind the look of fear. The pain had frozen his mind.

"I thought about doing this all the way down here on the plane," Napoleon said, "but it doesn't feel near as good as it should."

As if to punctuate his disappointment, Napoleon brought his right leg around sharply and kicked Jebediah in the thigh.

Jebediah gave an involuntary yelp like a puppy.

"You've got to be the dumbest motherfucker in the whole world," Napoleon continued.

Jebediah's coughing and sputtering gradually was replaced by a rhythmic whimper, and his body rocked back and forth like a baby in a crib.

"But beating you around ain't going to solve our main problem." Napoleon walked over and sat behind the desk in Brad's chair.

It took a while, but the fact that Napoleon had used the word "our" finally crept into Jebediah's consciousness.

"Stop your whining," Napoleon ordered. "You sound like a dog. What I want to know is who gave you the idea you could blackmail the Mafia?"

Jebediah couldn't or wouldn't answer, but his silence didn't seem to matter.

"Did somebody tell you you could do it, or did you just decide all by yourself? Shit. And you don't go out and pick on some little dirtball, you play big time and try to blackmail one of the bosses, Norman Calvado himself. Damn you."

Napoleon got up from the chair and came around to Jebediah. He raised his right leg, as if to kick Jebediah again, then with it in midair decided not to bother. Jebediah was still curled up, and now had his thumb in his mouth.

"You put us in one fine mess, Jebediah Stuart." Napoleon stopped and looked down at him. "You listening to me, asshole? And stop sucking your thumb."

Napoleon returned to Brad's chair. "One fine mess. The way I figure it is we give Calvado back the cigarette case we stole, we end up dead in one week. Guaranteed. And if we don't do as they say, my guess is that we don't live that long."

Jebediah moved now, painfully, and pulled his body into a sitting position against the door.

"So you tell me, what do we do?" Napoleon continued. "You're the planner, Jebediah. You got us into this mess, and now you're going to get us out of it."

They stayed in Brad's office for another twenty minutes, talking. Occasionally Napoleon's voice would bellow, but most of the conversation was quiet and sedate. When Napoleon left, a careful observer would have noticed that there was more spring in his step and the slight hint of a smile on his face.

"Well?" Teddy asked as Napoleon walked across Duke of Gloucester Street toward them.

"He says he'll bring the microfilm to us at the hotel after six."

"Where did you tell him we were going to be?"

"Williamsburg Inn, George Wythe Suite. That's where we staying, ain't it?"

"Where is the microfilm now?"

"He didn't say."

"You ask him, nigger?" Joey said.

"Yeah, I asked him," Napoleon said, turning away from Teddy to face him, "but I didn't press him because I knew he would get spooked.

That's the difference between us. I'll get results. You'd just bull right straight ahead and blow the whole deal."

"Oh, yeah?"

"Good comeback, Joey. I'll get you on the Johnny Carson show."

"Stop it, you two," Teddy said sharply. "Why do we have to wait until six o'clock?" he asked Napoleon.

"He doesn't have it with him."

"Why doesn't he go get it now?" Joey asked.

"'Cause the man's got to work. He can't leave."

Teddy was quiet for a minute, then turned to Joey. "One of us has to stay here to watch the shop in case his friend has a sudden urge to leave work early."

"Jebediah's too afraid to leave," Napoleon said.

"You rough him up a little?" Joey asked.

"Just enough to let him know we're serious. Didn't leave no marks."

Teddy turned and gazed intently at Napoleon. "I'll bet you didn't." He paused. "Does the bookshop have a back door?"

"No," Napoleon lied. He waited in the silence that followed, wondering if his nose would grow longer. He had taken a foolish risk. It was a simple matter for Teddy to check on the other side of the building and find the rear door himself.

Teddy turned back to Joey. "Your choice. One of us has to watch the shop, the other one has to go back to the hotel and baby-sit this one. I don't feel safe him being out in a public crowd like this all afternoon."

"Hell, I'm not going to stand out here in the hot sun all afternoon with you two back in the hotel downing a few brews. Anyway, I drove all night to get here. If he left and somebody had to tail him on foot, you'd be fresher."

"Fine, Joey, but don't fall asleep."

"Don't worry about me," Joey said defensively.

"Just go straight to the hotel and wait."

"No sightseeing?" Napoleon asked.

"Listen, don't make this any more difficult than it already is," Teddy said.

* * *

Napoleon and Joey walked up Duke of Gloucester Street, past the Bruton Parish Church, toward the Inn. As they walked past the Magazine, where they kept gunpowder and cannon in Colonial times, they saw a group of costumed fourteen-year-olds parading past as a fife-and-drum corps. "That's real nice," Napoleon said as he passed. Joey didn't even glance in their direction.

To Brad Parker the fife and drum had been a poignant scene ever since he had come to Williamsburg, but he saw it in terms of Viet Nam and other fourteen-year-old boys who fought there in black uniforms against slightly older boys from America. The fife-and-drum corps had reminded him that there was a link between war and children, one that had probably existed forever.

Back at the Inn, a prissy hotel clerk handed Joey the key to the George Wythe Suite with a practiced look of disdain. Napoleon wondered if the clerk knew what Joey did for a living, or if he treated everyone who looked like he didn't belong in the same way. Joey didn't seem to notice, and if he did, he certainly didn't care.

Once inside the suite Joey walked directly to the television set and turned it on. Flipping the channel changer, he finally settled on "The Flintstones." While Napoleon took off his leather jacket, Joey went over to the telephone and dialed room service.

"Yeah. I want two Budweisers. Send them up to the George Wythe Suite."

"I sure could use a beer," Napoleon said as Joey replaced the receiver. "Thanks."

"Thanks for nothing. I ordered both beers for me."

"You're a real son-of-a-bitch, aren't you?"

Joey took out his revolver and waved it in front of Napoleon. "Son-of-a-bitch or not, you better stay in line. You give me one excuse, I'll fucking kill you right here in the hotel room. You understand?"

"Everything's cool, man. Take it easy. We're both trying to get the microfilm back. We're on the same side."

"Same side. You'll never be on my side, nigger."

"You feel that way," Napoleon said calmly, "I'm going to take a bath."

"I never knew you people washed."

Napoleon turned and walked into his bedroom. The George Wythe Suite had a central sitting room and a bedroom off both sides. Each bedroom had its own bath. With the television set droning in the background, Napoleon began drawing his bath water. While it was running, he went back to the bedroom, saw Joey sitting in front of the television, and walked to the window on the far side of the room. The window faced the golf course at the rear of the hotel. The suite was on the second floor, and Napoleon opened the window quietly to see if the thin band of decorative brickwork he had noticed on the front of the hotel extended to the back. It was there, three feet below his windowsill.

Napoleon left the window open and went back to turn off the water. Outside, he heard room service knock at the door. Napoleon went to the bedroom door to see Joey sign for the beers, his undershirt hanging out of his trousers and his suspenders dangling loose by his knees. He had left his revolver on the arm of his chair, and for a second Napoleon thought about making a lunge for it. Then he saw Joey's key ring and wallet lying on the desk near where he was standing. Before Joey shut the door and got back to his seat, Napoleon had palmed the key ring.

"You got something here I can read in the tub?" he asked.

"Jesus Christ."

"Yeah, some of us can read too," Napoleon said, grabbing a Williamsburg tourist magazine from the desk. "Screw it," he said to himself, throwing the magazine back on the desk. "I'll just take a shower."

"Suit yourself."

In the bathroom Napoleon released the plug and let the bath water drain before turning on the shower. He directed the spray against the shower curtain so that it made more noise and silently walked out to the bedroom. As he passed the door, he saw Joey, drinking his beer. He was laughing at a rerun of "Three's Company." Napoleon climbed out of the window and stood on the thin row of protruding bricks, no more than two inches wide. He lowered his left leg until he could feel the top edge of the first-floor window directly below. Then he lowered his right leg and found new handholds on the bricks where he had originally stood. He took a deep breath and repeated the maneuver until he was standing on the first-floor windowsill, and then on the ground.

Napoleon looked up at the open window above and then hurried around the hotel to the parking lot in front. It didn't take very long to find the white Cadillac with Pennsylvania license plates that had brought them from the airport. Napoleon was looking at the car from a different perspective now, but he was certain that it was the same Cadillac that had slowly driven past him while he was lying under the panel truck in New York. Napoleon opened the door with Joey's keys and spent a few minutes behind the wheel adjusting the seat and making sure he knew what the different gadgets on the dashboard were.

Just as he was about to turn the ignition key, Napoleon glanced up and saw Teddy running down the driveway toward the Inn. Teddy was running as hard as he could, arms and legs akimbo, totally without form, a white man's run. Napoleon slouched down behind the steering wheel, keeping his hand poised on the ignition key just in case Teddy should see him. He waited until Teddy had burst through the main door, leaving a perplexed doorman in his wake, before he started the car. Driving slowly, Napoleon eased it out of the parking lot.

"Where is he?" Teddy shouted, the door to the room flying open.

Joey was sitting in front of the television in his undershirt and shorts. "Taking a shower," he said, barely glancing up.

Teddy ran into Napoleon's bedroom with his revolver drawn.

"Hey," Joey said. "What's the matter with you?"

Teddy opened the bathroom door and pulled back the shower curtain. "Fuck." Water sprayed out, soaking his face and the front of his shirt.

Teddy turned around, saw the open window on the far side of the bedroom, and ran to it, looking out in both directions. By then Joey was out of his chair and standing at the bedroom door.

"What happened?"

"Your Mr. Jones appears to have climbed out of the window."

"Oh, shit."

"Yeah."

"Don't look at me like that," Joey said. "It ain't my fault. What am I supposed to do? Stand there and watch him take a shower like a goddamn queer?"

"Damn it."

"And why aren't you at the bookshop watching what's-his-face?"

"He left. Went out the back door that Jones said wasn't there."

Joey sat down on the edge of the bed. "Do you want to call Mr. Calvado, or should I?"

# Chapter
# 18

"F reddy's Truck Stop?"

"You know where it is?"

"Yes, but I don't know anyone who's ever been inside."

"That's why I'd like us to have lunch there."

"To be the first on your block to get ptomaine poisoning?"

"No, I want to talk to you and not be overheard. Any other place I can think of, we're going to meet friends."

"All right," Samantha said. "Give me ten minutes."

Brad waited, sipping a cup of coffee at the Formica counter. When Samantha walked through the door, Brad swiveled on his chrome stool and stood to greet her.

"We'll get a booth," he said.

Aside from the waitress, Samantha guessed she was probably the only woman ever to walk into Freddy's unescorted. There were three men Samantha identified as truck drivers sitting at a table in the middle of the room. The largest of the trio, a bearded man who must have weighed over three hundred pounds, leered at her as she walked past. He looked like an aged Hell's Angel, and from the quick glance Samantha allowed herself, a toothless member of the species.

"You owe me one, buster," Samantha muttered to Brad as she followed him to the corner booth.

The waitress brought two plastic-covered menus.

"The eggs are a safe bet," Brad said, trying to be helpful.

After they ordered, Samantha asked, "Why all this cloak-and-dagger business?"

Brad told Samantha about his talk that morning with Peter.

"He's being interviewed?"

"For the twelve o'clock news. That's another reason I wanted to eat lunch here." Brad pointed to a television set blithering away high on a shelf facing them.

They watched as the "News at Noon" came on the air. There was a story about hostages in Lebanon, and a denial by the President that he had ordered the CIA to send Americans into Nicaragua. Then a local news story came on about a fire.

"Damn," said Brad.

"What's wrong?"

"This is a Richmond station. I want Channel Five, WMSB, in Williamsburg." He got up from the table, stood on a chair, and changed the channel. Peter was already talking.

". . . have proof that these books, all twenty-nine of them, were printed not at the time and place indicated on the title page but most probably by Carl Riesling of Williamsburg."

"Dr. Eastrovich," a young, female reporter asked, "why are these forgeries so important?"

"Well, undetected and thought to be genuine, these documents could mislead people about our literary heritage. Ever since the Renaissance, scholars have been attempting to accurately record the processes and circumstances surrounding the writing and publication of literature. These forgeries represent a vicious attempt to alter that history. Seen in the most positive light, they are merely a very unfunny practical joke. However, I look at them as a malicious attempt to defraud the academic community, and the thought of that appalls me."

"Dr. Eastrovich, do you think that Mr. Avery knew of these forgeries?"

"I think under the circumstances that it's a distinct consideration. After all, we are faced with only two possibilities. First, that Jonathan Avery, because of lack of discretion and gullibility, was duped into buying these books by the Rieslings. The other possibility is that he had a direct hand in creating this hoax. In either case he bears a certain degree of culpability."

"Now that the Avery Library is being given to the state tomorrow, do you have any advice for the governor?"

"Yes," Peter turned away from the reporter and stared directly into the camera. "Because of my discoveries, I firmly believe that the research value of the Avery Library is suspect—definitely tainted. I would strongly encourage the governor to initiate a comprehensive study of the library's collection—done by reputable bibliographers and scholars—before he opens it to the public."

"As we heard earlier, the police have now called Carl Riesling's death a murder. Do you think that there is a link between the forgeries at the Avery Library and this crime?"

"I'm glad you asked that question, Belinda. I want to make it clear that I have no evidence of a connection, but if I were the police investigating poor Carl's murder, I would concentrate my efforts on looking for one."

"Thank you, Dr. Eastrovich. Belinda Freemont, WMSB News, Williamsburg. And now back to you, Bob."

"Thank you, Belinda. Tune in to the six o'clock report for more details about this strange case of the Williamsburg forgeries."

Brad turned the television set back to the Richmond station and returned to Samantha.

"Peter's new suit is very nice," Samantha said. "It makes him look believable. Is he?"

"I don't know, but he certainly thinks he is," Brad said. "Which brings me to a question."

"Yes?"

"Do you have time this afternoon to do me a favor?"

"Are you feeling frisky?" Samantha said with a glint in her eye.

"A good idea, but not exactly what I had in mind. Remember six months ago, you told me you worked with a publisher from New York who was retiring here and wanted to build an addition to his house?"

"Morris Hausbach."

"Is he living in Williamsburg now?"

"Yes. I talked to his wife the week before last."

"When you told me about him, you said he was a real expert on printing."

"He has his own printing press. I had to design a studio for him. Did I mention he even makes his own paper? I had a terrible time finding room for two large tubs he needed to mix the paper glop."

"Do you think you could call him and ask if he would talk to me?"

"When? This afternoon?"

"Yes."

The waitress brought their lunch. They waited until she left the table to continue.

"Why do you want to see him?" Samantha asked.

"I need some information about these forgeries, and I want to show him the Xerox copy of the Melville pamphlet Jonathan gave me."

"It's possible. I don't have anything pressing this afternoon, and I'd enjoy seeing the Hausbachs again."

"I was hoping you'd say that."

They finished their lunch and stopped at the telephones by the door. While Samantha called Morris Hausbach, Brad dialed the bookshop.

"Parker's Rare Books," Mrs. Johnson said.

"Brad, Mrs. Johnson. How's everything going?"

"Where have you been?"

"I'm having lunch with Samantha." He noticed a strain in her voice. "Let me speak with Jebediah if he's handy."

"Well, he's not. He went home sick. Also that policeman, Tom

Egan, has been calling every ten minutes wondering where you are, and then there's Fleder."

"Little Fleder?"

"Little Fleder, nothing. That cat jumped up on my lap just five minutes ago. I was eating lunch and spilled my salad all over the floor. I thought I was going to have a heart attack."

Brad calmed Mrs. Johnson and agreed to have Fleder taken out of the shop as soon as possible.

"All set?" Brad asked Samantha.

"This afternoon is yours."

"The Hausbachs will see us?"

"In an hour."

"Another favor. Could you pick up Fleder and take her home, and while you're there, bring the Melville Xerox with you?"

"Where will you be when all this is happening?" Samantha asked.

"At K-Mart. I have a little shopping I have to do."

"Where?"

Brad and Samantha were driving slowly along a heavily wooded section of Queens Lake.

"The driveway's to the left, unmarked, just between those two trees."

Brad swung slowly onto a gravel path that curved and descended at a fifteen-degree angle toward the lake. The grounds were left in their natural, wooded state, untrimmed, even to the small branches that brushed against the car as it passed. The driveway ended in a small turnaround that also doubled for parking. A contemporary house was built to the left, with the lake beyond. The sides of the house that faced the driveway were windowless, and covered with cedar boards, stained gray.

Morris Hausbach greeted them at the door. "Come in. Come in. I see you've found the place."

"Morris, why don't you put up a sign?" Samantha asked.

"I simply tell people to look for the Allisons' mailbox. When they see that they know they've gone too far. Once you've met the Allisons you'll appreciate the humor of that remark."

"Samantha," said a voice from inside the house. "You've found our driveway."

"We've just been through that, Ruby," Morris yelled over his shoulder.

A slim, unpretentious woman in a loose-fitting housedress came to greet them. "No one ever finds our driveway, especially the first time."

"Samantha's been here before, dear."

"Of course she has. She designed the addition. What an odd thing to say."

"Ever since I retired, we don't get many visitors. Before, we . . ."

Ruby interrupted. "When Morris was working, we entertained almost every night."

"That was in New York, darling."

"And here. We entertained authors in Williamsburg, too."

"Not every night."

"Almost every night. At least it seemed like it."

As they talked, their words began coming closer together and soon cascaded with increasing speed until they were both speaking simultaneously—two conversations running on parallel lines. Brad tried to concentrate on Ruby, then Morris, but it was hopeless.

"I tell friends contemplating retirement," Morris said, "that they should be prepared for the phone to stop ringing."

"Samantha, your dress is so smart," Ruby almost yelled near Brad's left ear.

Morris subconsciously must have noticed Brad's distraction because he stepped directly in front of him. "When people used to call me for advice or to invite us to some function or another, I always thought that they wanted to talk to me, but I soon found out that it was my position, not me, they were really interested in."

Ruby grabbed Brad's wrist and began to speak as Morris continued.

Brad understood the words "tour," "drink," and "house special," little else. Ruby had her hand on Brad's wrist and was herding him into the living room. Morris walked beside him, still talking. Brad turned briefly to Samantha and gave her a look, helpless and forlorn. She followed with a devilish grin.

Brad found himself in the Hausbachs' kitchen, watching Morris assemble gin-and-tonics for four. "The secret is," Morris said, "to use a quarter of the lime and squeeze the juice into the glass first."

While he spoke, Ruby kept tapping Brad's shoulder, explaining Samantha's architectural designs. "When Morris first looked at the house, he called it a double-wide with extras. But we loved the view."

". . . good gin, Tanqueray. I used to serve cheap gin until I stayed with the Malls in North Carolina."

"Mills," Ruby interrupted, joining her husband's conversation. "Ed and Annie Mills in North Carolina, not the Malls."

Even without a drink Brad was beginning to feel lightheaded. Samantha grabbed two of the gin-and-tonics and motioned for Ruby to join her on the deck outside the kitchen.

"Morris," Samantha said, "why don't you show Brad your printing press?"

Brad and Morris went downstairs with their drinks. The room, which was large, light and airy, extended under the Hausbachs' living quarters. Because of the slope of the property, the room, a basement on the front side of the house, was all windows in the back, where it faced the lake. "As near as you can get to a true northern exposure," Morris said when he saw Brad glancing in that direction. "Bad for heating bills, wonderful for light."

A large metal printing press stood in the middle of the room.

"It's an early example of George Clymer's famous Columbian Press."

"When was it built?"

"This particular press, before eighteen twenty-four. We know because that was the year they changed the pivot on the bar the printer pulls to make the impression. I bought it about twenty years ago. Had it restored and reassembled in our New York apartment."

"You must have had a large apartment."

"Not really. It was just off the living room. I couldn't let anything I was working on stand overnight. Ruby would yell about the mess."

"Well, everything looks immaculate down here," Brad said.

"It's a clean workshop. It pays to be neat. The New York apartment was good training."

"Samantha tells me that you make books entirely by yourself."

"That's not exactly true. I don't mix my own ink, for one thing, and the type I use is bought. I could make ink, and I know how to punch and cast a font of type if I had to do it, but it's too much like hard work, and I'm supposed to be retired.

"I do make my own paper. Did Samantha tell you the trouble she had designing plumbing and drainage for my vats down here?"

Morris Hausbach continued for another five minutes, showing Brad the papermaking area. They ended in a corner of the room where Morris had a desk, couch, and two easy chairs.

"Well, the nickel tour's over," Morris said, motioning for Brad to sit down, "but you didn't come here for that. What can I do for you?"

"Did you happen to see the twelve o'clock news today?"

"No. We have a television in the bedroom closet, but I don't know when we turned it on last. Why?"

"A customer of mine, Peter Eastrovich—"

"The Special Collections Librarian at the College."

"That's the man. He was interviewed, claiming that several books in the Avery Library are forgeries."

"And you want to pick my brains."

"That's about the size of it."

"Tell me what Peter Eastrovich said." Morris leaned forward and listened intently as Brad repeated what he knew about Peter's theories. Then he sat back in his chair, his fingers intertwined behind his head.

"It sounds like a nice, plausible, academic theory to me," Morris finally said. "But in the real world, nobody forges books. First, it's very hard to do. And second, there's no money in it."

"Peter mentioned that the twenty-nine books were sold to the library for less than two thousand dollars."

"My point exactly. It would have cost more than that to print one of them."

"But what if someone wanted to make a book like that for other reasons, other than the money?"

"Theoretically speaking?"

"Yes."

Morris sat back and closed his eyes. After a few seconds he opened them and leaned forward again.

"You said these were late-nineteenth-century, early-twentieth-century books?"

Brad nodded.

"Let's concentrate on the nineteenth century. If a person wanted to print a forgery of a nineteenth-century book, he'd have to start by finding paper made back then. It wouldn't be as hard as finding paper from the fifteenth century, but it wouldn't be a terribly easy job either.

"Let's say our forger came across just the right paper. Maybe, since he was only going to make one copy of the book, he cut pages out of a large blank book. Then he'd have to solve the problem of ink."

Morris Hausbach stood up and went over to his bookcase. "If a person wanted to make ink like they did in the nineteenth century—" He paused, running his fingers along the spines of his books until he came to a small, thin volume and pulled it out. "—he would have to have a formula. This," he said, pointing at the book in his hand, "was the bible. William Savage, *On the Preparation of Printing Ink*. It's not an easy book to come by, but it does exist.

"Even if you have the right formula, you have to age the ink. I don't know exactly what happens chemically, but I understand you can put ink in a microwave oven and make it appear older. It changes the molecular structure or something, and the ink seems used. You have to fool one of those carbon-dating machines, so you have to experiment and find out how long to leave the ink in the oven for the precise 'age' you want. If you don't have access to a carbon-dating machine, you could just find old paper that age and burn it—use the residue for the soot—or carbon black. All the recipes for black ink called for it."

"You'd use the black ash from the burnt paper?"

"No, its not the right texture. I'd burn the paper in a beaker first and scrape the soot from the smoke off the glass. You've got to remember, ink is one of the weakest links if you're a forger. You have to take care of a lot of details."

"But it could be done," Brad said.

"Yes. We're talking theory now. But even then there are ways that scientists can tell how long ink has been on paper. There's a machine, for instance, at the University of California at Davis—"

"But people looking into forgeries wouldn't necessarily want to go to California and . . ."

"No, but it could be done—theoretically," Morris said. "Just for the sake of argument, say you solved the problem of paper and ink. The next thing to consider is type. Each font of type is different, like a fingerprint. If a person were serious, he would have to go back to old-type specimen books and find a type that was used when the book was supposedly printed. Even match types a particular printer used."

Brad could almost see the rows of type-specimen books that Carl Riesling had on shelves near his printing press.

"Once you find the type you want to use," Morris continued, "you have to find a source and buy some. Again, it's not impossible— theoretically—but whoever did it would need to have a considerable amount to gain, other than money, to make it worth all the work, and if he were buying the type commercially there would be a paper trail of bills and things."

"But you still hear of people forging documents."

"Documents, yes. Engraving twenty-dollar bills, writing someone's name on a sheet of paper, passing something off as Hitler's diary, even forging a seventeenth-century American broadside. This is all child's work compared to forging a book. We haven't even talked about glue, binding, design, finding the right printing press. There are a hundred details that could trip up even the most careful forger.

"The best-documented case I know of someone's forging a book—actually he did several—was Thomas J. Wise. I suppose you know all about that."

"Some," said Brad.

"Wise 'discovered' small books by Byron, Shelley, and other poets, all of which he printed many years after the dates on the title pages. But he was caught. Caught with nineteen-thirties technology, no less, by two young turks—John Carter and Alfred Pollard, who made quite a name for themselves."

Brad reached into his inside jacket pocket. "I have a Xerox copy of one of the books from the Avery Library."

"Is this one of the forgeries?" Morris asked, taking the copy from Brad. "Of course we won't be able to tell anything about the paper, the ink, or the binding by looking at—"

His last words hung in midair as Morris Hausbach stood up again and went back to his bookcase. "Jaspert, Berry, and Johnson," he said to Brad, pointing at a book he had pulled from the shelves, *The Encyclopaedia of Type Faces*. Morris looked at the Xerox of the Melville pamphlet again and flipped through the *Encyclopaedia*, stopping at a page for a few seconds and then moving on.

"Remember, I told you that a typeface is like a fingerprint?" Morris finally said, looking up at Brad. "Come here."

Brad walked over to where Morris Hausbach was standing.

"Look at this capital *Q* here on page three of your Xerox. That's a typical Goudy capital *Q* if ever I saw one. Here. Look at the *Q* in my book under Goudy Old Style."

Brad did.

"Now, look at the short descenders on the lower-case letters." Brad seemed confused. "The things that go below the line—the *y*'s, *p*'s, *j*'s. Notice how short they are. Look at the *g*'s."

"They do look like they're the same as those in the Melville pamphlet," Brad said.

"That's because they are. No mistake about it."

"What's your point?"

"My point is that Frederic W. Goudy created his Goudy Old Style typeface for the American Typefounders in nineteen fifteen. It couldn't have been used to print a book in eighteen forty."

# Chapter
# 19

J esus Christ!" Joey screamed.

Teddy ran into the living room with his revolver in his hand.

"The nigger stole the keys to my Cadillac."

Teddy dropped the gun to his side and began to laugh. It was the first time he had laughed in four days.

# Chapter
## 20

T hank you for steering Ruby out to the deck," Brad said to Samantha. They were driving down the Colonial Parkway toward Colonial Williamsburg.

"Did you get the information you needed?"

"I think so. I showed Morris the photocopy of the Melville pamphlet."

"Did he think it was a forgery?"

"He agrees with Peter. He said that the typeface in which the book was printed didn't exist until the beginning of the twentieth century. Which means, of course, that the book couldn't have been printed until after then."

"And he was sure about his facts?"

"Very confident. He even showed me the typeface in a reference book. Sam, I believe him."

Samantha gazed intently at Brad's face. 'Then why is it you have that look on your face?"

"What look?"

"The one where you find out from your doctor that you have an advanced case of Alzheimer's disease."

"Sorry. It's just—"

"What?"

"Doubts."

"You don't think that Carl Riesling printed that Melville book?"

"I don't know. I believe it's a forgery, from what Peter and Morris Hausbach told me, but there's something . . ."

"Go ahead."

"It's just that I'm surprised Carl would have made such an obvious mistake."

"I had a course in psychology when I was in college."

"They had courses in psychology back then?"

"Very funny. The professor gave a lecture about the criminal mind. He said that thieves start out doing something mildly illegal, like stealing a candy bar from a store. No one notices, which gives them a false sense of security. Then they go on to bigger and more outrageous things, and when they eventually get caught, they're surprised. Maybe Carl got overconfident."

"Maybe."

"But you doubt it."

"Yes."

"Or maybe he didn't have the reference books to check his facts the way Morris Hausbach did."

"That's a distinct possibility," Brad said with newfound energy, "and one that should be checked out." With that he turned off the Colonial Parkway and started driving through Williamsburg.

"Where are we going?" Samantha asked.

"To the Rieslings."

They drove east on Route 5 and took the turn to the house as they had done on Monday. This time, the parking lot in front of Carl's office was empty. Brad slowed down as they passed.

"Sam, turn around and check the driveway that leads up to the house."

Samantha turned around in her seat and looked back. "What am I checking for?"

"Police cars."

"None that I can see. Just a van next to the house."

"Dark blue?"

"Yes."

"That's Carl's."

Brad turned the car around in the next wide spot in the road and doubled back. When they reached the Rieslings', he pulled into the driveway, went all the way to the turnabout in front of the house and came halfway back, where he parked his car near the rear of Carl's office.

"What are you doing?" Samantha asked.

"You can't see the car from the road here." Brad opened his door. "Wait for me."

Brad circled through the brush behind Carl Riesling's cinderblock office. When he reached the building, he picked up a large rock and broke one of the rear windowpanes. He chipped away the jagged edges and then reached in and opened the catch and raised the lower half of the window. Inside, Carl had nailed a piece of plywood across the opening. Brad stood on the windowsill and began kicking at the plywood to loosen the nails. He was contorted, coiling his leg for one final kick, when he heard a noise behind him.

"Samantha," he whispered.

"I've observed," Samantha said, in her normal voice, "that the professional burglar doesn't whisper after spending five minutes loudly pounding on the building he's breaking into."

"What are you doing here?"

"I sat in the car and decided that I'd feel more comfortable with my feminist lawyer if I were arrested for 'breaking and entering' instead of being an 'accessory to breaking and entering.'"

"Give me a hand, then," Brad said.

He heard Samantha clapping behind him as he took his final kick, removing the last of the nails that were holding the bottom of the plywood panel.

"Cute."

"Thank you."

Samantha held the plywood back to make a hole for Brad to climb through. Once inside, Brad did the same for her. "Just watch the nails."

Warmed through the day by the sun, the room in the late afternoon was permeated by the musty odor peculiar to old books. There was enough light seeping through the cracks in the boarded windows and from around the doors that they could see without electricity. Brad walked over to the small bookcase by the printing press he had remembered at Morris Hausbach's.

He glanced over the spines until he came to a volume in the middle of the top shelf. "There it is," he said.

"What?"

"Jaspert, Berry, and Johnson."

"Thanks for sharing that with me."

"It's the book Morris used that showed him the information about the typeface."

Brad thumbed through the pages. "Here," he said to Samantha. She stood next to him. "This is the typeface, Goudy Old Style. And Carl put marks next to it."

"Are there any other marks in the book?" Samantha asked.

"Could you look? I want to see what else is here."

Brad went back to the bookcase and scanned the other titles. Besides fifteen or so type-specimen books, there were books on manufacturers' paper samples, printing inks, bookbinding techniques, and related subjects. Next to the bookcase was a flat filing cabinet with large drawers for maps or architectural drawings. Brad opened one of them and found stacks of unprinted paper. He couldn't be certain, but the paper looked old. Some sheets were beginning to brown along the edges. In a lower drawer he found cloth for bookbinding. Many of the sheets seemed to have been soaked from the covers of old books.

"Well, if we ever needed proof that Carl printed the forgeries, it's all here."

"There are marks next to other typefaces all through the book," Samantha said.

"Put it back. I'll tell Tom Egan he'd better impound it as evidence, the beaker too. Carl probably used it to make ink."

"Do you think that forging those books has something to do with the murder?"

"Of course." Brad looked around the room. "I wonder if Carl's telephone is still working."

"Simple breaking and entering isn't enough for you," Samantha said. "Now you're going to take on the telephone company."

"A local call." Brad picked up the receiver, got a dial tone, and placed his call. While it rang, Brad cupped the mouthpiece. "Can you find a pencil for me?" he asked Samantha.

Before she had a chance to move, Brad was speaking into the receiver.

"Mrs. Johnson, Brad. Could you call Tom Egan for me? Tell him it's important. I have to see him. A half-hour. At his office.

"Would you mind dropping me off at the police station?" Brad asked Samantha.

"Why are you going there?"

"To tell Tom what I know."

"Oh, the expert witness?"

"You don't approve?"

"That part's okay, but I know you. You're going to get involved and I don't think it's any of your business."

"None of my business? Whoever killed Carl Riesling broke into my shop and then tried to kill me. That makes it my business."

"You're not working for the CIA anymore."

"So?"

"So you don't have the right to go around doing anything you please."

"You think I'm wrong to pursue this?"

"If by pursuing this you mean breaking into places, yes."

"I didn't steal anything. I just wanted to get some information."

"I'm sure Richard Nixon said the same thing after Watergate."

"Ah."

"Don't 'ah' me. The law applies to you just as it does everyone else."

"I just want to nail the bastard that did all this."

"I'm sure you do. It's just that I don't like the way you're going about it." They were silent and a tear began to well in Samantha's eye. "And I don't want to see you get hurt," she finally said.

"I know. I'll be careful," Brad said quietly.

The Williamsburg Police Department was located in a new brick structure that formed, along with the library and fire department, a complex of city buildings near the colonial section of town. The small entryway faced a bulletproof glass window, behind which the receptionist sat.

Brad and Samantha gave their names and waited until a uniformed policeman came and escorted them back into a large workroom. Tom Egan sat in a prefabricated fishbowl of an office, set in the center of the larger room. Through the glass windows that banded the room on all four sides, Brad and Samantha could see him speaking into the telephone. He was animated and barely able to conceal his irritation with the person on the other end. The sound of his staccato bursts of speech wafted over partitions that walled his office, which did not reach the ceiling. There were four policemen in the room going about their business, making every effort not to appear to be listening. Tom Egan's office was not a private place.

The conversation ended and Egan slammed the telephone receiver down into its cradle and got up from his desk in one explosive motion. Not satisfied, he kicked his wastebasket and sent it crashing into the base of the partition.

Brad and Samantha waited while the rest of the staff busied themselves with paperwork and other chores that diverted their attention away from Egan. Finally he came to his office door and looked directly at Brad.

"Wonderful. Now I have to deal with you."

"If you want, I can come back later," Brad began.

"What I wanted from you was a little advance warning about this Eastrovich and his damned news conference."

"I only found out about it myself about a half-hour before the interview."

"But you never thought I'd be interested in knowing?"

It was a rhetorical question, and Brad kept silent.

"You have any idea what it feels like, just before an election, to get a microphone shoved in your face and be asked about a key point in a murder investigation that everybody else except you knows about?"

"I'm sure it wasn't pleasant."

"Neither was being chewed out on the telephone by the governor," Tom said, pointing behind him in the general direction of his desk.

"What does the governor have to do with all this?"

"He's going to accept a library as a gift to the state from Jonathan Avery tomorrow, but before he did he wanted to know if I was going to arrest Avery for murder during the ceremony."

"What did you tell him?"

"I told him I didn't know. Then he yelled at me."

"The governor?"

"Said I was trying to ruin *his* political career. Christ, I've never even met the man."

"Have you had the chance to talk to Jonathan Avery about any of this?" Brad asked.

"This afternoon. Another milestone in my day." Egan looked up at the ceiling and raised his hands slightly like an Old Testament prophet beseeching God. "Yes, I had a talk with Jonathan Avery, along with Jonathan Avery's lawyers and Jonathan Avery's personal FBI bodyguards. It was really a marvelous interview. With that mob advising him on his rights, I'm lucky I got him to tell me his name."

The three of them went into Egan's office. Brad quietly reported about discovering that his copy of the Melville pamphlet was missing, about how he came to have it in the first place, and about his conversation with Morris Hausbach that afternoon.

"Any luck calling Greta?" Brad asked.

"I dialed the number you gave me and asked for Greta Riesling; a woman answered and started talking German to me; I couldn't make myself understood. I told her I was a policeman from Williamsburg and she hung up."

"Next time, say it's Brad Parker. I think you'll find that the prospect of money can melt most language barriers. Anyway, there's enough evidence in Carl Riesling's office to prove that he was the one who printed the forgeries," Brad concluded. "In fact, you might be able to get some information on that point from my sales manager, Jebediah Stuart. He was the one Carl was teaching how to print."

"Did you ask him about this?"

"I called the shop a few minutes ago, but Mrs. Johnson told me he'd already left, went home, sick."

"Let me get back to one point. Did Avery know you had a copy of the Melville pamphlet?"

"Yes. He wanted to buy it from me."

"Did you agree to sell it to him?"

"It isn't mine to sell until I buy the library from Greta Riesling. Anyway, I had promised Peter Eastrovich I would sell it to him if it was an exact duplicate of Avery's. I don't see much sense in Jonathan's having both of the only known copies."

"And how did Avery react to that?"

"He still wanted to buy the book, of course. If you knew book collectors you'd understand that. But he was being reasonable about it."

"You and Avery are fairly close friends?" Egan asked.

"I'd say so."

"Do you think you could ask him some questions for me?"

"I actually came over here to volunteer."

"Good."

They remained in Tom Egan's office and talked for another ten minutes before Brad and Samantha left.

# Chapter 21

Jebediah and Napoleon sat in Joey's car at the Kentucky Fried Chicken parking lot eating three-piece chicken dinners from boxes. The parking lot had a separate entrance and exit. In an emergency, Napoleon knew, the Cadillac could jump the short asphalt curb that separated him from the next parking lot, and leave that way. The Teamsters had taught him about such contingencies.

"Sure would have liked to have been there when Joey found out I stole his white Cadillac." Napoleon finished gnawing on a bone and threw it into the back seat with the rest of the trash. "You think we should call him now?"

"Let them sweat for another half-hour," Jebediah said.

"They're going to come after us with everything they have after they get the microfilm," Napoleon said. His face wrinkled as he wiped his hands on the white suede patch on the inside door.

"You said yourself that we'd be dead if we just turned it over to them. You've got to have faith."

"Yeah," Napoleon answered without any enthusiasm.

"Listen, my plan for the robbery worked, didn't it?"

"Sure. I got twenty thousand dollars. Only trouble is, I can't touch it without getting killed."

"I went to the bank and gave you half of my twenty thousand, didn't I?"

"Yeah."

"So no matter what else happens, you're ten thousand dollars ahead of the game." Jebediah looked over at Napoleon and saw a wall of indifference. After the beating Jebediah had taken from him that afternoon, he didn't much care. All he wanted was to get the rest of the money and leave.

"What you going to do when they come stalking you like an animal?" Napoleon asked. "You know they will. The difference between them and the police is that the Mafia don't get overworked and forget. They just keep looking till they find you."

"I think you give them too much credit."

"You were brought up in the South. You don't know them like I do."

"They won't find me."

"What you going to do, disappear?"

Jebediah hadn't been going to tell him, but he felt it wouldn't matter now, and, anyway, it was too good a plan to keep secret. "They won't find me as Jebediah Stuart." He paused. "After we get the money, I'm going to fly to Canada and then to Denmark. I'm going to have a sex-change operation."

"Say what?"

"I'm going to become a girl. Maybe I'll even try to pick you up in a bar some night."

"You do that, you won't have to worry about no Mafia. I'll kill you myself."

"You got the microfilm on you?" Napoleon asked.

They were driving along back roads outside of town, killing time.

"No. It's hidden."

"Where?"

"In the bookshop. It's in a book in the glass case in the middle of the shop."

"What if somebody buys the book?"

"It's in Lawson's *A New Voyage to Carolina*, in the folding map. Mr. Parker put a price of twelve thousand dollars on it. It will be there for a long time. Trust me."

"But how are we going to get at it, now that you've retired?"

"We'll let your Mafia friends worry about that. We'll tell them where it is and if they really want it, they can buy the book."

"You think they going to give us four hundred thousand dollars in cash for a note that tells them where their microfilm is?"

"Not normally," Jebediah said. "But we're in charge now and we've got to play it for all it's worth."

# Chapter
## 22

**B**rad Parker peered down at the mound of mail that had accumulated. He didn't have the mental stamina to go through it, so he merely picked over the stack, sifting out the obvious junk and tossing it into the wastebasket. The smaller stack that remained made him feel that much less guilty.

"A command decision," Samantha said. She was waiting, with the telephone in her hand, while a maid went to find Fiona Avery. "I wish I could do that, but I'm always afraid I'll throw out the one that announces some distant aunt has died and I've just inherited the family fortune." Samantha abruptly shifted her focus to the telephone. "Fiona."

There were long periods of silence on Samantha's end before she could ask if they could come out to the house.

"Well?" Brad asked when Samantha got off the phone.

"Jonathan's been in meetings all afternoon, but Fiona said to come along, that you would get his mind off his problems."

In the car, Brad said, "I feel guilty taking you away from your work today."

"They gave me the day off, actually."

"Why?" Brad asked, already sensing her answer.

"The firm got the job in New York," Samantha said flatly.

Brad felt a tightness throughout his body.

"I should have told you before, but—"

"What are you going to do?"

Samantha met his eyes. "I don't know."

"I love you," Brad said, "and whatever you decide, I'm sure we'll work it out." He was glad he'd said the words, even though he wasn't sure he meant them.

Samantha reached over and squeezed his hand. Brad tried to smile but only managed a tight grimace.

"How did Fiona sound on the telephone?" Brad asked too intently.

"A little flighty. Reading between the lines, there must have been a lot going on there this afternoon after Tom Egan left."

As they neared the gate to the Avery estate, Brad noticed Anthony Patronsky standing next to the speaker system.

"Hi," Brad said, rolling down his window.

"Mr. Parker."

"I'm surprised to see you down here. Isn't the intercom working?"

"We had some reporters drive onto the estate earlier this afternoon. Mr. Avery thought it would be better if we screened all callers here."

"Going to shoot them?" Brad said.

"The law's very specific regarding unwanted trespassers," Anthony replied humorlessly. "But you're expected," he quickly added. "Mrs. Avery is at the house, and Mr. Avery is in his office at the library. My instructions are to ask you to take Mrs. Parker up to the house first and then go to the library yourself."

"Mrs. Parker," Samantha said after they were out of sight of the gate.

"It could be."

"Is that another proposal of marriage?"

"I guess it is."

"But I'd have to give up the offer in New York to accept."

"Not necessarily."

"Hm." Samantha paused. "That gives me something else to consider, Brad Parker."

The sun was providing its theatrical lighting to the house again as they approached. Fiona waited for them in the driveway.

"Did you see that reptile on television today?" Fiona asked.

"Just part of it at noon," Samantha answered.

"Jonathan had me record the six o'clock version on our VCR."

"Anthony told me Jonathan's at his office," Brad mentioned.

"He's also in one of his snits. Why don't you stay here? You'll find us much better company."

"There are a couple things I have to ask him," Brad said.

"Don't say I didn't warn you. He's been meeting with lawyers all afternoon. When he gets in one of his moods he likes to take it out on someone. I think he called the lawyers because he didn't want to abuse anyone human."

"It sounds serious," Samantha said.

"I don't even want to think about it."

Brad left them in the driveway and drove slowly toward the library. The sun had set by the time he pulled into the parking lot by Jonathan's office. Jonathan waited for him in the open doorway.

"Did you see that idiot Eastrovich on television?" Jonathan asked before Brad could shut his car door.

"A little of it."

"Come on in. I have the bastard on videotape."

Brad followed Jonathan into his office, and they watched a television set on the credenza behind Jonathan's desk. The "Six O'clock News" version seemed to be an expanded repeat of the "News at Noon," complete with "no comments" by the governor and Tom Egan. The report ended with Peter staring into the camera, saying that he "would strongly encourage the governor to initiate a comprehensive study of the library's collection—done by reputable bibliographers and scholars—before he opens it to the public."

"Cheeky little bastard," Jonathan said, flipping a switch that turned off the television set.

"He certainly seems confident about his facts."

"Well, he did enough homework. The damned little gnome spent months in my library scribbling down his crampy notes. If I had known what he was doing I would have thrown him the hell out the first day he came."

"How is this going to affect the dedication ceremony tomorrow?"

"That's in the hands of the governor."

"How?"

"I didn't build this collection and pay for the library building to have it closed until some snot-nosed punk gives his academic seal of approval to have it opened again," said Jonathan. "So I had someone call the governor this afternoon and tell him that I wanted written assurance by him that he wouldn't do that."

"Or?"

"I left the 'or else' open, but we called him over three hours ago, and still no word."

"It certainly isn't working out the way you'd planned."

"That's an understatement." Jonathan walked to the inside door of his office and looked out to the library. "He just sat there, day after day, writing his notes, Xeroxing pages from my books. I was so damned busy playing patron of the arts. I gave him free rein. Thought it would be bad form to pry and ask him what he was doing."

Behind them, Brad heard a light knock on the outside door.

"We thought we'd join you," Fiona said. Samantha was behind her.

Jonathan stared into the darkness of the library.

"I don't see what all the fuss is about," Fiona said. "It's no sin to buy a bogus book."

Jonathan turned to her. "You really don't understand, do you? Fiona, this man is implying that I had something to do with forging these

192

books. He claims that I knew about them in advance, worked with Carl Riesling to manufacture them; then killed him."

"Did you?" Brad asked.

"Et tu, Brutus?"

"I'm just asking a question."

"And Eastrovich was just using my library for 'research.'"

"A question you didn't answer," Brad continued.

Jonathan stopped pacing in front of his desk and glared at Brad.

"Damn it, Jonathan, that Melville pamphlet I took from the Rieslings' was stolen from my apartment the night I was hit over the head. Somehow these forgeries, Carl's death, my being mugged in my own apartment—they're all connected. I think I have a right to an answer."

"Now you're saying I hit you over the head and stole the Melville pamphlet?" Jonathan said, his voice barely under control.

"I'd like an answer to my question."

"And I'd like an answer to mine."

"Is this what you Americans call a Mexican standoff?" Fiona asked in the silence that followed. "Because we English are noted for our diplomacy, I would like to suggest that you, Jonathan, answer Brad's question first, since he asked it first." She turned to Samantha. "Am I making sense?"

"A great deal," Samantha answered.

"And then you, Brad, can answer Jonathan's question. You first, Jonathan."

Jonathan stood silent, then in an explosion of words he said, "Of course I didn't know they were forgeries."

"You see," Samantha said, "Jonathan was just a horse's ass for buying them in the first place."

They all looked at Brad.

"No," Brad said quietly, "I never seriously thought that you were the one in my apartment that night."

"Isn't that nice, Jonathan? Your best friend doesn't think that you're

Jack the Ripper. Now, don't you boys feel better?" Fiona turned to Samantha. "Let's go back to the house and let the menfolk kiss and make up."

Brad and Jonathan awkwardly exchanged grunts and apologies in the otherwise empty office.

"This has been a hell of a day," Jonathan said, "and tomorrow promises to be even more so."

"Do you think the governor will come through?"

"I'm not counting on it."

"What will you do, then?"

"In the game of bridge it's called reneging."

"Isn't it a little late for that?"

"Eastrovich and the governor changed the rules. So can I," Jonathan said. "Even my spineless lawyers agree—reluctantly. Apparently there's nothing in the papers we signed that could stop me. There might be a court case, but by the time that's over, we'll both be dead." He paused. "Not a word of this to Fiona. She still thinks that we're having a reception tomorrow. I'm going to have to tell her later tonight. I guess," he added, "I didn't really want to give it all away after all."

Brad tried to think of something positive to say, but he couldn't.

"There was a Tom Egan here today from the Williamsburg Police. He said he met you."

"At the Rieslings' just after Carl . . ."

"I think he's going to try to bring me in for questioning on Carl's murder." Jonathan frowned. "I wouldn't like that."

"They'd need a lot more than Peter's accusations before they'd arrest you," Brad said. "Just as a matter of curiosity, do you have an alibi for the night Carl was killed?"

"I was here on the estate, working in the library."

"Well, can't Larry, Moe, and Curly vouch for that—what with all the electronic surveillance on the estate?"

"To a degree."

"What does that mean?"

"If you wanted to go out at midnight and get a cup of coffee or something to eat," Jonathan began, "you'd just hop in your car and go. I can't do that. I have to wake up the team, tell them what I'm going to do, and one of them comes along for the ride. Does wonders for spontaneity.

"The result is that I never left the estate. But when we built the library building, I noticed that they didn't put sensors by the front door of the building. They put them on the outside door of my office to keep people from breaking into the estate, but nothing to keep me from breaking out.

"The library has its own alarm system, of course, but I could deactivate that from inside. There was always a company car for the library staff in the outside parking lot. I didn't use it much, but—you have to live a life like I do to really appreciate how good it made me feel, just knowing the car was there and I could escape. So you see I could have easily been at the Rieslings' that night, even though I wasn't."

"So you don't have an alibi."

"Nothing that a half-wit with a sixth-grade education couldn't break. I'm telling you this because I might be taking a vacation for a little while, until all this blows over. Life's too short to subject yourself to unpleasant things if you don't have to, and thanks to Uncle Sam, I don't have to."

"Where are you going?"

"To do a little computer work for the government, maybe a little something else." Jonathan hesitated. "The nice thing about working for our side in intelligence is that it doesn't matter if I'm a homicidal maniac or a lunatic, as long as I produce. You, on the other hand, are my friend. I care very much about what you think of me. That's why I want you to know. I'm sure I'll get a lot of bad press out of this." Jonathan walked toward Brad and embraced him. "It might be a long time before we see each other again."

# Chapter
## 23

I have tried to run this organization by modern business principles. I have given each and every employee responsibilities in the hope that he might grow and therefore make the organization itself stronger. Perhaps I was wrong." Norman Anastasius Calvado was in Williamsburg.

Both Joseph Sabatino and Theodore Simon sat quietly in front of him, their heads slightly bowed and their eyes moving occasionally to avoid direct eye contact with their don, who paced while he talked. Mr. Calvado had flown directly to Williamsburg after receiving the telephone call from Teddy. He'd had the Williamsburg Inn switch their accommodations to a separate eighteenth-century cottage at the edge of the historical district. It had three bedrooms, two baths, and a kitchenette just off a large living room.

"From now on, I want you to think of this as a military operation and yourselves as being under military law—mine. Is that understood?"

Joey and Teddy mumbled their yeses.

"This will be our command post. I have asked the Inn for a direct telephone line into this cottage. It will be installed tomorrow morning. You can reach me directly on that number, or through the Inn's switchboard."

"I still think that we should have called the police about them stealing my Cadillac," Joey said.

Calvado glared at him; Teddy just hung his head lower.

"Jeffrey," Calvado called.

Jeffrey emerged from the shadows near the brick fireplace.

"Where you able to hire some local help?"

"I have six men waiting at the Holiday Inn. All with rental cars."

"Excellent. You know we're probably going to need more tomorrow?"

"I've taken the liberty of bringing in people from New York, reliable people I've worked with before. They'll be here before eight in the morning."

"Excellent."

"What makes you think they'll call?" Teddy asked in a soft, unassured voice.

"Human nature, greed, street smarts. Take your pick. They knew we were going to kill them once they gave us the microfilm. I tried to make our meeting with Mr. Jones as nonthreatening as I could, but I'm afraid that not everyone on my staff understood that. Did they, Joseph?"

"That nigger started it," Joey said in his own defense.

"Jeffrey," Calvado said, abruptly turning away from Joey, "I'd like you to direct your six men to check every parking lot in Williamsburg for Mr. Sabatino's car. That's every parking lot: motels, restaurants, stores. Have them take a map and divide up the city, work in ever-expanding circles until they find it. Stress the fact that I don't want them taking any action on their own. Is that understood?"

"Yes, sir."

"Go out to the Holiday Inn and tell them in person. I don't want to tie up the telephone line."

Jeffrey left, and Calvado walked into the kitchenette and poured himself a glass of bottled water. "I'm going into the bedroom now," he said to Joey and Teddy. "When they call, let me know immediately. I'll pick up the extension in there." Calvado began walking down the hall

198

with his glass. "One more thing," he added. "Theodore is to answer the telephone. Nothing personal, Joseph, but under the circumstances, that's the way it will be."

Joey raised his right arm and pointed his middle finger in Calvado's direction as he turned and shut the bedroom door behind him.

Quiet hung over the room like a coating of lead. Five minutes passed, then ten. Breathing itself became noticeable, then difficult.

It was almost an hour before the telephone rang. Teddy picked up on the first ring. Joey was already in the hallway waiting for a sign from Teddy before he knocked on Calvado's door.

"Yeah," Teddy said into the phone, nodding his head to Joey.

"The rules of the game have been changed," a voice said. Teddy could hear the click as Calvado picked up his receiver, but he didn't think that the caller had noticed. The voice wasn't Napoleon's. "You get four hundred thousand dollars in small bills ready by tomorrow morning and put them in a suitcase."

"Four hundred thousand in small bills won't fit in one suitcase, asshole," Teddy said.

"Then get two. They'll fit in two suitcases, won't they?" The voice seemed confident on the surface, but Teddy knew the man was flustered.

"Sure," said Teddy. "I can arrange that."

"Well, you get the money ready, and I'll call you again at ten tomorrow morning with further instructions." There was a click and then the sound of a dial tone; finally Teddy heard Calvado replacing his receiver.

"Was it the nigger?" Joey asked.

"No. The other one," replied Teddy.

"Did he say anything about the Caddy?"

Calvado appeared in the hall. "Theodore. Call Dominic in Atlantic City. Ask him to have four hundred thousand in cash delivered to us here by nine-thirty tomorrow. Use my name. There won't be any problem." Calvado turned to go back to his bedroom, then stopped.

"And tell him to have it delivered in an armored car. That should impress our friends of our seriousness if they are watching." Calvado walked back into the living room. "By the way, that was a nice touch about the suitcase. Very revealing."

"Thanks."

"But for future reference, four hundred thousand dollars will fit in one suitcase, with room to spare."

# Chapter
# 24

"D id you learn anything from Jonathan?" Samantha asked during their drive back to Williamsburg.

"About the Melville pamphlet?"

"That's what I meant, yes. Why? What else did you two talk about?"

"The Avery Library. Jonathan's all but decided not to give it away after all."

"Why? Because of what Peter said on television?"

"That and the probability that the governor will close it just as soon as the state takes possession."

"Close it! On Peter's advice?"

"I'm sure the governor has advisers of his own that think it would be politically wise to do just that. At least until the dust settles."

"But Jonathan's not going to give him the chance."

"Precisely."

"Won't there be legal problems?"

"Jonathan has lawyers to take care of all that. I think his immediate concern is telling Fiona that there won't be a dinner party tomorrow night."

"She strongly suspects that already."

"Woman's intuition?"

"Fiona's lived with Jonathan for years. She knows that he's the type to take his bat and ball and go home if he doesn't like the game."

"The spoiled-brat theory?"

"No, more the little-boy-in-all-men scenario, if you have to label it. It's the one most of us women subscribe to."

"Well, no matter what name you put on it, it's going to make for an interesting morning tomorrow."

As they talked, Brad made a left turn off Jamestown Road, just past the colored neon lights of the Muscarelle Art Museum.

"Where are we going?" asked Samantha.

"I have one more thing I have to do before I call it a night."

Brad parked his car with the motor running and reached for his K-Mart bag.

"What is this?"

"A penlight," Brad said, putting it in the pocket of his knit shirt. "And some electrical tape."

"What do you think you're going to do?"

Brad put the car in gear and started forward again, turning into the parking lot behind Swem Library.

"Oh, God," Samantha sighed. "You're going to break into the library."

"I know how you feel about it, but I don't think there's anything to gain by rehashing it again. It's something I have to do." Brad turned off the car and left the keys in the ignition. "I'd like for you to wait for me. I'll probably be an hour, no more, but I'll understand if you leave."

"What are you looking for?"

"I'm hoping to find the copy of the Melville book that was stolen from my apartment."

"If Peter did take it, what makes you think you'll find it in his office?"

"He keeps his other files there—the research he did on the book. My guess is that the Melville pamphlet won't be too far away."

"Brad, he's probably destroyed it by now. I would have."

"So would I, but we're not librarians. A librarian can't throw away a book, even if it is incriminating evidence. It's just not in his nature, and if there's one thing Peter is, first and foremost, it's a librarian."

He took the roll of electrical tape she was holding, tore off two five-inch lengths, keeping the sticky side out, and wrapped them around the back of the fingers on his left hand. "If you decide to stay, and hear an alarm or a loud commotion, I want you to leave. Just drive away slowly. Do you understand?"

"Brad."

"No." Brad reached across the car and kissed her gently on the cheek. "I love you no matter what you decide. I wanted you to know that."

Before she could say anything more, Brad was out of the car and walking toward the library's service entrance, leaving her with a kaleidoscope of questions flickering in her mind. After a while she squirmed over into the driver's seat.

Brad walked up the steps to the loading platform and pushed the button under the sign that read "Night Service." After a few minutes a middle-aged black man in gray-green overalls opened one of the steel-faced doors.

"Yeah?"

"Sorry to bother you," Brad began, "but I'm a tourist and I got all turned around. Could you tell me how I could get to Merchant's Square from here?"

"Down that road till it ends, then hang a right. You'll run right into it."

"Down which road?" Brad asked.

"That road," the black man said, pointing, looking at Brad as if he were a retarded child. "That road." He leaned outside to be in a better position to point at the only road either of them could see. As he leaned forward, Brad moved between the man and the door, looking directly over the man's shoulders. Behind him, Brad felt for the door latch.

Once he found it, he firmly stretched the pieces of electrical tape over the protruding catches, keeping it in a permanently unlocked position.

Brad thanked the man for his help and started back down the steps. At the bottom he waited, counting slowly to thirty, before doubling back toward the door. He opened it, removed the tape, wadded it into a ball, and put it in his pocket.

He stepped into the library. Everything was quiet, and Brad shut the door softly, listening for the lock to click. Then he took a deep breath and began walking up the stairs to the next level.

From the top of the stairs there was still a long corridor between him and Special Collections. Brad went down it confidently, at a normal pace. Halfway, a cleaning woman came out of one of the offices with a green plastic garbage bag in her hand.

"Electrical inspection," Brad announced as he passed. "Notice any fluorescent bulbs not working properly?"

"No," she replied.

Brad walked on, not acknowledging her reply. She was used to being ignored, like the plants that sat in the corners of the offices she cleaned. The woman shrugged her shoulders and continued into the next office along the gray corridor.

At the end of the hall Brad turned into the exhibition area for Special Collections. The department had six different exhibits each year, with books and printed cards filling the glass cases. Exhibits represented a lot of work, especially since virtually no one ever stopped to look at them. "Exhibits are as much for the staff as for anyone else," Peter had once told Brad. "It gives us a chance to find the strengths and weaknesses in the particular collection we're showing."

Brad walked across the room to the maintenance closet on the far side, and turned on the light. He closed the door behind him and climbed up on the slop-sink. Overhead he removed the ceiling panel, took out his penlight, and looked inside. There was at least three feet of space between the false ceiling and the concrete floor above. Directly above him was a long I-beam that ran across the exhibition area, over the wrought-iron gates, and into the Rare Book Room beyond. Brad reached down for a small stepladder and placed it as securely as he could in the sink. Then he climbed up to the beam, gripping the base of the "I" with his hands and feet. Suspended from the beam he inched his way forward, headfirst, like a worm, bringing his feet and knees up to his hands, then walking forward with his fingertips until his torso was straight again.

The surface of the beam was coated with concrete, and Brad wished he had thought of buying a pair of gloves. He was halfway, or what he thought might be halfway, across the exhibition room when he realized he had not even counted the number of ceiling panels he had to crawl over before getting to the far side of the wrought-iron gates. Sloppy, he thought, but it was too late to go back and start all over.

The concrete was beginning to cut into his fingers, making them smart. On his right, he began to scrape against the side of a light-fixture set flush into the drop ceiling. He tried to adjust himself, placing both hands on the left side of the I-beam, but it was a greater strain than he had anticipated. After bringing his feet and knees forward and then straightening out again three times, he gave up this plan and went back to his original position. He cut his right forearm on his last thrust past the light, and then put a half-inch tear in his pants leg, but these were the least of his problems. His breathing was deeper and he could feel his heart pound. Sweat from his forehead began to trickle into his left eye, burning.

Brad felt every one of his forty-five years, and each of his two hundred and ten pounds. His shirt was soaked through and clung to his body. For a second, he saw himself impaled on one of the iron spears that rose as part of the baroque design on the gates. He even imagined the headline: BOOKSHOP OWNER FOUND DEAD IN LIBRARY.

"Enough nonsense," he said to himself. It was now a matter of will. "Five more," he said out loud, urging his body forward like a weightlifter finishing a set of repetitions. He reached out with his left hand, then his right, pulling his feet behind him until he was in a

jackknife position. "One," he said, repeating the movements. "Two."
At the end of five, Brad was finding it difficult to breathe deeply
enough to catch his breath. He reached down and lifted a ceiling panel
underneath him to see where he was. There, directly below, was the
card-catalog file, just inside the door. He had done it.

It took two more wormlike movements to bring his feet into a
position where he could drop down to the top of the wooden cabinet.
This he did, replacing the ceiling panel before jumping down to the
floor.

Brad walked over to the reading room, safely away from the view of
the exhibition area, and sank onto the carpet. He had been careless, first
in not buying a pair of gloves, then in not counting the distance he had
to travel along the I-beam. He was out of shape and lucky not to have
been seriously hurt. There was a time when he would have rolled an
operation like this over and over again in his mind, anticipating
everything. Now he was just a careless, middle-aged civilian.

It was ironic, Brad thought, sitting on the floor, trying to regain his
breath. Ironic, because living a normal life, having the freedom to be
careless, was a goal he had fervently wanted to achieve when he left the
Company. Moments before, clinging to the I-beam, he had suddenly
realized he had reached his goal, but at that moment it seemed like the
Dubious Achievement Award of the month. Life was like that, he
thought.

The reading room was dim, bathed in reflected light from the
exhibition area. Brad walked quietly to Peter Eastrovich's office. He
took out his penlight and sat down behind Peter's desk. He tried the
drawer that Peter had pointed to earlier that morning when he talked
about his files and notes about the forgeries. It was locked. Brad
reached into his rear pocket for his wallet. In a compartment behind a
leather flap were a series of six picks. "You don't throw away old
friends," he had told Samantha when she accidentally found them one
evening. It only took thirty seconds before the cylinder released. "Hot
damn," Brad whispered, feeling less the civilian now than he had a few
seconds before.

He took the files out of the desk drawer and sat on the floor in the knee-well of Peter's desk, where the penlight wouldn't reflect out the window. The notes were written in Peter's minuscule print, tiny and neat like that of a trained draftsman or engraver. The notes were detailed and concise—fastidious, in fact. Brad thumbed through the folders, paying particular attention to one labeled "Melville, Herman. *A Sermon for Sailors.*"

Peter's notes identified the typeface used to print the text of the pamphlet, just as Morris Hausbach had. Peter had gone further, however, and pointed out three typefaces used on the title page that had also been created after the Melville pamphlet was supposed to have been printed. Inside the folder, along with Peter's notes, was a laboratory report from the University of California's Research Library at Davis, giving an analysis of a small sliver of paper Peter Eastrovich had sent them. In marginal notes on the report Peter claimed that the paper was taken from the Avery copy of *Sermon*. The report went on to say that the paper analyzed contained esparto grass. Stapled behind the report was a photocopy from a book giving a detailed history of when esparto grass was used in papermaking and when the practice had stopped. The dates it was used were later than the date the pamphlet was supposed to have been published.

Brad returned the files to the drawer and sat again in Peter's chair, his elbows resting on the arms and his fingertips supporting his chin, lost in thought. He swiveled the chair, sitting very still, looking at the room in the dim light. If he had it, and he did hide it here . . . He let the thought hang in the stillness. Someplace accessible. He had mentally divided the room into sections. First, the obvious, he thought, and went over to the bookcases. It took ten minutes to go through the volumes, taking the larger ones off the shelves to see if something were laid inside the covers. He looked at his watch. Fifty minutes, ten to go. He stood still, but his mind was racing.

"The desk," he said out loud. He sat down again in Peter Eastrovich's chair. Motionless for a minute or longer, Brad finally reached down and felt beneath the center drawer, above the knee-well. Then he got down on his knees, flashed the penlight on the lower surface, and turned it off. Nothing. He was getting back to his feet when he noticed that the drawer rested on an outer panel. He got back down on the floor again and opened the drawer. There, securely taped underneath, was a brown manila envelope. Brad tore it off the drawer and put the package on the top of the desk.

He unfastened a metal clip and pulled out a copy of Herman Melville's *A Sermon for Sailors*. He had no way of knowing if it was the one from his apartment, but that was a moot point. He didn't have time to examine it in any case, or even to put it back where the police could find it later with his help. Outside, he heard noises in the exhibition area. Brad quickly locked Peter's desk, stuffed the Melville pamphlet into its envelope, and slipped it under his shirt and belt, over the small of his back.

He heard a key slip into the lock on the wrought-iron gates that led into the Rare Book Room. There were two voices. One was Peter's, the other was female and giggly. Brad couldn't place it. He walked to the door of Peter's office. Someone had turned on the light in the entrance area. Next to Peter's office was another door. Brad opened it and found a small closet. He deftly slipped inside.

Less than ten seconds later the lights went on in the reading room, forming a yellow glow along the outline of the closet door. With the increased light Brad noticed an old wooden coatrack to his left with Peter's overcoat and umbrella hanging on it. Brad moved it slightly so that it stood between him and the door.

The voices were clearer now. They both had a lilt of drink tiptoeing through their inflections. The woman's voice especially was noticeably slurred, but even so Brad recognized the professional tones of Belinda Freemont, the reporter who had interviewed Peter on television.

Peter was cooing softly to her. Then Brad heard the woman giggle and say "Oh, no!" without conviction or thought. There was a rustling sound, then another. Brad listened to her sporadic giggles as they gradually lowered an octave, from playfulness to lust.

Brad heard Peter say the word "couch," and the light from under the door dimmed perceptibly.

"But the cleaning people—" the woman protested.

"Belinda, they do this area first. Nobody ever comes back here."

So Brad was right. It was Belinda Freemont on the couch with Peter. The air in the closet was stale and warm. Brad looked at the luminous dial on his watch. His hour in the library had passed fifteen minutes ago.

"I have a bottle of champagne chilled just for tonight," Peter said. "I'll only be a minute." Peter's voice seemed to drift away to the entrance. Brad remembered a refrigerator in the makeshift lunch area in the room behind the reception desk.

On the other side of the closet door, Belinda hummed some nameless tune to herself and, to Brad's amazement, opened the door to the closet. Brad froze behind the coatrack. Silhouetted in the soft light of the reading room, Belinda hung her white silk blouse on a peg a few inches from Brad's nose. She stood there, perfectly relaxed, humming, a pretty black-haired woman in her late twenties, stark naked, her two small breasts undulating like unhurried ripples on a peaceful lake.

Just as she was closing the door, her eyes focused on Brad standing behind the coatrack. He returned her gaze. The skin on her face perceptibly tightened. Her entire body seemed to freeze—everything, that is, except for her eyes, which grew wider and wider until Brad could see white completely around their edges.

"Hi," Brad said.

"Ahhhh—" Belinda screamed, and screamed again.

"What's wrong?" Peter yelled from somewhere in the stacks. From behind his coatrack Brad saw Peter race into the main reception area, his tie loose and his shirttails over his trousers. By then Belinda was already at the wrought-iron gates, her blouse clutched firmly in her left hand.

"Ahh," she bleated over and over again, in short, shallow breaths.

Peter was only ten paces away from her. He hesitated for a second, staring at the open closet and the darkness that hid Brad. The hesitation was a critical mistake. Belinda was now outside in the exhibit area, and from the sound of another door opening, Brad guessed that she was starting down the long hallway toward the rest of the library. Peter looked from the closet to the iron gates and then followed Belinda at a dead run.

Immediately after Peter made his decision, Brad made his. He ran across the reading room and slid into the exhibit hall. He looked fleetingly at the maintenance closet, rejected the idea, and began running toward the emergency exit door. He hit the handle on the door at full speed, snapping the lock open. As he did, the loud, clanging alarm sounded. The force of impact jolted the door open and just as quickly caused it to spring shut behind him, muting the sound of the alarm.

Outside, Brad ran toward the parking lot. There was no sense in a forty-five-year-old man's trying to look inconspicuous on a college campus in the dark of night with alarms sounding behind him. When he reached the parking lot, he saw his car stopped at the entrance. It was just starting to pull out. Brad broke into what he hoped would be one final sprint, pumping his arms like a high-school track star. He caught up to the car in the middle of the road, less than a hundred feet from where it had left the parking lot. As if he were breaking a tape at the end of a race, Brad raised both hands above his head and brought them down hard on the trunk of the car to get Samantha's attention.

Samantha instantly slammed on the brakes, sending Brad across the trunk and over the right rear fender. She reached and unlocked the passenger door. "God! Are you all right?"

Brad wasn't sure, but he quickly got off the ground and leapt into the car. Behind them Brad could hear human noises and a man yelling, "Hey, stop there!"

"Let's get out of here," Brad said.

Samantha jammed the accelerator to the floor and kept her foot down, driving the car through a stop sign and making a full right-hand turn without a hint of deceleration. After a few blocks she took her foot off the gas pedal and the car slowed to a normal pace.

"You scared me to death back there," Samantha said.

"I scared myself."

"What happened?"

"You wouldn't believe it." Brad felt his back. The envelope was still there.

"Try me."

Brad did as they slowly drove west on Richmond Road.

"So Peter did steal the book from your apartment," Samantha finally said when he was finished.

"It certainly looks that way."

"Are you going to the police with it?"

"With what? Peter would just deny everything. Damn. I only wish I'd had the time to put it back."

"And tell the police where it was?"

"Direct them to it, maybe." Brad looked at the side of Samantha's face as she drove. "I'm glad you waited for me, Sam."

"I almost left, several times. You were longer than an hour, you know."

"I know."

"I almost panicked when I saw Peter going into the library with that television reporter."

"Did they see you?"

"From the way they were fondling each other, I would guess that they were both too preoccupied or drunk to notice, especially Belinda Freemont. She took her shoes off in the parking lot. For a while I wondered if she would make it to the library with any clothes on at all."

"She's cute naked but really not that great."

"Damn it, I was worried about you, and you're trying to turn it into one big joke."

"Not really."

"I'll never understand you," Samantha said.

"At least I learned something about myself tonight."

"What's that?"

"The older I get, the more excitement makes me randy."

"Oh, for Christ's sake."

"So do you want to spend the night in a cheap motel with a burglar?"

# Chapter
## 25

I t's nine forty-five," said Napoleon. "Time to make the call."

"You understand what you're supposed to do?"

"Jebediah, I'm big and I'm black, but I ain't dumb. We been over this fifty times already."

"Okay." They were sitting in a rented gray Toyota in the parking lot at Merchant's Square. Joey's white Cadillac was in the Patrick Henry Airport lot, just a few cars from where they'd picked up their Toyota. As a parting gesture, Napoleon had bought two pounds of limburger cheese at a local supermarket and spread it over the Cadillac's rugs and upholstery. He'd left the motor running for almost an hour, with the windows closed and the heat turned up as high as it would go, while they filled out forms for their new car.

"You want to call, or do you want me to?" Napoleon asked.

"I'll do it. They know my voice now."

"Let's go, then."

They both got out of the Toyota and headed for a pay telephone set against a brick wall at the back of one of the shops. Jebediah dialed the number for the Colonial Williamsburg Foundation and was connected with the Inn.

"Joseph Sabatino," Jebediah said.

There was a click, then ringing.

"Yes," said a voice at the other end, one Jebediah hadn't heard before.

"Joseph Sabatino," Jebediah repeated.

"This is Mr. Sabatino's supervisor," the voice said.

"I want to talk to Joseph Sabatino," Jebediah said nervously.

"Doesn't four hundred thousand dollars give me the right to talk with you directly?" the voice said coolly.

"You have the money?"

"Right here with me. It was delivered this morning."

"In two suitcases?"

"We were able to fit it into one."

"Good."

"I hoped you'd be pleased."

"All right. In fifteen minutes I want you to take it to the gate in front of the Governor's Palace. Not the gate in front of the Palace itself. The gate alongside that leads to the gardens."

"Yes."

"You know where I'm talking about."

"I see it on the map. Yes."

"Good. Now I want you to send one man. No more."

"And who is going to make the exchange for your side?"

"Napoleon."

"Ah," Calvado said. "Mr. Jones."

"Your man is to give him the money."

"And he will receive the microfilm in return?"

"Not so fast. I have to have time to count the money. If it's all there, I'll call you this afternoon and tell you where the microfilm is."

"Wouldn't it be a little foolhardy of me to give you four hundred thousand dollars in cash and not receive anything in return?"

"That's the way it's going to be."

"If you were me, would you do that?"

"If I wanted the microfilm badly enough. And I think you do."

"I'm uneasy about this transaction," Calvado said, savoring the silence that followed.

"*You're* uneasy? Once you get the microfilm in your hands, you're going to try your best to kill us."

"That's quite true."

Jebediah hesitated, surprised at the casualness of the man's reply. "So you see," he stammered, "we can't bring the microfilm with us."

"I understand your predicament, and I assume you understand mine. What can we do about it?"

Jebediah stood with the telephone in his hand. He had that same uncontrolled sinking feeling he had had standing in front of the bus during the robbery.

"You okay?" Napoleon asked him.

From the telephone Jebediah heard the voice say, "Do you want to call me back after you've had a chance to think this through more clearly?"

"No!" Jebediah shouted. "You just bring the money, or I'll take the microfilm to the FBI."

"If I were you, I wouldn't want to have to explain how I happened to come into possession of the film, but that's your affair."

"Goddamn it. You bring the money in fifteen minutes, or else." Jebediah slammed the receiver into its cradle.

"Christ, Jebediah. What happened?"

"The man didn't want to give us the money," Jebediah said. Napoleon could see the craziness in his eyes and in the peculiar set of his jaw. "I think I straightened him out, though. You just go to the Governor's Palace as we planned. Wait half an hour. If they don't bring the money by then, come back here and we'll figure out some other plan."

There was nothing else Napoleon felt he could do, so he shrugged his shoulders and began walking across South Henry Street and up Duke of Gloucester Street toward the Palace.

When he had disappeared from view, Jebediah went back to the pay telephone and called the Williamsburg Inn again.

"Yes," Calvado answered.

"New plans," Jebediah said.

"And what might they be?"

"I want three hundred thousand dollars put in the suitcase and I want you to bring it to the Visitors' Center in fifteen minutes. You know where the Visitors' Center is?"

"It's where I got my map of the colonial area."

"Good. Again, I want one man to bring the suitcase. Have him stand on the pavement near the entrance to the Center. When a gray Toyota stops, have him put the suitcase in the passenger's side, front door. He's to wait until I have a chance to count the money. Then I'll give him an envelope explaining where the microfilm is."

"That's much more satisfactory," said Calvado. "But out of curiosity, who will be picking up the money? You, or Mr. Jones?"

"Me."

"I see. And where will Mr. Jones be?"

"Standing in front of the Governor's Palace, I imagine."

"And the change in your ransom demand?"

"I figure under the circumstances there would be an extra one hundred thousand dollars for me and a savings for you."

"Delightful. I like the way you think, sir," Calvado said, motioning to Jeffrey, Ted, and Joey to come over to the kitchen counter, where he had his map of Williamsburg unfolded.

# Chapter

# 26

Black wires snaked in all directions across the Avery Library parking lot. Television workers from two of the local stations yelled back and forth trying to get their remote cameras, lighting, and sound working in synchronization before their live coverage of the dedication began. Peter Eastrovich's moment as an instant celebrity had turned a simple local story into a media event with implications of forgery and murder.

Between the cords and cables the invited guests stepped gingerly to avoid falling on their way to the library's entrance. Brad and Samantha did the same. The opening had an aura of a traveling circus's midway. Brad touched Samantha's shoulder and pointed to Peter Eastrovich being interviewed in the parking lot by Belinda Freemont, "Williamsburg's top investigative reporter." Belinda's raven hair gleamed in the television lights. She wore an outrageous, wide-brimmed hat and a low-cut dress that made her seem worldly and confident, far from the screaming woman Brad had met the night before. The hat was causing problems for the lighting man, but he would have to adjust since it was her trademark.

Brad and Samantha watched the interview from a distance. Brad noticed that Peter wore the same blue suit he had had on for his first television interview, the day before. He had changed his tie, however, from a conservative rep stripe to a muted paisley. When several other guests stopped to watch, Samantha tugged on Brad's suit jacket and they began walking toward the library again. From a small mobile television monitor one of the technicians was holding, Brad tried to get a quick glimpse of Peter's face, wondering if the camera could pick up the veins of red he was certain streaked through Peter's eyes from the drinking and all that had gone on the night before. If the red was there, Brad couldn't tell.

The front of the library that faced the parking lot outside the Avery estate was an imposing stone facade, devoid of windows. The entrance itself began a hundred feet from the building, where blocks of granite, bordering the path, seemed to peep out of the ground at first, rising slowly and thickening at the base the nearer they came to the building itself. Soon, without warning, they became walls on both sides of the walk that led to a pair of large, carved wooden doors. As it neared the building, the path became dark and foreboding, like an entrance to the tomb of some ancient pharaoh.

It had been Jonathan's idea. An architectural juxtaposition between an ancient entrance and the modern, airy interior of the library itself. Once inside the door, everything was light and expansive. Brad and Samantha passed a long information counter and desk, made of natural ash with a white marble top. Dotted throughout the entry room were glass display cases filled with some of the treasures from the collection.

Beyond this was the main reading room, its sheer glass walls making it a room in a spun-sugar palace. The rear wall, facing Brad and Samantha, was floor-to-ceiling glass. It looked out on a magnificently manicured Japanese sculpture garden beyond.

The room had been temporarily rearranged for the dedication. Rows of aluminum and plastic chairs faced a specially constructed dais with its own row of chairs and a podium and microphone for a speaker.

Brad and Samantha sat in the back, on the far aisle nearest the

Japanese garden. The room was flooded with light. The billowy curtains that normally covered the sloped glass roof were pulled back, showering the room with sun. Brad looked over the crowd. The room was filling nicely, due more to Peter Eastrovich's television appearance than to the ceremonies themselves, Brad thought. Even the balcony over the entrance was filling with people.

Out of the corner of his eye Brad saw Tom Egan trapped in a corner by a newspaper reporter and photographer. When he noticed Brad, he politely brushed the photographer's camera to one side and came toward them.

"Any luck seeing Mr. Avery last night?"

"Yes."

"Good, but later. This isn't the time for us to talk."

"I agree."

"How about two o'clock?"

"Where?"

"Is my office okay?"

"Sure."

Tom turned to go back to his reporter, then stopped.

"One thing, though," he asked. "Have you heard from your shop manager? We've been trying to reach him for questioning."

"No."

"I have to get back," Tom said, pointing to a reporter.

"Just a second. I'd better share my news with you. If I don't tell you, you'll accuse me of withholding information."

"What is it?" There was a ring of impatience in Egan's voice.

"Jonathan's not giving his library away today."

"What?"

"It's true," said Samantha. The sunlight seemed to Brad to dance in her light brown hair.

"No wonder the governor didn't come."

"He's not here?"

"Sent a last-minute replacement."

The noise in the room changed. Brad looked up and saw people filing toward the row of chairs on the dais. People in the audience were beginning to take their seats too.

"Thanks for the warning," Tom Egan said.

"There's the president of William and Mary," Samantha whispered in Brad's ear. "And, oh my, Warren Burger's with him."

"Who's the replacement for the governor?" Brad asked.

"I think it's the man over there," Egan said.

"That dowdy, bald-headed man in the gray suit?" Samantha discreetly pointed at him.

"That's the one."

"No one can snub someone quite the way a politician can," said Samantha.

The door to Jonathan's office opened, and Dewitt Hughes walked out. Hughes was Jonathan's chief lawyer, an ex-United States senator, whose social contacts were as impeccable as his clothes and haircut. There was a slight murmur from the guests when the door to the office shut without Jonathan and Fiona's appearance.

Hughes was alone. He walked directly to the podium and put a sheet of typewritten paper on the lectern.

"May I have your attention," he began. "I have a prepared statement to read to you." With a flourish he brought out a pair of half-lens reading glasses, adjusting them until they seemed to sit almost on the tip of his nose. On a less distinguished man they would have appeared silly, but on Dewitt Hughes, you could sense the beginning of a new trend.

"Mr. Jonathan Avery has been greatly disturbed during the last twenty-four hours over certain allegations made by a Dr. Peter Eastrovich of the College of William and Mary concerning the alleged forgeries Dr. Eastrovich said he found in the holdings of the Avery Library. Since the validity of Dr. Eastrovich's claims still must be studied by trained bibliographers and scholars, we do not want to comment on them today. It has been Dr. Eastrovich's contention that the Avery Library should be closed, even before it is officially opened to the public, which is of immediate concern to Mr. Avery.

"In order to put these concerns to rest, several conversations have taken place between representatives of Mr. Avery and the governor of Virginia during the past twenty-four hours. It was Mr. Avery's wish to gain certain assurances from the governor before handing over the operation of the Avery Library, the assembling of which has been of great personal interest to Mr. Avery.

"Such assurances were not forthcoming."

Dewitt Hughes paused for a moment to take a sip from the glass of water by his right hand. A small murmur from the guests subsided, and he continued.

"When Mr. Avery originally planned to offer his research library to the Commonwealth of Virginia, he did so because he felt that it would assure efficient, long-term use by the academic community. Now that the assurance of this actually taking place has not been confirmed by the governor, it is with great reluctance that Mr. Avery now withdraws his offer to donate his collection and this library building to the Commonwealth."

Dewitt Hughes glanced over his reading glasses at the assembled guests and reporters until the new wave of murmuring passed.

"The Avery Library will remain, as it is now, Mr. Avery's personal property. This will continue until some other, more suitable arrangements can be made that will ensure its continued use.

"Until then, access to the library will be given by Mr. Avery only to those scholars who in Mr. Avery's judgment have legitimate scholarly purposes in using the collection."

Dewitt Hughes removed his glasses and returned them to his inside jacket pocket. As if on cue reporters started yelling questions at him.

"Does this mean that Dr. Eastrovich won't be allowed to use the collection—"

"Mr. Hughes, how does this affect the murder investigation into the—"

"Is Avery going to destroy the forgeries?"

"What—"

"Gentlemen," Dewitt Hughes said into the microphone. "And ladies too, of course. I was asked not to entertain questions at this time."

That remark started another outburst.

"Where is Jonathan Avery?"

"Does Avery think he can—"

Dewitt Hughes turned and walked back toward Jonathan's office. After he went through the doorway, the office door was closed behind him. Anthony Patronsky stood in front of the door. Several reporters rushed over to him, but Patronsky was oblivious to their questions. Another man, whom Brad thought he recognized as Jonathan's chauffeur, stood by Patronsky in case a reporter became too insistent.

Brad looked around the room for someone else from Jonathan's staff, but he couldn't find anyone. The general clamor was over. Guests had started to file out of the building. Brad saw Belinda Freemont in a corner of the reading room with her arm wrapped firmly around Peter Eastrovich's elbow, holding him in place while the television crew adjusted their sound and color. Peter was not as animated as he had been earlier, but he was not tugging to get away from her either.

Belinda finally freed her captive, made a quick move with her head that shook out her hair and nearly dislodged her hat, and took a microphone from one of the grips. Without missing a beat, a plasticized smile appeared on her face. Someone pointed a finger at her and yelled, "Go."

"This is Belinda Freemont, WMSB News. Standing here with me in the Avery Library amid a stunned crowd is Dr. Peter Eastrovich, Special Collections Librarian at the College of William and Mary. Dr. Eastrovich, what was your reaction to the prepared remarks made on behalf of Jonathan Avery?"

"I'm flabbergasted, Belinda."

"Do you think Mr. Avery is trying to hide something with this action?"

"Yes. I can only urge the district attorney and the law-enforcement officers in charge to impound this library immediately as possible evidence in the murder of Carl Riesling."

"Are you suggesting that Jonathan Avery has some connection with the Riesling death?"

"I think Mr. Avery's actions speak for themselves."

"You heard it here. Are the Williamsburg forgeries, the Avery Library, and the death of Carl Riesling interconnected? Dr. Eastrovich seems to think so. This is Belinda Freemont, WMSB News, Channel Five, reporting, hoping to bring you further details in this fast-moving story on our next news broadcast."

"It's a wrap," one of the technicians yelled. Belinda Freemont's body visibly sagged.

Brad walked toward Peter, agilely avoiding a man already starting to pack the television equipment.

"Have you met Belinda Freemont, Brad?" Peter asked when he saw Brad approaching.

"I've seen quite a bit of her lately."

"Oh, where was that?" Belinda asked.

"Don't you remember?"

Recognition came in a single tidal wave. "Why—why—Peter! That's—" Belinda sputtered, at a loss for words for one of the few times in her life.

"You do remember, after all." Brad said, beaming.

Peter stood aside smiling politely, realizing something more was expected of him but not knowing what.

"Peter! Why—Peter! That's the man! Last night. The closet!"

Peter was beginning to understand.

"He's the one I saw!"

"What?"

"Aside from Miss Freemont, I saw some other interesting things there last night."

"What?" Peter said.

"Like an item taped to the bottom of your desk drawer."

Peter blanched. He had begun to open his mouth again when another television crew surrounded him.

"Dr. Eastrovich." Someone leaned forward with a microphone.

"Your public awaits," Brad said, and turned to leave.

"But—?"

"Peter. What's going on?" Belinda asked. She tried to get to Brad, but the television cameraman was already between them.

When he reached the doorway, Brad looked back on the scene. He was too far away to be certain, but he felt that Peter was giving a less-assured performance than he had in his past interviews.

# Chapter
## 27

Napoleon waited outside the gate to the gardens at the Governor's Palace. He watched the large, billowy clouds drift across the light blue sky and he was afraid. Even though they were making the exchange in a crowded area, the fact that people were passing by didn't make him feel any less wary. Jebediah had said that they would be unharmed until Calvado knew he had the microfilm in his possession. He even suggested that Calvado might try to put a homing device in the suitcase they would bring to Napoleon, but they were smarter than Calvado. They would transfer the money into the two suitcases they had bought the previous night before making their call to let Calvado know where the microfilm was hidden.

Somehow, leaning against the brick wall, Napoleon felt dumb, like a kid in school asked to stand up and answer questions about homework he had never read. He had allowed Jebediah to talk him into this plan—after all, Jebediah was the planner—but Jebediah had never played the game against pros like this. He didn't know the Calvados of the world like Napoleon did. They were like crazed prize fighters who would stop fifty punches with their face only to get one clean shot in at you. You couldn't beat people like that.

Tourists passed Napoleon with tickets in their hands. A lady in a colonial costume validated and marked them at the garden entrance. The tourists were all shapes and sizes: families, young couples, older people, gays. They all looked freshly scrubbed and laundered to Napoleon. Mostly they were white—learning about white man's history. Napoleon felt grimy and rumpled after spending the night in the car, out of place in this tourist world. He always felt out of place except in large cities. He had never been to Europe, but he wanted to give that a try sometime.

Napoleon concentrated now on watching the tourists, looking for a man with a suitcase or someone who just stared at him strangely. God knows how many men Calvado will really send, he thought.

Then he saw him. Joey was walking across the green in front of the Governor's Palace with a suitcase in his left hand. He walked with a gingery bounce. Napoleon focused only on him. He knew something was wrong, but he didn't know what. Maybe it was the little grin on Joey's face. Maybe it was because he doubted that Calvado would trust Joey with anything more valuable than a subway token. Napoleon stared, noticing the way Joey stood straight—not leaning toward the weight of the suitcase—the way the suitcase seemed to float as Joey bounced along.

"That sucker's empty."

Joey was still fifty yards away when Napoleon turned and started running in the opposite direction. The colonial lady, stamping tickets, tried to step in front of him, but Napoleon just put out his left arm and threw her to the ground. He heard a shout from behind him—one of Joey's growls—and then he heard high-pitched screams from tourists and the word "gun." Napoleon ran.

Joey had opened the suitcase behind him and had pulled out a sawed-off, twelve-gauge shotgun. He threw the suitcase to one side and took aim. They had showed him his car after Jeffrey's men had found it the night before. It all had become personal again. He was too far away to stop Napoleon, but he shot anyway, discharging one barrel, then the other. He cursed under his breath, drew out his pistol, and yelled as he started running toward the gates.

As Napoleon sped past the wheelwright's shop, he heard the percussive sound of a pistol shot behind him. He turned slightly and bolted down the gravel path, salted with crushed oyster shells, that led to the formal gardens. There were high hedges on his left. He could sense that Joey was not far behind. Napoleon ran past two tourists who were ready to yell at him when they all heard the sound of another gunshot boom from behind them.

Napoleon saw an opening in the tall hedge and cut sharply to his left. He ran straight along the path on the other side of the hedge, through a tall wrought-iron gate, and into the formal sculpture gardens behind the Palace. As he ran, he heard a third shot and sharply juked to his right, leaping over a knee-high bush.

There were a lot of people screaming now, both in front of Napoleon and from behind. He could see the look of terror on an elderly couple's faces as he turned, to his left stumbling, to avoid crashing into them. He went zigzagging through the gardens, trying to keep the tall shrubs between him and where he imagined Joey would be. He reached the far side of the garden and ran through another wrought-iron gate, the twin of the one near the entrance. A fourth shot was fired, and Napoleon heard the bullet graze the metal bars of the gate near his head.

On the other side, Napoleon chose the path to his right. There was a tall brick wall on his right and a high, impenetrable hedge on his left. He hoped Joey was far enough behind him not to be able to take a shot here. At the end of the path were several steps that angled down to an open garden cubicle where grapevines grew. He ran to the steps like a runner lunging for the tape, leaning forward, almost diving across the steps and into the lower level of the garden at the bottom. Just as he hit the ground he heard a fifth shot.

He landed at the base of the steps on all fours and scrambled to his feet again without losing time. The grape-arbor garden was small, and on the far side was a tall brick wall with an open wooden gate in the center. He ran straight for it.

In front of him was a formal maze of shrubs and hedges—built for the delight of children and garden-club members. Napoleon attacked it like Alexander untying the Gordian Knot—he cut straight ahead, through the walls of hedges, directly into the maze's center. Lunging forward, he reached the far side of the maze. His arms and face were cut from the bushes, but he didn't seem to notice. In front of him was a short series of stairs. He would be exposed if he ran up them, but there was no other place to go. Just before he reached the top of the steps Napoleon heard a sixth shot from behind and the dull thud of a bullet striking the ground to his left. Without thinking, he lurched to the right and found himself on a short path with a sign pointing in his direction that read "Ice House."

The path curved, and as it did, Napoleon saw a low brick wall in front of him. On the other side was a highway eight feet below. Napoleon climbed over the wall quickly, landing off balance on the other side. As he did, he stumbled out onto the road in front of a car. The driver swerved into the lane of oncoming traffic and then swerved back again, narrowly missing both Napoleon and a white Honda. He slammed on the brakes and got out of his Pontiac Trans-Am, leaving it parked at an angle in the center of the road. Traffic stopped in both directions as the young man began walking toward Napoleon, shaking his fist and screaming epithets.

Napoleon didn't hear what he said, he didn't notice the Greek letters on the fraternity T-shirt, or see the young man's fist quiver from delayed fright. Napoleon just ran straight at him, head up, arms slightly in front and to his sides.

Five paces away, the young man stopped screaming and stood with his mouth wide open, watching Napoleon execute a perfect open-field tackle. The big man hit him high, just above the waist, sending the youth back into the side of the Trans-Am with an impact that stunned his senses. The sudden jolt stood Napoleon upright. With an old street-fighter's move, he grabbed the dazed driver by the armpit and crotch and threw him across the back of his car.

People were now getting out of their cars to watch as Napoleon got into the Trans-Am. He was searching for the lever that would allow him to push back the bucket seat from the steering wheel when a seventh shot shattered the window on the car door, next to him.

Napoleon shut the door, jammed the gearshift into first, and released the emergency brake, sending the car fishtailing down the road past spectators who jumped to get out of its way. The car's owner had picked himself up off the ground in time to hear a grinding sound as Napoleon, his stomach tight against the steering wheel, threw the car into second.

"Noooo," the kid yelled in a primal voice, like a mother bear seeing her cubs being taken away—helpless to do anything about it.

# Chapter
## 28

Jebediah sat nervously in the Visitors' Center parking lot. The doors of his gray Toyota were locked and the windows rolled up, making the inside hot and uncomfortable. He regretted that he had told the man on the telephone what kind of car he was driving, but it was done now and worrying about it wouldn't help. Seeing other Toyotas in the parking lot made him feel slightly more secure.

His mind wandered to the three hundred thousand dollars, a payoff worth the risk. He wasn't joking when he told Napoleon about the sex-change operation. He had thought about doing that ever since he was a teenager, but he'd never had the money to make it a serious consideration.

Jebediah had a plan. After he picked up the money, he would get rid of the suitcase it came in, with all its potential bugging devices, and drive the back roads to Petersburg. There he could rent another car and drive west through Virginia, then north to West Virginia, Pennsylvania, and New York, on into Canada. He had never been to Montreal, but he thought that would be a nice place to catch a plane for Europe. Jebediah wished he had thought in advance to get another passport, under an assumed name—Stuart Something, he didn't care what—only now it was too late.

After the operation Jebediah would still have enough money left over to open his own rare-book business. Nobody would suspect him as an unmarried woman. It was the perfect business for a sedate, scholarly girl, although the list of desirable heterosexual booksellers was abysmally short.

Having his own business, though—that was the payoff. Not having to deal in books someone else bought, not having to fullfill someone else's fantasies—that would be the real reward.

Jebediah looked at his watch. It was five minutes past the deadline and still there was no man with a suitcase standing at the entrance. Then he thought of it—the other entrance on the opposite side of the building.

"Christ."

He started the car and forced himself to drive slowly around the Center to the far side. His heart was beating faster and the perspiration welled on his forehead. Then he saw him, a thin man in a light gray suit, with a large cloth suitcase. The suitcase had little wheels underneath that allowed you to pull it behind you. Three hundred thousand dollars must be heavy, Jebediah thought. The man held it by a leather strap that extended from the corner of the suitcase.

Jebediah drove the car into the semicircular driveway where passengers were picked up and dropped off. The man in gray seemed to notice Jebediah immediately and started walking toward the car. Jebediah leaned over to roll down the window on the passenger's side.

"Where do you want this?" Teddy asked.

The suitcase was obviously too big for it to fit in the passenger's seat next to Jebediah. Jebediah looked at him blankly. It had to go in the back seat, but Jebediah didn't know how he was going to count the money from there.

"The suitcase, where do you want me to put it?" Teddy asked again, thinking he might have approached the wrong car.

"In the back," Jebediah finally answered.

Teddy tried the rear door. "It's locked."

"Christ."

As Jebediah stretched across the car to open the rear door for Teddy, a station wagon with two children jostling each other in the back seat pulled behind Jebediah and waited. Jebediah didn't notice it. Nor did he see a black Chevrolet Citation that was backing up toward his Toyota.

Teddy opened the car door and put the suitcase on the back seat. Then he picked up the suitcase slightly and pushed it across the seat until it was directly behind the driver. Jebediah was just about to say something when he felt the Citation tap his front bumper lightly. He looked around, caught a glimpse of the station wagon in his rear-view mirror, and realized that the car was sandwiched in the driveway. By then Teddy had reached across the car. Jebediah didn't even have time to raise his arms to protect himself. He didn't see the small needle, the size of a thumbtack, that Teddy had taped to the inside of his middle and index fingers, and he hardly felt the prick of its tip on the back of his neck.

The rushing sound came into his ears so quickly. Then he was picked up—rolled—he couldn't remember which, but however it was done, he was sitting in the passenger seat and the car was moving. He couldn't drive the car from the passenger seat, could he? This was a question that floated through his mind before the darkness came, and with it, sleep.

# Chapter
## 29

Y ou're right. I've been a bad boy."

"Yes, you have, and your bad-boy routine isn't going to get you off the hook this time."

Appeasing Mrs. Johnson was not going to be easy. It never was.

"Jebediah left yesterday, and I've been watching the shop by myself since then," she continued.

"I know, and I appreciate it."

"But I'm not going to do it forever. It's not my job."

"Did you call Edna?"

"She can't come in until Monday, her daughter's home from college for the weekend."

"Louis?"

"I didn't call him yet."

"Maybe he can give you some relief on Saturday."

"Are you going to fire Jebediah? I would."

"I'd like to find out what happened to him first."

"I called his apartment. His roommates haven't seen him, and he wasn't admitted into any of the hospitals."

"You called the hospitals?"

"I worry about him too. Just leaving like that after talking to his Negro friend."

"What Negro friend?"

"I told you about him."

"No, you didn't."

"Well, you haven't been around much. It must have slipped my mind," said Mrs. Johnson. "Anyway, yesterday a big Negro came in. Jebediah said he was an old friend and they had to talk—would I mind watching the store for a few minutes?"

"I said yes. What could I say? Then they went up to your office. I don't know what went on up there, I had forgotten my hearing aid, left it at home. I thought they would be five minutes, but it was more like an hour. The big fellow came down first, then Jebediah. He said he was sick and left me with the shop for the rest of the afternoon."

"Did you ever see Jebediah's friend before?"

"No, but I'd recognize him. He was big, like one of those football players or a Sumo wrestler."

Brad brought papers from his office and worked behind the desk in the shop to keep Mrs. Johnson company.

At two o'clock, he called Tom Egan.

"Egan."

"Tom, Brad Parker."

"I'm glad you called instead of coming over. All hell's broken loose and I don't have time now. I do want your advice on something since you got a chance to talk to Avery last night."

"What do you want to know?"

"On the basis of your talk with Avery last night, do you think I should arrest him for the Riesling murder?"

"I don't think you'd have much of a case."

"I have to make a decision in an hour."

"Why in an hour?"

"I got a call from the governor again this morning. We're getting to be real bosom buddies. He told me if I didn't arrest Avery by three o'clock this afternoon, he would get the state police to do it."

"What's gotten into him?"

"He's a political animal, and he senses a kill. It will make good headlines for a while, take the pressure off of him in other areas."

"What if he's wrong?"

"That's why he wants me to make the arrest. Meanwhile he's meeting with this Eastrovich fellow. They're making plans to take possession of the library as evidence in the murder case."

"What are you going to do?"

"I was really waiting to get your opinion."

Brad sat back in his chair. "I don't think that Avery had anything to do with the murder," he said, "and I guess my advice to you, politically, would be to stay away from it. It might grab a few quick headlines, but in the long term I think it might be embarrassing."

"You have any facts to back this up, or is it a gut reaction?"

"A little of both. I think the governor's going to be sorry he listened to Peter Eastrovich."

"Why?"

"I can't prove it now, but I'm convinced Peter's the one who stole the Melville pamphlet from my apartment. At least he had it in his possession last night."

"Where did you get this information?"

"I'd rather not say on the telephone."

"Eastrovich, huh? I did a routine background check on him myself. Ph.D. from the University of Indiana. The Terre Haute police gave him a clean bill of health, but there's *something* there."

"What does this something involve?"

"All I could get out of phone call was that there were funds missing from the university library when Eastrovich worked there. Fifty-thousand dollars. The police arrested an Archibald Hershey. He was Eastrovich's boss."

"Was Hershey convicted?"

"Committed suicide before the trial, but I got a real good feeling that the police suspected Eastrovich took the money and set Hershey up to be the patsy."

"They never pursued it?"

"Not after the suicide. The university was insured. Nobody cared, least of all Hershey."

"How sure are you?"

"Call it a gut reaction. I don't get one often, but when I do, you can usually take it to the bank."

"There's more I have to talk to you about. Can you come over to the shop?"

"I guess you haven't heard. As if this whole Avery thing wasn't enough, I got a minicrisis here. Some lunatic started playing cowboy and indians near the Governor's Palace this morning. The asshole had a sawed-off shotgun and a pistol."

"Was anybody hurt?"

"Not seriously, thank God. Oh, a few people got scratched from the shotgun pellets, but we really could have had a disaster. Seems the nut was trying to kill some black man."

"A big man, about the size of a professional football player?"

"Yeah. Just what do you know about this?"

"Jebediah Stuart, a man who works for me, left the shop yesterday after talking to someone that meets that general description."

"Has Stuart reappeared? I still haven't been able to contact him."

"No. He hasn't been back to the bookshop at all, and apparently he hasn't been to his apartment either. Mrs. Johnson tried to reach him there."

"I'll run an APB, see what that dredges up. But what about the black guy? Did you see him?"

"No, only Mrs. Johnson."

"I'll send someone over to get a description, both of him and this Jebediah Stuart."

"We have a photo of Jebediah, but I don't know how detailed Mrs. Johnson will be about the other man."

"Whatever. It'll be better than what we got now: an untraceable shotgun thrown out in the grass in front of the Governor's Palace, and a cheap suitcase. Did I mention that this cowboy was carrying the shotgun in a suitcase?"

"No."

"I'm going to have to ask him what that was all about if I collar the sonofabitch. By the way, did a middle-aged, fat Italian come into the shop with the black man?"

"Not that I know of, but you'd better ask Mrs. Johnson. Why? Is that the description of the shooter?"

"Yeah. A real cutey. Tries to kill the black man, then follows him out to the street and they both steal cars and drive off in opposite directions. You tell me."

"I hope Jebediah isn't involved in any of this."

"Stranger things have happened." Tom Egan cupped the telephone for a few seconds, then came back on the line. "Look, I've got to go. Belinda Freemont, WMSB News, wants an interview."

"Good luck."

"Just so you know, I used your name and got Greta Riesling to the telephone. When I told her who I really was, she hung up. I'm going to need the State Department to extradite her."

"Good luck. Can you stop by the shop later?"

"See you when I can."

"Try the back door. I'll leave it open. If it's locked, I'll be at my apartment."

The phone rang seconds after Brad hung up.

"I've been trying to call but your line's been busy." It was Samantha. "You ought to get another line, like a real business."

"I know."

"Listen, I was wondering when we could get together to talk."

"How about right now?"

"I can't come over—work, emergency meeting."

"What do you want to talk about?"

"Not over the telephone."

"Oh. Serious talk."

"Yes."

Brad slumped in his chair. "Okay. When can you come over?"

"Is six or seven too late?"

"I'll be at the shop."

"Leave the back door open. The last time I had to pound for five minutes."

"Sound doesn't carry well from downstairs to the office."

"I personally think you're starting to grow deaf."

# Chapter
# 30

Gerald Hamilton sat watching his house in Bryn Mawr from behind the steering wheel of his BMW. He was parked on a side road in the development, under the protective branches of two large maples. He glanced at the clock on his dashboard. It was two in the afternoon already. He had been sitting there for three hours. Gerald Hamilton hated to waste time. Time was money.

A middle-aged woman in a pants suit passed. She had walked in the other direction a half-hour before and was now returning with a small bag of groceries. The woman gave Gerald a long, distrustful stare as she passed. Gerald assumed that she was one of his neighbors, although he didn't remember seeing her before. In fact, he didn't know anyone in the development. The well-appointed houses were owned mostly by executives of large- and middle-sized corporations. They moved into the community, using their houses for sleep and personal entertainment, and then moved out again. If they didn't have children, like Gerald and Deborah, they rarely met each other. Their movements were chronicled by "For Sale" signs that suddenly appeared on their neatly manicured lawns, only to vanish again. Such was life in the suburbs.

During the three hours sitting in his car Gerald had thought about that. He remembered growing up with friends, classmates whose parents were friends of his parents. Now he was living with a wife who he was convinced was sleeping around and no longer loved him. He could forgive the first, but not the last. Too many key people in his life, starting with his mother, had not taken the time to love him, and three hours alone in a car had given Gerald Hamilton time to think soberly about all that had happened to him since birth. Materially life was everything he had wished and planned for it to be. Unfortunately, in his list of goals and aspirations, he hadn't thought to include personal relationships, and now everything had somehow turned empty and he was afraid.

Gerald didn't like thinking these thoughts. He would rather have been working, but, he convinced himself, there was a considerable amount of money involved if he succeeded here. "Spec work," he often called it. If he could actually catch Deborah in one of her little trysts, the difference in his divorce settlement would be substantial, and more and more, divorcing Deborah was rising to the top of his crumbling list of goals. He had hired a private detective to watch her a few months before, while he was away on a business trip. The detective's bills were staggering and his reports uneventful. So much so that Gerald was convinced the detective was sleeping with Deborah himself.

Nothing had happened in the three hours Gerald sat watching. Then he noticed a black Cougar ride slowly past, make a three-point turn, double back, and park on the street directly in front of his house.

A tall man got out from the driver's side. Gerald picked up the binoculars from the seat next to him. The man had an olive complexion, Gerald noted, and dark hair. He had rugged features and high, chiseled cheekbones. "A definite Guido." Deborah's type, he thought. Typical of her.

Then Gerald noticed a second man, ten years younger than the driver. He climbed out of the passenger's side. He couldn't have been more than twenty-five, Gerald thought, and he was carrying something long in his right hand. Gerald jerked the binoculars with a nervous twitch and didn't get a good look at it. The two men confused him for a moment. Then he remembered back, early in their marriage, something Deborah had told him about her fantasy of having sex with two men at the same time. Perhaps, he thought.

The men walked toward the door. The older man rang the bell. After a few seconds, the door opened and they both went in quickly, closing the door behind them. There was something furtive about the way the older man looked back into the street before entering the house. Gerald was looking for signs, and this was the first positive one he had seen. In the back of his mind he realized that the men could be there on legitimate business—salesmen perhaps. In which case, he would look very foolish.

Oh, hell, he thought. I'll give them three minutes. If she's screwing around, fine; if not, I've just come home to pick up some papers I forgot.

The three minutes Gerald arbitrarily set for himself passed more slowly than the three hours before. Gerald felt his stomach muscles tighten and he wanted to use a bathroom, badly. Turning the ignition key, he forced himself to swallow as he pulled his car in front of the black Cougar. He reached for the Polaroid camera on the seat next to him and put it in his jacket pocket. Then he took a deep breath and walked to the door, telling himself over and over again to be natural.

At the door, he heard Deborah's voice from inside and strange scuffling sounds, sounds of bodies pushing together, dead, muffled noises. Gerald was convinced. His latchkey was in his right hand, the Polaroid camera poised in his left. Yeah.

He unlocked the door quickly, letting it fly open. Gerald Hamilton was thinking of the alimony payment, how much he could save with evidence like this, when, puzzled, he saw the younger man from the car raise an Uzi automatic rifle and fire as Gerald took his picture. Gerald's last thought was of the lowest possible amount his lawyer could offer Deborah to make it a clean divorce, but the Uzi's first short burst completely severed his head from his body. He never did arrive at a final figure, but friends of Gerald's, if asked, would have been surprised if it was over twenty thousand dollars. Whatever the amount, it was academic, because on the floor, next to Gerald's body, lay Deborah, in a most ungainly position, dead.

# Chapter
# 31

**M**rs. Johnson left the shop at two seconds after five, and Brad locked the front door behind her. Fleder sat impassively at her station in the front window, watching people walking up and down Duke of Gloucester Street. After turning off the shop lights, Brad took the remainder of his unfinished paperwork upstairs to his office.

He called Jebediah's home number again and talked with one of his roommates. No one had heard from him since Wednesday.

"If he calls, or gets in touch in any way, let me know," Brad said.

He sat back in his chair and looked at the pile of unsorted papers that had been dumped from the filing cabinets. It was something he wasn't up to tackling just yet.

He walked over to the row of file cabinets along the back wall of his office. He opened the third drawer from the top of the second cabinet, and gripping it firmly just above the drawer, began inching the cabinet away from the wall. Once the back cleared on both sides, he pivoted the cabinet on its front corner, swinging the back out to the middle of the room where he could reach it.

There, taped to the metal, was a flat box, which he removed and put on his desk. Then he pushed the filing cabinet back into its place against the wall.

Brad sat down in his desk chair and opened the box carefully. Inside was his .38 service pistol with two clips of ammunition. He had kept it behind the filing cabinet, out of sentiment, instead of returning it. It was in a safe place there, and sufficiently difficult to get at that he would never have been tempted to use it without giving the matter serious thought for a long time. The pistol felt heavy and strange in his hand. The smell of the oil on the metal brought back memories that he quickly repressed.

Brad took off the safety and held the gun level in his right hand, his left hand supporting the right wrist, and squeezed the trigger until he heard the familiar metallic click. Then he jammed a clip into the handle and put the pistol into his desk drawer.

Again he tried to put thoughts of Samantha out of his mind. Deep inside, "in the gut" as they used to say at the Company, Brad knew she was going to accept the job in New York. In terms of her career, he couldn't have been more pleased. Samantha, when she talked about it, stressed that the job would only last for a year, but Brad knew that work like that tended to extend. Then there was the problem with their schedules. Samantha worked Monday through Friday. The shop had its biggest day on Saturday. How many of these could he afford to miss? That left Sunday. Brad was feeling the importance of time and didn't want to spend it sharing Samantha with a telephone. Brad also knew that Samantha was too alive not to find new interests and friends in the city. The thought of her starting another life without him etched itself in the dark side of his mind. Brad knew his attitude wasn't mature, not very "eighties," but he felt what he felt and wondered if a quick ending to their romance wouldn't be preferable to the long, slow death he imagined.

With a deep sigh, he turned to the mail that had accumulated during the week. Catalogs from other book dealers, want-lists from customers, offers of books, orders, trade magazines— "If you like to receive mail,"

Brad had once begun a speech to a local librarians' convention, "you might want to consider the antiquarian book business." The remainder of the week's pile was sprawled out over his desk. He went through it, piece by piece, making subpiles and noting on a separate yellow sheet the things he had to do.

Then Brad sat back. He made a few telephone calls, sold some books, and waited.

# Chapter
# 32

Norman Anastasius Calvado sat in the library chair wearing his pleated scarlet lounging jacket from Paris and sipping from a glass of Perrier. Calvado glanced languidly into the adjoining bedroom, where Jebediah's mutilated body lay unconscious on the bed.

"I want him kept alive until we have a chance to check out his story," Calvado said to a figure moving about in the shadows of the bedroom.

"What he told you about hiding the microfilm is the truth," the man replied in a thick Eastern European accent. He was a short man, with the sure, deft movements of a person used to living in small confined spaces. Calvado thought of him as being in his mid-sixties, but he remembered having the same thoughts about the man's age when they had first met almost twenty years before. The man called himself Dr. Morarto, and Calvado employed him professionally to extract information from people who otherwise might not wish to share it. Dr. Morarto used a combination of drugs, pain, and fear in his treatments, all of which he inflicted with great clinical skill.

"All the same, I want to be certain this time. There have been too many blunders already in this affair."

"I will keep him alive if you wish. He will sleep for eight hours. If you want to speak with him then, you may. Otherwise, I give him another injection."

"Good."

The telephone rang. "Theodore," Calvado said, and Teddy came out from the kitchen area, where he had been hiding, to answer it.

"Yes," Teddy said. He listened for a few seconds and replaced the receiver.

"A man left a message. He told me to tell you that Philadelphia called and that everything went as planned."

Calvado took another sip from his glass. "One less loose end to worry about," he said to no one in particular. "We still haven't had any word from our Mr. Sabatino yet, have we?"

"No, Mr. Calvado," Teddy said.

"That's a matter we must address. Theodore, when he calls, I want to speak to him personally."

"Yes, sir."

"Even if I'm sleeping."

"I understand."

Calvado picked up his copy of *The Letters of E. B. White*, which lay next to him. "I'm going into my bedroom to read now."

"Mr. Calvado?"

"Yes?"

"Let me go after the microfilm?" Teddy's voice was almost a whine.

"No, Theodore. But not to worry. You will have your chance for redemption, but I have something else in mind for you."

"What is it?"

"Not now."

"Whatever it is, anything, just ask."

"I intend to do just that," said Calvado, turning away. "Doctor," he said into the darkened bedroom. "Stay with our patient, will you? I don't want him left alone."

"His vital signs are normal, but, *ja,* I will do what you ask."

"Thank you."

Calvado shut the door to his bedroom, leaving Teddy alone with his thoughts. They were dark thoughts. Teddy had spent the afternoon watching Dr. Morarto at work on Jebediah. There was one point in the afternoon, just after the doctor finished making incisions around Jebediah's eyes with a razorblade, that Teddy had to leave, rushing into the bathroom to vomit into the toilet. When he had splashed his face with cold water and was blowing his nose into a wad of toilet paper, he had glanced up at the mirror over the sink and saw Calvado standing in the doorway staring at him.

"You don't have to watch, Theodore," he said. "I won't think any less of you if you want to go out and take a walk."

"I'm fine now," Teddy replied.

"Usually I let Dr. Morarto do his work alone—unobserved—but this time I thought there might be a valuable lesson in it if you saw him."

Teddy didn't want to guess at what Calvado was talking about, so he remained silent.

"There are two lessons, really. First to observe the ingloriousness and baseness to which human life can descend. For that lesson, however, I could have brought you to any hospital cancer ward in this country.

"The second lesson, Theodore, is that I love my family, the people I work with and am responsible for protecting. If someone threatens their safety—I wanted you to see the extent I will go to in dealing with that person."

There was nothing for Teddy to say.

"This fool was an outsider, and he confronted me and our organization without proper respect. You, Theodore, are an insider. You have been a loyal and good worker, but on this last assignment, you made serious and incompetent mistakes. This, too, can threaten my family. Do you understand what I'm telling you?"

"Yes."

"Theodore, our organization is expanding, and I strongly encourage you to give your work serious attention and grow with us. If not, you become as serious a threat to me as Jebediah Stuart in the other room."

*  *  *

Teddy sat by the telephone thinking about that conversation. The smell of urine and excrement, so strong a few hours before, had diluted with time, mingling with the smell of pine from the room deodorant that Dr. Morarto had prissily sprayed into the air. Traces of human stench did linger, however—enough to serve as a reminder.

The telephone rang and Teddy picked it up on the first ring. "Yes."

"Christ, is that you, Ted?" It was Joseph Sabatino.

"Hold on a minute, he wants to talk to you."

Teddy put the receiver down on the table and ran down the short hall to Calvado's bedroom.

"It's him."

Calvado positioned the inner flap of the dust jacket to mark his place in the book and put it down on his bed. He picked up the telephone.

"I understand you ran into some difficulty with your assignment," Calvado said.

"Hey, Mr. Calvado, I—"

"Conversations are so much more pleasant without names, don't you agree?"

Joey exhaled deeply.

"Just tell me what happened."

"I walked down to the Governor's Palace with the suitcase just like you said. I was going to give him the suitcase and do him like the plan, but I didn't get close enough. When he saw me, the bastard started running the other way. So I had to run after him."

"Someone mentioned gunfire to me."

"I thought I had a good chance to waste him, or at least make him stop, but Christ, that nigger can really run."

"But you've managed to escape, yourself, without anyone following you?"

"People saw me. I stole a car."

"I'm glad you weren't caught."

"I think I'd be better off back in Pennsylvania, but I don't know if I can drive my car back without puking. Limburger cheese!"

"Joseph, first I have one more thing for you to do."

"Sure, I only—"

"I was initially disappointed that our mutual friend got away from you, but we had some good fortune and have learned from his partner where the missing package is located."

"Where?"

"I'm going to send Theodore to meet you. He'll fill you in on the details and give you instructions." Calvado put his hand over the mouthpiece, smiled tightly at Teddy, and said in a low voice, "Redemption is at hand."

Calvado talked with Teddy for fifteen minutes after the telephone call was over. They reviewed every detail, every contingency the don could think of that might happen.

# Chapter
# 33

Napoleon stood outside the rear door of Parker's Rare Books. He had taken several picks out of his wallet and was about to insert one when it occurred to him to try the doorknob. He did, and stood watching while the door lazily swung open. He quickly went inside and closed the door silently behind him.

It was dusk and the light inside the shop was gray. Inset spotlights illuminated the window display, and from the bottom of the steps Napoleon could see the reflected whiteness of fluorescent tubes from the second floor. There was also a faint murmur of a man's voice coming from upstairs. Napoleon couldn't hear the words, but from the intermittent periods of sound and silence, he guessed that the man was talking on the telephone.

Napoleon glanced around the shop. On top of the counter he spotted a telephone in the semidarkness. A little button on top of it was lit, and Napoleon knew that as long as it glowed, the man upstairs was still occupied and he was safe. Once the light went off, Napoleon was on his own, just like he had been when he played on the defensive line in football. "Wait and react," he'd coached himself. "Expect anything. Wait, then react to it, and when you react, damn it, you better do it fast."

In the center of the room Napoleon saw the glass display case where Jebediah had said he'd hidden the microfilm—safely, in one of the books. When they were talking about this, Jebediah had told Napoleon what the book's title was, but now Napoleon had forgotten it. All he remembered was the price: twelve thousand dollars. "A hell of a lot of money for one book!" he had told Jebediah at the time. Now that Jebediah's plan had gone sour, Napoleon sensed that finding the microfilm somehow was his last chance for a long life. They had come after him twice and nearly killed him. Bad things came in threes, and Napoleon didn't feel that he had enough residual luck to survive a third attempt. His chief fear now was that Jebediah had already removed the film.

After the shooting incident with Joey, Napoleon had been too afraid to use the contingency plan and wait for Jebediah in the parking lot. Instead he spent the afternoon drinking in a WASPish bar on Second Street, surrounded by plants and polished oak, watching the soaps on their television. He left a little after four and found a gun shop, where he paid for a cheap .38 special with some of Jebediah's cash. He had to spend a half-hour filling out the necessary forms and permits, all of which the salesclerk stamped and signed, but never read.

Now, in the bookshop, Napoleon walked over to the glass case and tried to slide open one of the doors. There was a clank against the panel, and Napoleon saw the small metal lock that held it closed. He stood back and thought about breaking the glass. There were only six books in the entire case. Three under each arm? Then he thought of the man upstairs and looked around the room again. There was only one desk, behind the sales counter. After a few seconds of searching he found a tangle of keys in the center drawer. Each key was attached to an identification tag by a piece of string, the strings were knotted and intertwined with each other. In the dim light he found the paper tag marked "glass case" and was following the string through the maze to locate the corresponding key when the telephone light flickered off.

Napoleon froze, sitting at the desk in the darkness with his left hand encasing the wad of keys to stop them from jingling. He heard the man upstairs stand up and walk across the room. Then there was silence. In the dark and the quiet, Napoleon became aware of something behind him and turned quickly to his right, where he saw Fleder sitting on the counter, grooming herself. She calmly met Napoleon's stare. Then she stood, stretched, and without warning jumped down onto Napoleon's lap.

In another time and place, Napoleon, who hated cats, probably would have thrown her against the wall, but now he forced himself to relax and run his right hand down Fleder's spine from head to tail, hoping to keep the cat quiet. Fleder, for her part, seemed to accept this and settled on Napoleon's thigh, gently purring, a noise Napoleon mistook for asthma.

Suddenly the back door of the shop opened. "Brad?" a man yelled.

"Upstairs," answered a voice from above.

Napoleon sat motionless and watched the man bound up the stairs.

"You damn son-of-a-bitch," Peter said in a rage. "You broke into my office last night."

"You bet." Brad had decided at the dedication ceremonies how he wanted to play this conversation.

"You're not going to deny it?"

"What's the point? You're right."

"What's the point?" Peter continued. "What you did is a crime. It's called breaking and entering."

"Not to mention coitus interruptus."

"Belinda said you were the one in the closet."

"I heard her tell you. Don't you think you're a little old for her?" Brad said, sitting behind his desk and looking up at Peter with a half-smile on his face.

"That is not the issue."

"What is the issue, Peter?"

"You broke into my private office, rifled through my personal files, and stole one of my books."

"Feel free to call the police if you want. In fact, I'd like to hear your explanation of how you happened to have my book in the first place. I was just taking it back."

"What? You think that was the copy of the Melville someone stole from you?"

"Yes."

"Well, it wasn't. I bought that copy myself from Carl Riesling months ago."

"Really? It's funny you never mentioned that to me when you were persuading me to sell you my copy of the book. And if I were to believe you, then why did you tape it underneath the desk?"

"So that Jonathan Avery wouldn't send one of his goons to steal it from me. That's why. Quite frankly, I didn't think that you would be the one to do Jonathan Avery's dirty work for him. I'm appalled."

"That's bullshit, Peter, and you know it."

"Bullshit?"

"Bullshit." Brad raised his hand to fend off another tirade. "Peter, I marked my copy of the Melville pamphlet before it was stolen. I wrote my initials in pencil on the inside margin of page fourteen. The copy of *Sermon* I found underneath your desk had those initials in it. That was the copy you stole from my apartment." It was a lie—he hadn't marked the copy—but Brad thought he delivered the line with assurance and a complete lack of guile.

Peter looked intently at Brad's face, like a gambler trying to decide if his opponent had actually filled an inside straight. After a few seconds he said, "That would be your word against mine in a court of law. I'd say that you were planting that copy in my office as evidence to help Jonathan Avery. That Belinda and I caught you red-handed."

"It's a good story, but we're not in a court of law here," Brad said, gesturing at the room. "It's just you and me, Peter."

"What do you want, Parker?" Peter's defiance was starting to return. "If you already know it's your copy, why are you still bothering me with questions?"

"Because I want to understand why."

"Why what?"

"For starters, why you felt compelled to nearly kill me just so that you could have that copy of the Melville pamphlet."

Peter stood silent for a considerable time. Brad let him think for as long as he wanted. He had conducted interrogations before.

"I didn't mean to hurt you," Peter finally said. "I hope you believe that. I hope you can understand just how much this work I've been doing with the Avery Library and the forgeries means to me. I guess I was temporarily insane."

Peter kept on talking about the copy of *A Sermon for Sailors* he had taken from Brad's apartment, and how much the publication of his book exposing the forgeries would help him and his career, but Brad wasn't listening. Brad had expected it was going to be tougher getting Peter to confess. Up until then, Brad had only had his theories. There had been a part of him that didn't want to believe that Peter would actually have attacked him. He had been Peter's friend, and he felt betrayed. Now emotions welled up inside him. He had to keep them in check so that he could play his subject a little longer, wear out his fish before he dragged him into the boat.

This was no time to get cocky or crazed. Brad realized he had nothing yet that could be used by the police, but he did know that once a man starts confessing to sins, he will continue to do so until something stops him. If that wasn't one of Newton's Laws, it should have been.

Brad waited as Peter droned on, and then, when he felt the moment was right, he interrupted. "But I don't understand why you needed to see a copy of the pamphlet, Peter. After all, you were the one who created it. You were the one who asked poor Carl Riesling to print it for you."

"Are you crazy? It was . . ."

"Just like you had Carl print all the other forgeries you said you discovered in Jonathan Avery's collection."

"Brad?"

"And now that Carl is dead and Greta is safely in Germany, you're about to become a famous literary detective. Did Jebediah help him print it? I'm curious."

Peter stood by the door, trying to compose himself, but fidgeting, shifting his weight from foot to foot. "You're crazy. You know that? All those years you spent in the CIA warped your mind."

Brad pretended not to hear. "What confused me at first was how careless the forger had been." Brad talked in a calm, even voice. "The mistakes he made could have easily been avoided. At first I just assumed that Carl Riesling was a fool and didn't know what he was doing. Then, when I knew more details about the forgeries and had a closer look at Carl's reference library, I suspected I was wrong. In those reference books Carl had all the information he needed to correct his mistakes. He even marked the pages. It puzzled me. Why did he continue to screw up?"

Peter was quiet and didn't try to answer. He kept rocking back and forth.

"Then I began thinking that Carl actually made those mistakes on purpose. I asked myself, Why? Who would benefit? The more I thought about this, the more I thought about you. Your name kept rising higher and higher on my list. Here we have a moment in the sun for Peter Eastrovich, a new book, celebrity treatment by the governor and the local press, professional recognition, and the most important thing of all: revenge on Jonathan Avery, who had the audacity not to hire you as his librarian. Am I close?"

"You have no proof," Peter answered, his voice a choked sob.

Brad knew Peter was right, but he sensed that the man was near his breaking point. Brad decided to gamble.

"It's all a pattern, Peter. It's Terre Haute, Indiana, all over again." Brad wished he knew what had happened in Terre Haute but he trusted Tom Egan's instincts that something had.

"You know about Terre Haute?" Peter was the color of ivory.

"Not only me, Peter, but the police."

"Stop it!" Peter screamed, his hands squeezed tightly over his ears.

"Did Carl ask you to stop it, Peter? Did Carl plead with you, before you killed him?"

"Nooo!" Peter screamed like a wounded animal. He reached into his jacket pocket and took out a snub-nosed revolver, pointing it shakily at Brad.

He had underestimated Peter. For too long Brad had been with people who didn't carry guns, and it surprised him. He could only continue with his questions if he pretended that the gun didn't exist.

"Tell me, Peter, why did you kill Carl Riesling? It's the one piece of the puzzle I haven't quite figured out."

"Why?" he asked, his voice cracking and barely under control. Brad looked directly at Peter's eyes, which didn't appear to focus. They were like the eyes of a sleepwalker.

"Yes, why? Was Carl blackmailing you?"

"Blackmail? No, not blackmail."

"What was it, then?" said Brad, trying to keep Peter talking, trying to keep both of their minds off the revolver in Peter's hand.

"Money. He was going to sell copies of the books to other people for money. I went to his office. I told him no. I told him no, that we were too close."

"And what did he say?"

"He laughed at me. He showed me a whole box of *Sermons*. Said he could get five hundred dollars apiece for them, even if they were forgeries. He said collectors would pay the money, just like they did for the Wise forgeries."

"But that wasn't the way you planned it," Brad answered sympathetically, inching his hand closer to the desk drawer and his own gun.

"No. I told him. I couldn't let him do this. But he wouldn't listen. He laughed at me. Then I picked up a composing stick. It was filled with type. I hit him with it. What else was I going to do?"

"And then you tipped over the bookcase on top of him to make people think it was an accident."

"Yes."

"And the box of *Sermons?*"

"I put them in storage. You'll never find them."

"Why didn't you destroy them?"

"They would be valuable some day. Carl was right about that. And you don't destroy books."

A true librarian to the end, Brad thought. "Then why did you need my copy?"

"I needed them all." Peter was leaning toward the other side of madness, and Brad tried to bring him back.

"How many were there? How many forgeries did you make?"

Peter looked confused and then started to talk about his forgeries like a young father describing his children, telling Brad how he had conceived each of them in turn, each one with a flaw that only he could expose.

Downstairs, Joseph Sabatino peered into the darkened bookshop through the opened rear door below. He drew his gun and walked inside. He heard the two men talking upstairs, but went straight toward the glass display case in the center of the room. The copy of Lawson's *A New Voyage to North Carolina* (London, 1709) sat inside on the top shelf. Joseph tried to slide the glass door open, saw the metal lock that held it shut, and shattered the door with the butt of his revolver.

Just as Joseph reached into the case for the book, Samantha Frye opened the back door of the shop and called, "Brad!"

"*Run!*" a voice from upstairs screamed.

Samantha froze, silhouetted by the doorframe, as Joey leveled his revolver and took aim at a spot between Samantha's breasts. At that moment Napoleon stood up and, in one fluid motion, threw Fleder across the room like a softball pitcher arching a slow ball toward the plate. Fleder landed just above Joseph's knee, sinking her claws deep into his skin and scampering straight up his trousers to his shirt and face before she leaped behind him into the darkness. Joey's gun discharged wildly, and his screams from shock and the clawing blended with Samantha's. Napoleon now was standing, his own gun drawn and pointed. He confidently squeezed three rounds into Sabatino.

In the shadows he watched Joey shudder but remain on his feet. Joey sent a second shot toward Samantha, who was now running up the stairs. It missed.

"Brad!" she screamed, and screamed again when she saw Peter standing in Brad's office with a gun in his hand.

In the confusion Brad had managed to open his desk drawer and grab his own pistol before Peter became aware of what was happening. Samantha had run into the room and stood between them. Peter grabbed her arm, and then her waist, pressing her body in front of him as a shield. Brad used the time to duck behind his desk, avoiding Peter's first shot, which struck the wall above and behind him.

"Throw the gun out or I'll kill her," Peter demanded.

Brad was on his hands and knees trying to think, trying to be calm, and failing on both counts. A flash of his first wife's face shot through his mind. He remembered the vacuum that surrounded him when she died. "Samantha," he cried. Terror paralyzed him. Then, in the time that Brad thought was forever, he heard Peter grunt in surprise.

Peter had heard a noise and had swung around still holding Samantha in front of him. There, they both stared at Joseph Sabatino, standing in the doorway to the office, bloodied, ashen, and otherworldly, with his revolver pointed directly at them. Samantha brought her left heel down sharply on Eastrovich's foot, loosening his grip on her. Seizing the moment, she flung herself to the floor. Brad lurched from behind the desk in time to see Peter's body jerk as Joey's shot struck him in the chest. He dropped the gun. Joseph Sabatino, standing there without seeming to move, shot again. Peter crumpled to the floor in a pile, and Brad watched from his crouch as Joey listed forward and fell like a dead tree in the middle of an ancient forest.

Teddy waited outside until he heard the gunfire. His orders were to make sure Joey had gotten the microfilm and then kill him. His instincts told him to leave, but instincts were no match for his memories of Dr. Morarto. Without thinking, he started running forward—uncontrolled—toward the bookshop. When he reached the back door, he had his gun already drawn. Inside, he heard shots from upstairs and turned toward the steps, wondering how in God's name Joey had screwed this one up. Behind him, in the darkness, Napoleon stood and aimed his first shot for the center of Teddy's back, outlined as it was against the light of the steps. He squeezed the trigger and then raised his arm for a second shot that struck at the base of Teddy's skull. Theodore Simoneste was no longer bothered with thoughts of Norman Anastasius Calvado or the sinister Dr. Morarto, but for the first time since his childhood, he wondered briefly whether or not there was a heaven and if it looked like a playground in New York City.

Napoleon paused for a second and thought about trying to recover the microfilm, but decided it would be smarter to leave. Fleder watched him from her hiding place in the shadows as he walked out the back door.

# Chapter
# 34

There were a good many people in Parker's Rare Books that night who wished that they were somewhere else, and Tom Egan was no exception. He had stopped by on his way home, minutes after Napoleon had escaped into the darkness. Before that he had promised his wife that he would be there by nine. Their kids had gone to bed early, and she was waiting for him in her black-lace babydoll nightie, "compensation for your hard day at the office," she had whispered on the phone that afternoon. Now he didn't know whether to call her and tell her what had happened, or wait. Either way, he expected it would be a cold and frustrating week for him at best. Perhaps a long, frigid winter.

The shop was as crowded as a Navy bar on payday. The local police had called the state troopers, and they had sent down what must have been their entire police lab, because officers with cameras and tape measures were walking in every direction.

Brad sat silently on the leather couch in his office, holding Samantha in his arms.

"How's she doing?" Egan asked.

Brad just looked up at him.

"Dr. Ellis said it would probably be better if she went home now and tried to get some sleep. Eileen O'Rourke's one of my officers. I'll get her to drive Samantha there and stay with her for a while."

"Fine," Brad said without feeling.

"She must have had quite a shock tonight."

"Yeah."

"I'm sure," Egan grunted helplessly.

"I assume you want to talk with me tonight and not tomorrow morning."

Egan looked down at Samantha resting in Brad's arms and thought of his own wife. "Yes. Sorry."

"It's fine," Brad said again, gently shaking Samantha. "Someone's going to drive you home now."

"What about you?"

"I have to stay and answer some questions."

"We never talked," Samantha said to Brad as he helped her to her feet.

The pills Dr. Ellis had given her earlier that evening were having their effect. Samantha's speech sounded the way it would have after three martinis on an empty stomach. She walked uneasily, with Brad's help, through the team of crime-lab technicians who were still photographing and measuring.

"Tomorrow," Brad said softly in her ear. "We'll talk tomorrow."

Together, Brad and Tom Egan gently seated Samantha in the police car and watched as it drove through the parking lot until it was out of sight.

"We have a lot to discuss," Egan said to Brad.

"We certainly do."

"I'll tell them inside that we're going to my office."

On their way to the police department, Brad said, "There are two stories, one unofficial, the other for the record. Which do you want to hear first?"

"Let's drive out to Fred's Truck Stop. I've got to hear the unexpurgated version—whether I can use it or not."

Over three cups of very bad coffee, Brad told his story about Peter and the forgeries. Tom Egan sat silently except for an occasional "Christ!" until Brad had finished.

"So the son-of-a-bitch confessed to killing Carl Riesling."

"Yes, and to breaking into the store and to the incident at my apartment."

"All to cover up his involvement with the forgeries?"

"He had his entire career as a librarian at stake, so he was careful. He planned everything to the last detail, creating each of his forgeries so that it could fool Avery and any other unsuspecting person who would look at it. But each forgery had its own flaw, something that Peter could point out when the time came, to the applause of his peers. He asked Carl to print the books for him, under his precise instructions, and had Greta set up fictitious book businesses that would in turn sell the forgeries to Jonathan."

"I imagine Eastrovich would have been a hero if it worked."

"In the academic and bookish circles he lived in, yes. John Carter and Graham Pollard exposed Thomas J. Wise, a similar forger in the thirties, and it seemed to help their careers. Peter was hoping for a better job at a major library and a chance to do a little public speaking and bask in the limelight. I think he would have been successful at it."

"Did that sales manager of yours help Carl print the forgeries?"

"He didn't say. Jebediah certainly had the literary bent to help with the texts, but I don't know if Peter would have trusted him."

"I'm glad Eastrovich is dead," Egan said. "I doubt whether we would have gotten very far with this in court."

"You might have gotten a confession from Greta, but it would have been his word against ours. Now I think you'll find that box of Melville pamphlets—and there has to be other evidence. The man was a librarian to the end."

"And the governor is about to get a black eye in the press. I never had a chance to tell you. He tried to have Jonathan Avery arrested this afternoon. Insisted on full media coverage."

"What happened?"

"Nothing. Jonathan Avery wasn't there. Apparently the feds had him flown out of the state by helicopter earlier in the morning—before the press conference. All the governor found at the estate was a nest of Avery's lawyers."

"That must have been a sight."

"It was. My opponent for chief of police, Sam Ellington, was invited along for the arrest. He was so frustrated that he put his fist through the plaster wall in Avery's living room. One of the reporters took a wonderful photo of it. For the first time in weeks, I'm looking forward to reading tomorrow's papers."

After they stopped laughing, Egan said, "You took one hell of a chance pressing Eastrovich the way you did."

"I miscalculated. I never thought he'd have a gun."

"Guns are a reality in our society."

"Yes, but they're not so terribly common among book collectors or other gentle people."

"The dead man upstairs answers the description of the gunman at the Governor's Palace."

"I never saw him before."

"What about the man downstairs by the door?"

"Not him, either."

"A customer in the shop?"

"I don't remember him if he was."

"Well, in any event, you're lucky you didn't get yourself killed, or your girlfriend."

"Speaking of Samantha, I'd like to get back to her."

"She's probably asleep, and I still have to get your formal statement now."

"What do you want me to say?"

"You made an appointment to confront Peter Eastrovich with

268

theories you had about his involvement with the Avery forgeries and the Riesling murder. He confessed to the killing and the break-ins at your shop and apartment, said he masterminded producing a series of forgeries that he sold to the Avery Library through the Rieslings, and committed the murder and the rest of it to cover up his involvement. After he confessed, he made an attempt to kill you and Miss Frye—at which point he was shot by persons unknown. I think we can leave out the part about your visit to the library. Too many facts tend to confuse people."

"Are you Tom Egan?" a trim young man asked.

They were back in the bookshop.

"Matthew Gillespie, Lieutenant, State Police. I've been looking for you."

"You've found me."

"Right." He shuffled through a folder he was carrying. "We've identified your two corpses through their fingerprints. The one upstairs, who matches the description of the Governor's Palace gunman, is a Joseph Sabatino. The one downstairs is Theodore Simon. Both very well connected in organized crime, two big-time hoods, in fact."

Tom Egan laughed. "I'm sorry, Lieutenant, but I haven't heard anyone referred to as a 'hood' in over twenty years."

"You put on your own labels. This is my report."

"Let's see what you have," Egan said, pointing to the folder in Gillespie's hand.

"It's them, no doubt," Gillespie went on. "Twenty points of comparison on Sabatino's prints; twenty-three on Simon's."

"Ever hear those names?" Egan asked Brad, showing him the folder.

"No." Brad glanced over the reports. "Active, weren't they? There's quite a string of prior arrests and convictions in here."

"I already called the federal organized crime unit," Gillespie said proudly.

269

"You what?" Egan exploded. "Don't you want to get home tonight?"

"I'm going. This is your jurisdiction. They'll want to talk to you."

"Thanks."

"Always happy to be of service."

Napoleon Robespierre Jones stood at the reception desk of the Hilton Hotel.

"This your best suite we're talking about?" he asked the desk clerk.

"Yes, sir. I'm sure you'll be very happy with it."

"Good."

"Can I get someone to help you with your luggage, Mr. Sabatino?"

Napoleon took back the credit card he had found in the glove compartment of the white Cadillac.

"No, I'll get it later. You got a car that can take me to the airport tomorrow?"

"Yes, sir, compliments of the hotel."

"Good."

"Enjoy your stay with us, sir."

Napoleon looked up at the young desk clerk and smiled. "I'm going to give that my best shot, young man."

At the police station Brad read his statement into a tape recorder, and one of the clerks in the outer office took it away for typing.

"And you're sure nothing was stolen from the display case tonight?" Tom Egan asked one more time.

"I distinctly remember that there were six books in there before the shooting, and there are six in there now."

"It doesn't make any sense. Why would two strong-arm boys, heavy into organized crime, come into a bookshop, break into a glass display case, and not steal anything?"

"Maybe they were interrupted," Brad said. "Being shot dead can have an effect on your concentration, I've been told."

The FBI finished their work at four o'clock in the morning. When

Tom Egan finally got home he found his wife asleep in their youngest girl's bedroom. She was wearing her long flannel nightgown and white athletic socks. Tom went into the kitchen and found the last can of Budweiser in the refrigerator. He drank it slowly in front of the television, watching a rerun of "The Mary Tyler Moore Show." He didn't pay attention to the story, and the laugh track droned on without him.

Brad and Samantha spent the entire weekend together. Brad even asked Mrs. Johnson to bring them some food from the local supermarket so they wouldn't have to leave Samantha's house.

"And here's your cat, too."

"My God, I completely forgot about Fleder."

"I found her at her place in the front window when I came in, but the poor thing was frightened to death. She didn't leave my side all day. Did you, Fleder?"

Samantha looked at Brad and shrugged her shoulders as Mrs. Johnson let Fleder out of her carrying case and scratched her gently behind the ears.

"And Clubman came over from the rental office. He just wrung his hands and kept saying what a tragedy all this shooting was for Colonial Williamsburg. He told me he thought it was a mistake to have an antiquarian bookshop as one of the tenants—too much of a bad element. I told him he ought to replace us with a nice upbeat disco."

"What did he say to that?"

"Clubman's not your quickest wit. He has the sense of humor of a warthog. Anyhow, he just wrung his hands again and walked out."

"One point for you, Mrs. Johnson," Samantha told her, and they all said their good-byes.

Samantha talked about working in New York.

"I'm happy for you. As far as we go, we'll take it one day at a time," Brad said.

"It'll work out. You'll see." Samantha squeezed Brad's hand.

By the time Brad took Samantha to the airport on Monday morning, she had regained some of her bounce and sparkle. They held each other closely for fifteen minutes, until her final boarding call was announced.

"Until Friday," Samantha said.

"Friday, but I'll call you at the hotel tonight."

"Last week you had a copy of Lawson's travel book on North Carolina in your case," a dapper gentleman said to Mrs. Johnson at the bookshop. Brad was sitting at the desk sorting mail. He stiffened enough to wake Fleder who was dozing on his lap. Odd that the man should be asking for the Lawson.

"The case got broken over the weekend," Brad interrupted. "I have the book in my safe in the back."

"If it wouldn't be too much trouble," the man said softly, "I'd like to take another look at it. There was a young man here last week who was kind enough to show it to me."

"Oh, him," Mrs. Johnson grunted.

"The young man left without giving us any notice," Brad explained, bringing the book out from the back. " You know: 'Good help is hard to find'!" Brad handed him the book, and the man thumbed through the pages briskly and then stopped at the map.

"May I help you open that?" asked Brad.

Norman Anastasius Calvado had a glimpse between the folds and saw a corner of the microfilm. "It's not really necessary. The young man last week spent a considerable amount of time with me going over the particulars."

"He explained that this was a large-paper copy, of course?"

"Yes."

"In a contemporary binding."

"It's beautiful. It looks as if it were new—it's not worn, I mean."

"I've never seen a better copy."

"And, if I remember, the price was twelve thousand dollars?"

"Yes."

"Firm?"

"I'm afraid so."

"I'll take it anyway," the man said after a reflective pause.

"Have you been collecting books long?" Brad asked, taking the book from him and handing it to Mrs. Johnson with a nod.

"I'm just a beginner, but one with a growing interest." Calvado went on to say that he was fascinated by early American travel.

Mrs. Johnson returned with the book and the invoice.

"How would you like to pay for this?" Brad asked.

"Cash?"

"If you're out of state and we ship it to you, we won't have to charge you tax."

"That's all right. I'd like to take it with me."

Brad talked with Calvado for half an hour about the joys and pitfalls of collecting rare books. He gave Norman several of Parker's Rare Books catalogs and *How to Buy Rare Books* by William Rees-Mogg to read on his way home. Calvado seemed expansive and appeared to be enjoying himself. He bought three other colonial American pamphlets for an additional five thousand dollars and left. Because of all the police in the shop the previous night, the thought lingered in Calvado's mind that the FBI had already found and copied his microfilm, replacing the original.

Whatever, he said to himself on the flight home, contemplating the end of his political friendships and the beginning of a new hobby, collecting rare books.

# Epilogue

The police put out an APB for a man answering Jebediah Stuart's description, but there was no response; the report was filed with several inches of similar forms in police stations across the state and the country. No one made the connection between Jebediah and a partially mutilated body that was found in a drainage ditch on the edge of a small North Carolina town, although its discovery made headlines in the local papers for months. Brad replaced Jebediah in the shop two weeks later with a retired army colonel who loved books and was good with people.

Belinda Freemont did a series of special reports on Peter Eastrovich for WMSB that helped to clear the mystery of the Williamsburg forgeries. Through interviews with Tom Egan, Brad, and Morris Hausbach, she was able to explain how Peter had created a string of books that existed only in his mind, and how he was able to have these printed by Carl Riesling and then sold to Jonathan Avery for his library. In each of the forgeries, there were conscious mistakes and subtle errors that Peter had planned to reveal at the appropriate time to what he hoped would be the applause and awe of the academic community. The enhancement of his own career was to be made even sweeter by the fall of Jonathan Avery, who had snubbed him when he didn't offer Peter the position of head librarian.

The shooting in front of the Governor's Palace was "solved" by the reported death of the gunman in Parker's Rare Books. It was described by Belinda Freemont as being a power struggle within organized crime, the gunman and Teddy Simon having shot each other in the bookshop—a convenient lie manufactured by Tom Egan, who was elected Williamsburg's chief of police by a landslide.

Jonathan Avery maintained a cold war with the Commonwealth of Virginia over his withdrawal of the library, occasional legal briefs serving as ammunition in their skirmishes. It took two years, but he eventually won his court battle, further justifying the participation of high-priced lawyers in legal wars with overworked public prosecutors. Jonathan never returned to Virginia; his book collecting career had ended.

There was a slight mystery in how Joseph Sabatino could have charged $475.68 to his VISA card in a Williamsburg hotel the evening after he was murdered. He was described by hotel personnel as a large black man, of the same general description as the one whom Sabatino had chased through the gardens of the Governor's Palace earlier that day. This was never reported to the press, but Brad Parker was told the details three years later, by Napoleon Robespierre Jones himself.

But that, as Jonathan Avery would have said, is another story for another time.

Fleder, incidentally, found a new friend in Mrs. Johnson, who began bringing freshly poached fish in plastic containers for the cat's lunch.